A Highlander in a Pickup

A Highlander in a Pickup

LAURA TRENTHAM

St. Martin's Paperbacks

This is a work of fiction. All of the characters, organizations, and events portrayed in this novel are either products of the author's imagination or are used fictitiously.

First published in the United States by St. Martin's Paperbacks, an imprint of St. Martin's Publishing Group.

A HIGHLANDER IN A PICKUP

Copyright © 2020 by Laura Trentham.

All rights reserved.

For information, address St. Martin's Publishing Group, 120 Broadway, New York, NY 10271.

www.stmartins.com

ISBN: 978-1-250-31503-8

Our books may be purchased in bulk for promotional, educational, or business use. Please contact your local bookseller or the Macmillan Corporate and Premium Sales Department at 1-800-221-7945, ext. 5442, or by email at MacmillanSpecialMarkets@macmillan.com.

Printed in the United States of America

St. Martin's Paperbacks edition / March 2020

10 9 8 7 6 5 4 3 2 1

Chapter One

Anna Maitland was waving the toddler class out the door of her dance studio, the strains of "The Wheels on the Bus" still resonating in her head, when her phone buzzed. Not an unusual state these days with the Highland festival three weeks away. Anna was doing her best to keep everything and everyone on track while the Buchanan ladies were seeing to an even bigger project—the birth of a baby.

Even though she tried to temper it, her voice retained the singsong tenor she used to cajole the toddlers into behaving. "Hello. Anna Maitland here."

"Howdy there, I got 'em." The male voice was double-battered and country-fried and held the peculiar familiarity of a born-and-raised Southern man of a certain age.

Anna had attended and been part of the festival for years. In fact, no one had won Lass of the Games, awarded to the best dancer, as many times as she had, but she'd never been in charge of anything but her dance troupe. This year, she was in charge of everything.

She'd had no idea *everything* ran the gamut of getting the stage set up and organizing the vendors, to verifying the number of portable potties and parking attendants needed.

All the while, Anna was trying to wrap her head around the fact her best friend, Isabel Buchanan, was having a baby. It didn't seem real. Maybe because she hadn't seen her best friend beyond a few video chats for almost a year. Just last summer, Izzy had embarked on a two-week fling with Alasdair Blackmoor and ended up falling in love. Now, she was married and having a baby. It was crazy-scary how fast life could deliver blessings and, for that matter, tragedies too.

Izzy had been put on bed rest a month earlier, and Rose Buchanan and Gareth Blackmoor had flown to her side to await the birth of the next heir of Cairndow, dropping the festival in Anna's lap earlier than they'd anticipated.

At first, Anna had relished being in charge of the festival. She was ready to prove herself. Anyway, it's not like she had a life outside the studio. No boyfriend. No hobbies. No family. At least, not since the winter, when her mother announced she was selling Anna's childhood home and moving into a retirement community in Florida.

While it had been a shock, Anna was used to people leaving. She was out to prove she could do it all—and then some—on her own. She needed no one's help.

She cleared her throat and tried her best to sound professional. "Who am I speaking with?"

"You will," the man said.

She switched hands and pressed the phone tighter

against her ear as if that would help deciphering his words. "I'm sorry. What will I do?"

"I said, this is *Ewell* Hightower." The man spoke slower and louder as if he'd gotten the town idiot on the line. "From down around Macon."

She riffled through her mental files for a vendor in Macon and came up empty. "What can I help you with, Mr. Hightower?"

His laugh was nasal but good-natured. "Call me Ewell. I gots your animals."

"What animals would that be?"

Now it was his turn to pause and consider. "Have you talked with Gareth?"

As a matter of fact, she hadn't. Rose and Izzy had been her contacts since they had spent the last decade planning the festival together on the grounds of Stonehaven, the Buchanan family home. "No. Should I have?"

"He leased a Scottish blackface ewe and a Highland cow for the festival you'uns is putting on up there."

The phone grew slippery in her suddenly sweaty palm. While there had been talk of incorporating animals into the festival, she assumed those plans had been on hold until next year when Gareth could oversee the new venture. The man Gareth had promised to send to help out wasn't expected for another week, and Anna feared he'd be more hindrance than help anyway.

"I see. I'll need to discuss the matter with Gareth and get back to you. We may have to cancel."

"You'uns would be out a fair amount if you cancel. 'Sides, I'm already on my way. Got the paperwork. Can you meet me out at your place to take delivery?"

The background sounds parsed itself into a combination

of the radio and road noise. Anna grimaced and mouthed a curse. "How far away are you?"

"Just passed that fancy WELCOME TO HIGHLAND sign. Are you out at the big house now?"

The big house could only mean Stonehaven. "I'm not."

"I'll need someone to sign off and take possession of the girls." It was a statement and an assumption someone would be there to handle the deed.

The girls. Ewell made it sound like they were arriving for a carefree sleepover. "I'll meet you there in ten minutes."

"Good enough, then." Ewell disconnected.

The surprise put Anna's thoughts into a tumble. Izzy had warned her there would be unexpected hurdles; she just hadn't counted on stumbling over so many this early in the race. She scrolled through her contacts and hit a name.

Keisha answered in her usual chipper voice. "What's up, Teach?"

"I need a favor. I have to run out to Stonehaven and take a delivery for the festival. If I'm not back, can you and Gabby run the girls through the routine a couple of times?"

"Sure thing. You know I love to boss everyone around." The laughter in Keisha's voice was usually infectious, but Anna was too stressed to join in.

"Thanks, sweetie. Try not to turn into a dancing despot. I'll buy you a coffee or some ice cream down at the Brown Cow after class."

She hit the end button then climbed into her black VW Bug and peeled out of the parking lot behind the studio, heading toward Stonehaven. Gareth was going to get an earful. What time was it in Scotland? It didn't matter. Gareth deserved to get dragged out of bed for this. She hit the call button. No answer. The butt chewing was on hold.

She pulled onto the pebbled lane to Stonehaven. Trees on either side of the lane offered a brief respite from the sun. Her AC hadn't even had enough time to cool her off when she parked by the row of pine trees between the house and barn next to Izzy's old truck.

The house's facade was stone and it had a castle-like feel with a turret even though the inside was straight out of a *Southern Living* magazine with a comfortable, breezy elegance that epitomized Rose Buchanan. Stonehaven provided the perfect backdrop to the festival that was held on the grounds.

She slid out of her car and paced next to Izzy's old truck. Pollen muted the tartan-painted hood and stripes down the side. Had it even been driven since Izzy left a year ago? Like a medium, Anna laid her hands on the truck as if she could somehow connect with her best friend a thousand miles and many time zones away.

A pine cone thudded next to her hand and bounced to the ground, making her jump. She gave a little laugh at her unusually whimsical thoughts. Maybe she was channeling Izzy after all, considering her friend was in the middle of writing a fantasy novel.

The rattle of a trailer brought her back to reality. An enormous double cab truck towing a horse trailer approached, passing her and parking close to the barn. Ewell swung himself out of the driver's seat and hopped to the ground from the running board.

With a weathered, worn face that could have been anywhere between sixty and eighty, Ewell was short and bowlegged and reminded Anna of a cheerful garden gnome.

"You Miss Maitland?" He spit tobacco to the side and offered her a gnarled hand.

She shook it and nodded. "Nice to meet you, Mr. . . . I mean, Ewell."

He pushed a sweat-stained Atlanta Braves baseball cap off his forehead with a thumb and grinned at her with tobacco-stained teeth. "Weren't expecting you to get all gussied up for me."

Anna looked down at herself and smoothed her tutu made up of lengths of different colored tulle. Her young kids loved the rainbow vibrancy. "I'm a dance teacher, but that's not important. I only drove out to say that you need to take these animals back with you."

"Cain't." Ewell sauntered to the trailer and lowered the gate to form a ramp.

Musky animal scents hit her like a slap in the thick air. The large trailer rocked with the shuffling of hooves, punctuated by grunts. Were they doing something X-rated in there? She squinted, but the trailer was shadowy inside compared to the bright day.

"Of course you can." Anna waved a hand, wishing she could spirit the entire problem away. "Just leave the creatures in there and drive away. Keep the deposit. How much was it again?"

"Not about the money. Got two steer in there to deliver south of Nashville, and I'm picking up a full load of milking cows. Ain't got room." The first animal out of the trailer was a sheep with a black face and luxurious white coat. "I left her unsheared in case Gareth wanted to demonstrate."

"That's what I've been trying to tell you. Gareth isn't here."

Ewell spit another stream of brown tobacco to the side. "Obviously."

He handed her the rope lead to the sheep, clopped back into the trailer, and pulled out a hairy brown animal with a set of curved horns. It tossed its head, less docile than the sheep. The cow wasn't at all like the ones she saw grazing behind fences on the side of the road or the one that jumped over the moon in picture books. Although, honestly, she'd never been this close to one before.

The Highland cow had long, silky-looking brown fur and stubby legs. Hair flopped into its eyes like an adolescent pop stars. The cow seemed to have an attitude to match. It shook its head as if trying to free itself from the harness. Or maybe it wanted to gore one of them with its horns. She took two steps back.

"Gareth is not just not at Stonehaven; he's not in the country. He's not here to care for the animals." Desperation crept into her voice.

Ewell held out the cow's lead, and she took the rope instinctively. Immediate regrets surfaced while he closed the trailer and walked back toward the cab of the truck. She tried to follow, but the Highland cow refused to budge. All she could do was hang on the end of the tether, putting as much space between them as possible.

Ewell returned with a clipboard and pen. He tapped a blank space at the bottom of the paper held in place on the clipboard. "Sign there."

She skimmed the paper. It was a lease agreement with a clause to buy at the end of the lease if both parties agreed. The leasing amount would be deducted from the final sale price.

"I can't sign this," she said.

"Here. Lemme hold 'em, so you can sign." He exchanged the leads in her numb fingers with the clipboard and pen. He squinted at the sun. "Not to rush you, but I gots a long drive and an appointment to keep."

Feeling backed into a corner Gareth had built, she sighed and signed.

Ewell touched the brim of his ball cap with a forefinger. "Thank you, ma'am. Now this here is Ozzie." He held out the lead of the blackface sheep. "And this'un here is Harriet." He held out the cow's lead.

"Ozzie and Harriet?" she murmured. Innocuous names for such large animals. They looked more like a Bonnie and Clyde. She took the leads with a feeling of overwhelmed exasperation. "What the heck am I supposed to do with them now?"

Ewell nodded toward the barn. "That's what a barn's for, ain't it?"

Was it? She thought barns were for drinking and smoking and making out. At least, that's what they'd been good for in high school.

Ewell swung himself back into his truck and hollered, "Good luck!" out his window as he rolled down the lane toward the main road. Anna was left holding the leads.

"Come on, then. Let's throw you in the barn while I call for reinforcements." Anna prayed Holt had time to help her out. It was a busy season for him on his family farm, but he was always willing to lend a hand. The Piersons were avid supporters of the festival, and Holt was training for the athletic competitions, like the stone throw and caber toss, to win Laird of the Games.

Ozzie the sheep followed her with a good-natured, docile attitude Anna appreciated. Harriet, on the other hand, was being a real bitch.

"Move, you foul creature from hell," she muttered, pulling on the lead. The cow cast a baleful eye in her direction and jerked her horned head. A game of tug of war had commenced, and Anna was losing.

She wasn't a country girl. She had never owned an animal, not even a dog, and she'd certainly never had to maneuver a cow into a barn. Trying a different tack, she circled around to the cow's haunches to push. Except, Ozzie's position put her too far away and now the sheep had turned stubborn and refused to move.

Anna dropped Ozzie's lead, pointed at the sheep, and said in the voice she reserved for especially rambunctious classes, "Don't you dare move. Not a step."

When Ozzie just blinked and stuck her tongue out to work her jaws, Anna turned her attention back to Harriet. Very slowly, not sure what to expect, Anna put her hands flat on the cow's rump. Her fur was surprisingly soft and springy and felt like a padded cushion. Anna nudged the cow, but she didn't move. Then, she put her weight into the effort. Nothing.

The cow's tail twitched up. The plopping sound registered before the unmistakable earthy smell. Anna reeled backward while Harriet left a steaming pile of poop on the driveway. "That's just lovely. Real ladylike, Harriet."

The deposit seemed to be what Harriet had been waiting for, and she finally lumbered forward. Anna turned with relief to get Ozzie's lead and froze. The sheep was gone. Anna turned in a full circle, scanning and seeing nothing that resembled a sheep or a path left by a sheep.

A trickle of sweat ran down her back and into the low

scoop of her black leotard as she tried to steady her discombobulated thoughts. First thing she had to do was secure Harriet in the barn, then she would go in search for her lost sheep like Bo-Peep. If she were going to be dropped in the middle of a fairy tale, she would have preferred one with a hot prince.

Fleeter of hooves now that she'd dumped her load, Harriet rambled toward the barn. Anna peeled the doors open and blinked to adjust to the sudden shadows. It was much cooler inside the barn, and Harriet quickened her step to reach the shade. Water and some sort of food would be needed soon, but the most pressing concern was finding Ozzie.

Anna closed the door and made sure it was latched securely before circling around through the line of pine trees and the field behind the barn. She shielded her eyes from the sun and scanned for movement. A shot of relief made her feel dizzy.

Ozzie had made it farther than Anna had expected, but there she was at the edge of the patio, plucking the heads off the flowers in Rose's prized flowerpots and eating them.

"Get away, you scallywag!" Anna hollered, waving her arms in the air.

Ozzie did move but only to the next pot to decapitate a burst of yellow pansies. If she'd been in boots, she would have stomped across the field, but she was in thin-soled ballet slippers and pranced rather than marched with a full head of steam powered by frustration.

At this rate, Anna was going to have to cancel her intermediate ballet class. The tall grass irritated her bare legs and left her itching as she quickstepped closer. Ozzie looked up from her flower munching and regarded Anna with bland amusement. Or at least it seemed that way.

"Oh, is that how we're playing it? You don't think I can handle you? You've never seen me corral a bunch of four-year-olds." Anna sidled closer, her hands out and ready to grab the lead.

Ozzie shuffled to the side and made a sound that Anna hoped didn't mean she was ready to attack. Anna stopped moving. What were the statistics on sheep-related deaths? She didn't want to end up on the news as an amusing freak accident. "Little Bo-Peep Trampled by Sheep."

Anna and Ozzie were at an impasse.

A loud clang roused Iain Connors out of his jet-lagged stupor. The unnatural sound shot enough adrenaline into his veins to make going back to sleep impossible. Sun sliced through a narrow opening of the curtains, and he stared at the dancing dust motes. For a moment, he was adrift, and it took a few blinks around the room to place himself in the universe.

Highland, Georgia. Stonehaven. He'd arrived late the night the before after a long flight. The shuttle he'd taken from the airport had been loud and bumpy, and besides the brightly lit road signs, he'd seen little beyond shopping centers and then tree-lined roads as they'd left the city.

A muffled voice outside sharpened his focus on the window, and he hauled himself out of bed to peel the curtains all the way open, squinting at the brightness. He shook his head and blinked at the unexpected sight greeting him.

A blackfaced sheep munched on flower heads while a lass in a rainbow skirt taunted it. Had the lack of sleep left him addled? The woman was lithe with wavy, red hair escaping from what may have once been a neat bun. Was he dreaming? Was he still in Scotland? He squeezed his eyes shut, then opened them again. The lass was still there.

He unlatched the window and raised the sash. The sharp cry of a blackbird greeted him along with the trills of other songbirds. A blast of humid heat left him feeling slightly braised. No, he was definitely not in Scotland, and if he needed further proof, the woman's accent was husky and honeyed and all Southern. Her voice reminded him a bit of Rose and Isabel, but sexier. Much sexier.

"You are not endearing yourself to me, Ozzie. Don't you want water and something to eat besides flowers?" The woman had her hands on her hips and spoke like she was berating a small child. Unless American-born blackface sheep were smarter than Scottish ones, the beastie would be unmoved by her words.

Sure enough, the blackfaced sheep merely turned to a fresh pot and beheaded more flowers.

The woman's voice grew more strident. "If you don't quit eating flowers and move your heinie toward the barn, I'm going to give you a real embarrassing haircut. Everyone is going to laugh at you."

Amusement bubbled up and built a pressure in his chest. Ach, he felt lighter than he had in ages, as if his sleep had been enchanted.

"Bo-Peep, I presume? Or did you spring from a Rabbie Burns poem?" He cleared his throat and recited:

"Ye wild whistling blackbirds in yon thorny den,

Thou green-crested lapwing, thy screaming forbear,
I charge you disturb not my slumbering fair."

The woman whipped her head back and forth, then spun in a circle. The airy fabric of her skirts swished like a kaleidoscope. She wore a tight black leotard with a deep scoop along her back. Her reaction triggered laughter he did his best to smother. He suspected she wasn't in a place to appreciate the farcical nature of the scene.

Finally, she tilted her head back and homed in on him like a falcon. "You!" She imbued the word with recrimination and accusation.

"Me? What have I done?" He leaned farther out of the window, the wood scraping along his bare stomach. He'd fallen into bed wearing nothing but his underpants the night before.

The sheep circled around the woman as if resentful her attention had shifted to another animal and bumped her in the bum. The woman yelped and high-stepped a few paces closer to his window and away from the sheep.

He was having a hard time controlling his laughter. "*Ahem* . . . do you need a hand?"

"Does it look like I need a hand?"

His sarcasm meter registered atomic. How to answer? With politeness or the truth? Because the lass obviously needed help, yet her ire was at combustible levels.

While he dithered, she precluded his response with an eye roll and a toss of her head. "Yes! I need a dadgum hand. Get down here."

"Aye, then, I'll be down in a tick." He pulled clothes out of his rucksack and put on the first thing at hand, an olive-green utility kilt and a black T-shirt. With no socks materializing in the mound he drew out, he decided to forgo his boots, which he'd left at the front door last night.

He wound his way through the unfamiliar home, unlocked the set of doors that faced the flowering field, and stepped outside. Amazingly, the air-con had blunted the effects of the heat when he'd been at the window, and he felt the brunt of it now. The atmosphere was thick and humid and starkly opposite the chilly morning air at Cairndow he'd breathed in the day before.

"You're Iain Connors, I suppose?" The woman was both smaller (in stature) and bigger (in personality) than he'd expected.

"Aye, and you are Anna Maitland." No reason to frame it as a question. Isabel had sketched out her basic bio for him. Anna owned Maitland Dance Studio and had been left with the task of planning the Highland festival. At least until now. It seemed he'd arrived not a minute too soon by the look of things.

Of course, Isabel had left out some fundamental information, like how her friend's rich red hair glinted in the summer sun like embers ready to catch everything around them on fire. Or the way her movements were graceful but vibrated with energy. Or the fact that her expression radiated intelligence and challenge.

"Were you aware these . . . these . . . *creatures* were being delivered?" she asked.

Her tone had him looking around for said creatures until he realized she was referring to the docile blackfaced sheep happily munching on flowers. "Creature? She's hardly on par with old Nessie."

"Nessie? Her name is Ozzie."

It took a few blinks to follow the path of the conversation. "I meant, Nessie the Loch Ness Monster. Here, allow me." He walked up, grabbed a hank of wool along Ozzie's flank to keep her still, and retrieved the dangling lead.

Anna shook her head. "Why wouldn't she let me get close?"

"Probably because she sensed weakness." Animals reacted to alphas. To the sheep, Iain was an alpha and Anna was not. A simple dynamic.

"Excuse me? I'm not weak. I was merely unprepared to take delivery of two unruly animals today. Gareth didn't even give me a heads-up. If it was your responsibility, then you should have been here." His assessment had unintentionally offended her and applied accelerant to her attitude.

"The delivery wasn't supposed to take place until tomorrow," Iain said.

"Be that as it may, Gareth should have filled me in as I am in charge of the festival until they return, which doesn't seem like it's going to be imminent." Her expression softened from granite to clay. "How's Izzy?"

"Quarrelsome. Her ankles are . . ." He made a circle with his hands, knowing better than to use a negative adjective like "fat" or "sausage-like." Isabel had thrown a pillow at his head when he'd compared her propped up, swollen ankles to something on display in the butcher's window. He had been thankful a cleaver hadn't been within reach.

A shadow of something familiar passed over her face. "I miss her."

The admission was barely audible, and Iain wasn't sure whether to acknowledge the sentiment or ignore it.

In a voice as brisk as the wind off the loch, she asked, "What's the plan for Ozzie and Harriet?"

Ignore the shot of emotion it was. "I assume Harriet is the Highland cow?"

"Yep. I got her into the barn after she took a giant crap on the driveway." The smile cresting her face had no relation to amusement or happiness. It was pure devilish glee. "Which you will need to clean up, by the way."

He didn't acknowledge her prodding remark. The primitive deposit of one Highland cow hardly filled him with disgust, considering he was used to managing hundreds of sheep and dozens of cows. Instead, he started toward the barn, Ozzie following docilely.

Anna fell into step beside him, taking two steps to his one. "A kilt on a weekday, huh? You take being Scottish seriously."

He raised an eyebrow and shot her an up-and-down look. "A rainbow tutu on a weekday, huh? You take being a fairy sprite seriously."

A laugh stuttered through her surprise before she muffled it. "A sprite? Nothing so magical. Just a dance teacher."

"I'll bet you're magical to the kids you teach." He opened the door to the barn and blinked, sun blind. The cow made a sound that bordered on distress. It was hot even in the shade of the barn. Better ventilation wouldn't go amiss, but water was the top priority.

He let go of Ozzie's lead, confident she would remain in the shade, and went in search of anything he could use as water troughs. Two large plastic buckets were stacked in the corner. Beating back the cobwebs, he hauled them to the middle of the barn. Inside one was coiled a green hose.

"There's a faucet out here, I think." Anna disappeared

around the side of the barn and he followed. A pipe came directly out of the ground with a valve.

They worked together to attach and unroll the hose, then filled the two tubs. Ozzie and Harriet fought to drink as soon as the water hit the bottom of the first. Iain spoke to them in Gaelic, and it seemed American stock wasn't much different than Scottish. Both animals calmed, and soon each was drinking out of her own tub. He gave each animal a scratch behind the ears.

Anna was looking at him with an expression absent the heat from earlier. "What are you telling them?"

"Basically that they're safe, and I will care for them."

"Interesting," she said in a way he wasn't sure meant "fascinating" or "strange."

Probably the latter. He'd been called strange and weird and a host of other things since he was a kid. His childhood had been unconventional. Not many lads were raised in the shadow of a castle and fed Robert Burns for breakfast. Iain's da could recite every poem the long-dead Scotsman had written. And now, so could Iain. Sometimes another man's words were easier than formulating his own.

He was at a loss for any words at the moment. Iain shot a glance from the corner of his eye toward Anna, trying and failing not to stare. More of her hair had come loose, and she wiped her forehead with the back of her forearm. Curls wisped around her face. Closer now, he could see the light freckles sprinkled across her thin, straight nose and the red slashes the sun had left on her fair cheeks. She was younger than Isabel had led him to believe, yet her dark blue eyes reflected a wisdom gained only through the crucible of painful life experiences.

The silence was deafening. It was his turn to say something. He understood the basic mechanisms of conversation, even if his gears often got stuck. Although Iain hated to butcher a perfect quote from a British treasure, it was a truth universally acknowledged that Iain was utter rubbish with women. His army mates had teased and tortured him about his tied tongue and awkwardness around bonny lasses.

He hadn't been gifted even a percent of Sean Connery's suave confidence. In fact, he would have been more likely to be cast as a Bond villain than the hero. While he wasn't an ogre under a bridge, he might pass as a distant cousin. His dark looks were intimidating, and the scar he'd acquired as a lad bordered on plain mean. A fact he'd used to his advantage when faced with snot-nosed village lads and in Her Majesty's service, but which didn't serve him well face-to-face with the fairer sex.

"Er . . . I guess I'll take things from here," he said.

"I guess you will." She turned toward a car that appeared more like an overgrown toy, then spun back around, her skirt swishing. "Wait. What exactly will you take from here?"

"I'll shepherd the festival to a successful conclusion and let you get back to your . . ." Dance seemed more of a passion than a job. ". . . work?"

The questioning waffle in his voice had been unintentional. Her blossoming anger transfixed him. Yes, beauty resided in her flushed cheeks and sparking eyes, but even more apparent was her spirit. She didn't seem fazed by him in any way. Not his size or his scar or his inability to formulate coherent thoughts.

"I have everything under control." She put her hands on her hips and stepped toward him.

"Of course you do, Bo-Peep." The words came out with a teasing edge that surprised even him.

Anna arrowed her pointed gaze on him. "You stay in the barn out of my way, and I'll stay out of yours. Understood?"

His brusque nod seemed to appease her. She turned, slipped into her car, and threw gravel on her tight turn around the driveway. While he had understood her, he hadn't actually agreed to stay out of her way. He had promised Alasdair to do whatever was necessary to make sure the festival ran smoothly. The last thing Isabel needed to worry over in her condition was a festival thousands of miles away.

Anyway, selfishly, he needed this time to away from Cairndow to figure out his life. He loved Cairndow and his da, and he couldn't wait to get home after leaving Her Majesty's service, but he hadn't slipped seamlessly back into his old life. An odd dissonance had wrecked his expected contentment.

He was no longer certain if he wanted to take over as groundskeeper of Cairndow. Maybe he did, but he needed time to figure it out. He'd tried to voice his doubts to his da, but they'd lodged somewhere around his heart when he'd seen his da's happiness and pride in having him home. Anyway, the Connor men weren't known for their loquacious natures.

His future was a bridge to be crossed, but for now, he would enjoy the respite life had given him and consider his options.

He'd assumed Anna Maitland would be more than happy to relinquish control of planning the festival. Why wasn't she? He hadn't a clue, but what he did know was he and Anna were sure to lock horns like two Highland cows during mating season. A zip of energy went up his spine.

Mating season. He tried to banish the images the thought inspired, but failed spectacularly.

Chapter Two

Anna arrived back at the studio as her high school class broke up. The girls moved toward the door in a scrum, laughter buzzing over talk of boys and the festival and the imminent start of the school year. Anna had taught most of the girls for years. She'd seen them through their first pimple to their first heartbreak. This time next year, many of the girls would be packing for college or pursuing their dreams as Anna had attempted at eighteen. She wished them better luck.

Keisha patted her face with a small towel, her braids pulled up into a sagging bun on top of her head. The chatter of teenagers faded as they made their way out the door to enjoy the last days of summer.

"Thanks, Keisha." Anna glanced around. "Where's Gabby?"

The smile Keisha wore like a favorite T-shirt slipped into a worried line. "A no-show. I texted her, and she said she didn't feel good, but . . ."

"But?" Anna prodded.

"She was fine yesterday. The problem is her dad. I don't think he's going to let her compete."

Anna's stomach swooped. Gabby's dad was a conservative Christian who had tolerated but never supported his daughter's love of dance. It had been Gabby's mother who had loved to watch her daughter on stage. But she was gone now. Passed away over the winter after a two-year battle with breast cancer. Since then, Gabby had seemed to channel her grief into hard work in the studio.

Anna regathered her unruly hair and twisted it off her neck into a clip. "If her dad doesn't want her competing, there isn't much I can do."

"It should be Gabby's decision, not his. It isn't fair!" The teenage refrain of the ages rang out and echoed back. "Can't you go talk to him?"

"I suppose so, but I doubt it will do any good."

"Thank you, Anna. You're the best." Keisha leaned in to give her a hug.

Anna loved dance and loved to watch her pupils improve and get stronger, but this was why she had taken over the dance studio. She wanted to give the girls something she hadn't had. Encouragement. A place where they could laugh together, work hard, tease one another, but ultimately build one another up, never tear them down.

Anna's mother was beloved in Highland. She had founded the studio as a single mom with a small business loan. She had pulled out the best from her dancers through an exacting work ethic. "Tough love" more than one person had said with a nostalgia that never failed to make Anna recoil.

Tough love. An apt way to describe their mother-daughter relationship. Her mother's love had been tempered in fire. Hardened. Unbending.

Anna had worked diligently for her mother's approval in the dance studio and had excelled. But she'd paid a price. All of her self-esteem had been tied to dance, and when she had failed to make it in New York City, something inside of her cracked. It had taken years to super-glue herself back together, stronger than she had been. At least, that's what she told herself.

When her mother couldn't physically keep up with the studio and the students, Anna had jumped at the chance for a do-over. She was molding the studio into the space she'd longed for as a young girl, unsure of herself and her place in the world.

Gabby reminded Anna of a younger version of herself, except more talented. Gabby danced with a vulnerability that couldn't be taught. She was born wanting—or needing?—to communicate through dance. What would happen if her dad silenced her ability? Keisha was right—it wasn't fair.

Anna retreated to her closet office and called Gabby.

"Hello." While Gabby was more serious than some of her friends, hearing the flatness of her voice made the seeds of worry Keisha had planted flourish in Anna's gut.

"Hey, Gabby. It's Anna Maitland. We missed you today. How are you feeling?"

"Fine. I mean, not great." A fake-sounding cough echoed in Anna's ear.

Anna swiveled back and forth in her office chair, not sure what tack to take with the girl. "Have you been to the doctor?"

"It's nothing serious. Allergies probably."

"Does that mean you'll be at the next practice?" At the lengthy silence that followed the question, Anna leaned forward and set her elbows on her knees. "Is there anything I can do to help?"

"With my allergies?" Gabby ranked around a seven on the teenage sarcasm scale.

"With your allergies or your . . . situation." Anna hoped her directness didn't blow up in her face.

"Look, I'm not sure about dancing anymore. It's not proper and stuff."

"You forget that I know how much you love to dance. I see it every time the music starts. You're talented. You can win Lass of the Games if you want it enough." Anna waited.

"Maybe I don't want it enough. I gotta go. Dad needs me." Gabby disconnected and Anna was left to wonder if she'd blundered by calling at all. While Anna was generally good at navigating the teenage minefield, Gabby's problem was more like an atomic bomb with an unseen trip wire.

Thankfully, she had her next classes to distract her. They flew by with the speed of enjoying a task. Finally, she was able to retreat to her small apartment above the studio for a shower, where her mind wandered into the brambles she'd managed to avoid. Mostly.

Iain Connors.

While he wasn't suave or handsome in a *GQ* model sense, he was arresting. His features were rugged and made more so by the jagged white scar trailing from his forehead over his left cheek and into his beard. A beard which couldn't hide the stubborn jut of his chin. Something about him struck her as primitive and elemental.

He was intimidating in both stature and demeanor. And ridiculously jacked.

Izzy hadn't mentioned how inconveniently hot the Highlander was. She had talked about how quiet and shy he was. How competent. A wizard with his hands, Izzy had said. *That* Iain had sounded perfect. Exactly the sort of man Anna could delegate menial tasks to while she handled organizing the Highland festival.

The Iain who had greeted her didn't seem quiet or shy. The jury was still out on competent, but he had taken charge of Ozzie with ease.

He'd called her Bo-Peep, but when he'd called to her from the window, her first thought was that she'd stepped into a reverse Rapunzel fantasy. Naked man in a high tower? *Yes, please.*

She'd tried not to squint to get a better view of his bare chest. Once he'd appeared outside, she'd tried to stop herself from staring at the way his black T-shirt had clung to muscles she was sure hadn't been covered in her high school biology class, but she'd never possessed the kind of puritanical self-control needed not to look.

Now, to torture herself further, she wondered if he was truly a wizard with his hands. If she continued down this path, she was going to need the shower wand for more than just washing away the day's sweat.

A plan. That's what she really needed. Or did she? All she really needed was for Rose and Gareth to keep their errand boy penned with the beasts.

After pulling on a tank top and shorts, she opened her laptop ready to compose the email she'd drafted in her head. Waiting in her in-box was a note from Rose informing her Iain was arriving to take delivery of a sheep and cow Gareth had leased, and reminding her to water her pots of flowers since they would be used on the stage as decoration during the competitions.

The information was too little, too late. She groaned. Rose's prized pots had been decimated by Ozzie. For a brief moment, she considered emailing Rose and going off about the inconvenience of the unexpected delivery, the shock of Iain appearing, and the destruction of her flowers. But she didn't.

Rose had enough to worry about. Instead, Anna returned several emails and made a couple of calls to vendors, then grabbed her keys. If she hurried, she could hit the nursery before they closed, and fix Ozzie's rampage of destruction.

An hour later, with her floorboards full of flowers and the sun setting behind the trees, Anna pulled onto the narrow lane to Stonehaven, her headlights a stage for the swarming, dancing bugs. She pulled to the side of the house so she could make her way around to the patio.

Lightning bugs rose in the field, and beyond them, the woods stretched like an endless black pool. Even though she had grown up in small-town Highland, she didn't consider herself a country girl. The silence and darkness had never inspired solace and calm, but a fear of the unknown.

The breeze played against the old house like a musician, the tinkle of the wind chimes accompanying the creaks. Sometimes it felt as if Stonehaven were alive. Or inhabited by ghosts.

Either way, Anna was creeped out. A shiver went through her, raising the hairs along her arms, in spite of the mild evening. If she hurried, she could be gone before full dark descended. She peeked in the barn, hearing the shuffle and snuffs of the animals. No sign of Iain.

With any luck, jet lag had caught up with him and her stealth flower planting would go unnoticed.

It took three trips to move the flowers from her car to the patio. She replaced the beheaded flowers with the new flowers pot by pot, working up a sweat by the end and wiping her face with the back of her arm as she surveyed her work. They looked good, but not as good as the originals. Hopefully, if she kept them watered, they would grow exponentially by the festival and provide a colorful backdrop for the dancers and pipers.

She gave the nearest pot a thorough soaking with the hose so the plant in it could make it to the next day without wilting. Her mind wandered to her fridge, where a slice of pecan pie from the Scottish Lass restaurant waited for her mouth. Pecan pie as dinner wasn't a bad thing, was it?

She moved on to the next pot and sighed, rotating her stiff neck. Every spare minute of her day was taken up by festival planning. She'd wasted too much time fumbling around the Buchanans' shorthand notes and learning the ins and outs. What might take Rose or Izzy fifteen minutes took Anna three times as long as she checked and double-checked, afraid of making an error.

In fact, first thing in the morning, she needed to verify the number of portable potties needed. The intestinal needs of hundreds of festivalgoers had never crossed her mind. Until now. Doing some quick math in her head, she tallied up one day's attendance and multiplied—

A noise had her spinning around, the water arcing around her in a weak defense. More than half the sun had fallen behind the trees now. Overhead, the orange streaks were being overtaken by a purpling sky. Gazing outward, she had to squint to see the shadowy monster looming in the middle of the field.

Her grip on the hose tightened and crimped the water into a spray. Logic inserted itself like a sliver. It wasn't Bigfoot; it was only Iain. She had nothing to fear, yet her jumbled insides sent flight impulses to her brain.

He drew within a few feet, and her heart stuttered for a different reason altogether. He was bare chested and barefoot, with a kilt covering the rest of the good parts, but if one believed the old sayings about the size of a man's feet, then his good parts were very good indeed.

"Anna." His rumbling brogue turned her name into something exotic.

"What are you doing here?" she asked.

His gaze narrowed. "I'm staying here, remember?"

She gave herself a mental kick. "Yes, of course. I meant, out here. And why are you wet?"

"I found a bonny glen in the woods with a stream. Perfect for a swim. It was hot as Hades today." He rubbed a hand through his hair and droplets slid over his shoulders and chest. She followed the path they made all the way down to the waistband of his kilt.

His very dry kilt. Which meant . . . "Were you skinny-dipping?" Her voice was squeaky and radiated outrage. Which wasn't at all how she felt. She felt like a blowtorch had been aimed at her body.

"Are you trying to finagle an answer to the age-old question of what a Scotsman wears under his kilt?" He crossed his arms over his chest, and while his expression remained serious, she sensed he was teasing her.

"What? No! I don't care what you have on—or don't have on—under there." Except now all she could think about was what was under his kilt. She needed a fan. Or a dunk in an ice bath.

He stepped closer, and Anna took a step back, keeping

distance between them. He halted, any humor emanating from him gone like a candle being snuffed. Between his thick black brows, dark beard, frown, and scar, he easily classified as formidable. Add in his height and he was downright scary. While she wasn't exactly afraid, neither could she name the emotion making her heart tap dance and her insides launch into a do-si-do.

Silence held them in limbo before he cautiously broke it. "I'm glad we ran across each other. We need to discuss the festival."

Already tired, her concentration was shot, faced with his partial state of undress and general demeanor. He, on the other hand, didn't seem thrown by her. Why would he be? The nicest thing she could say about her old tank top and ratty shorts was that they were comfortable.

"What about the festival?" She turned away to shut the water off and gather her wits. "We agreed you wouldn't involve yourself in the bulk of the planning."

"No. I understand you don't want me involved, but you obviously need help."

She wavered and hated the feeling. She possessed unparalleled confidence when it came to the dance studio. If kids sensed weakness, they would pounce with the swiftness and brutality of a mountain lion. Plus, her instincts in business hadn't steered her wrong. Her risk in taking out a loan to modernize the studio had paid off several times over.

It was other aspects of her life where she fought doubts. The people she'd grown up with in Highland expected her to be a certain way—comfortable in the spotlight and always ready with a quip—and usually she delivered. Sometimes, though, a lack of faith in herself snuck through the backdoor of her subconscious.

Not today, though. She refused to answer the knock. She'd faced down enough toddlers in tantrums and preteen angst to handle a single man. In fact, she could handle men like a blacksmith handled metal. "What exactly is your expertise beyond scooping poop?"

"Organization. Planning. Execution."

It could have been taken off a company logo, it was so generic. "I am in charge of the organization and planning. I could possibly use some help with the execution," she added the last so grudgingly as to be rude.

"In other words, you want a grunt to boss around."

"You got a problem with a woman in charge?" Anna narrowed her eyes, her upper lip curling.

"Not a bit, but I was given different instructions. The next three weeks are integral to the success of the festival. I plan to spend tomorrow getting myself up to speed, then I'll be happy to sit down over a cuppa and discuss my plans."

"*Your* plans?" She matched his stance, crossing her arms. "I have been intimately involved with the festival since I was a child. The plans to be put in motion will be mine."

"I plan to become *intimately* involved as well." Was that a tinge of humor she heard in his otherwise grumbly, unruffable attitude? "You need me."

"No I don't." Her knee-jerk response had shades of "I know you are, but what am I?"

Her disquiet with the situation was virulent, yet she wasn't sure why. Half-stitched costumes for the girls spilled out of the closet at the studio for her to tackle. The application to run for mayor of Highland still sat blank in her desk drawer. She was running herself ragged and could use the help, yet relinquishing responsibility felt too much like surrendering.

She'd watched her mom rely on her dad's promises and be disappointed over and over until finally her mom gave up. Anna had learned she could only count on one person. The one facing her in the mirror every morning. Everyone left for greener pastures, and if they didn't, Anna did a bang-up job driving them away.

One of his eyebrows quirked up in a way that conveyed dry sarcasm even as his rich brogue remained emotionless. "In that case, can I assume you'll be here at five tomorrow morning to see to Ozzie's and Harriet's needs?"

Five seemed an outlandish time, but she couldn't say it wasn't necessary. She made a throaty sound and wished she could pull out a set of 4-H credentials, but alas, she'd been a dancer and cheerleader in high school. Her knowledge of a cow extended only to how she liked her steak cooked.

Slapping on a "bless your heart" smile, she said blithely, "Ozzie and Harriet fall into the pooper scooper's domain. That would be you. The P.S."

Finally, he seemed ruffled and with gritted teeth said, "I am not a pooper scooper."

She raised her eyebrows leadingly and glanced away to hide her satisfied smile. "Whatever you say."

"Why don't we make plans to meet and discuss how we can divvy up the workload?" His voice brooked no argument.

Anyway, she couldn't come up with a single reason to shuffle him off. Rose and Izzy apparently expected them to work together as mother and daughter had for years, but Anna had no desire for her and Iain to become a well-oiled partnership. He would be gone in a matter of weeks. Even sooner, if Izzy had the baby in short order.

She would meet Iain, but on her terms and in her territory.

Iain braced for an argument or, even more unsettling, further teasing.

"You'll have to come to me. I have a toddler dance class first thing in the morning, a Mommy and Me movement class at eleven, and my teen girls in the afternoon." Anna ticked off her schedule on her fingers.

"Time and place." His clipped tone was due more to surprise at her acquiescence than any annoyance on his part.

"Twelve o'clock. Maitland Dance Studio on Main Street." Her tone was equally as brusque.

She set the hose down and ran a hand through her hair. It fell in a riot of waves a few inches past her shoulders. Her gesture left a smudge of dirt across her cheek.

Without considering the wisdom or the consequences, he brushed the dirt off with his fingertips. She jerked her head to the side as if his touch burned. He drew his hand into a fist and forced it to his side.

"What was that for?" she asked.

Not sure if it was fear or outrage coloring her voice, he could only produce some "achs" and "uhs" like a dobber before finally saying, "Dirt. Cheek."

She scrubbed her cheek with the heel of her hand as if trying to remove the layer of skin he'd deigned to touch.

"I apologize if I scared you." His brogue was thick with embarrassment. It was inevitable that he would make a doolally out of himself in front of her. She was just the sort of lass—beautiful, witty, and sharp-tongued—who ran circles around him.

"You surprised me is all. Why would you think I'm scared of you?"

"Because I could break you in two." Only when her eyes widened and she put a lounge chair between them did he recognize his joke had fallen short. Actually, his joke had taken a swan dive off a cliff. To a woman alone in the gloaming with a near stranger, he could see how his teasing declaration might come off as a threat. He attempted to backpedal, but stumbled over his words. "I wouldn't actually . . . I mean, yes, you're tiny and I could . . . but I would never hurt you. Or anyone, for that matter."

"I should hope not," she said smartly while maintaining her vigilant stance.

They entered a silent face-off for longer than was comfortable. He wanted to look away, but couldn't peel his eyes off her. She finally took a sidestep from behind the chair toward the line of pine trees separating her from her car.

"Alrighty then, I'll be going now. I'll see you tomorrow?" She cut him a look from the side of her eyes he couldn't interpret and muttered, "In public with witnesses."

He shuffled backward to give her space to escape. Just to make sure she got away safely, he trailed her to the trees and watched her taillights fade from view. Next on his agenda was an attempt to kick his own arse.

The only way he could have made a worse impression on Anna Maitland was to have— No, it couldn't have been worse. He muttered a string of Gaelic curses on his way to check on Ozzie and Harriet. Gareth had left him a bag of feed, but he would need more and soon.

While his expectations of a businesswoman with a stereotypical dancer's severity had been shattered, her coiled strength, vibrancy, and superhuman grace was undercut by a sense of exhaustion even her bravado couldn't mask. Navigating Highland would be easier with Anna's help, and whether she wanted to admit it or not, she needed him too. A sense of purpose lent a spring to his step.

He'd been adrift for more than a year and had thought—hoped—Cairndow would prove to be his rock, but only now did he feel like land was in sight.

Chapter Three

Iain overslept and blamed a combination of jet lag and dreams populated by a wild red-haired dancer in a tank top and short shorts. He wasn't proud of the romp his subconscious had taken while he'd been asleep and vulnerable. Would she take one look into his eyes and see the etchings left by his imagination?

It wouldn't do. He wasn't sure yet if she would be adversary or partner. Friend might have already been struck from the possibilities considering the events of the previous evening. He needed to have his wits in battle lines for their meeting.

Iain had spent time in deserts during his deployments, so the Georgia heat wasn't entirely foreign, but the humidity was like a boggart sitting on his chest and made it difficult to take a proper breath.

Isabel had insisted he drive her truck while he was at Stonehaven. It was a piece of . . . work. A red-and-black tartan pattern covered the bonnet and tailgate as well as two thick stripes down the sides. The rest of the truck was gunmetal gray with rust spots marring the fenders. While both admiration and horror arose, mostly he fought regret for not springing for a rental coupe.

Sliding onto the driver's seat, he opened the visor and caught the keys Isabel had left. The truck started with a grind of the engine that made his ears tilt toward the unharmonious sound. A well-tuned engine was like an orchestra. This was more like a garage band. He'd take a look under the bonnet later, but for now, he prayed the thing would carry him into town and back.

His regret took an exponential rise when the air-con did nothing to combat the heat. The air being pumped into the cab was sun scorched. He flapped his dark blue kilt and rolled down the windows. Even the shade was uncomfortable.

The tires crunched pea gravel on the truck's stuttering start. Trees lined the narrow private lane and dappled light danced across the arm he had crooked out the window. Rich scents of verdant greenery and wildflowers filled the cab. While pleasant, his nose twitched as if in search of the loam and salt of home.

The sea had been his lodestone and his anchor. While he relished and appreciated the life his da had given him at Cairndow, he wasn't sure he wanted the same. His da's expectations of passing the care of Cairndow to Iain as Gareth would pass the earldom to Alasdair had turned claustrophobic, and he didn't know how to extricate himself from his birthright without breaking hearts.

Iain took a deep breath, smelling freedom and opportunity. Had the Scottish settlers of generations past felt the same? Away from the rigid caste system of the aristocracy, the poor immigrants had had a chance to make their own way.

He turned onto the paved main road toward town. The trees gave way to scattered houses. One even had a stereotypical picket fence. The squeals of children playing in backyards and biking on side streets reached him and made him smile.

A decorative hand-painted sign with a cartoonish Scotsman playing the pipes welcomed him to Highland: THE HEART OF THE HIGHLANDS IN THE BLUE RIDGE. Beyond a four-way stop stretched a long street lined with colorful Scottish-themed restaurants and shops and pubs. Alasdair had done his level best to describe the place, but hadn't done it justice. It was over-the-top and ridiculous, and Iain couldn't decide whether he was appalled or bloody well loved the place on sight.

He traveled almost to the end of the street before finding a parking place in front of the Dapper Highlander. The mannequins in the window were kitted out in full Scottish regalia, signaling it was a tailor's shop.

He turned the truck engine off and sat in the cab for a few minutes taking in the vibe. Flowers overflowed baskets hung from wrought-iron light poles. People strolled up and down the sidewalks, some sipping on drinks, others licking ice-cream cones. They ducked in and out of shops. Almost everyone carried a shopping bag. Highland was a bustling little village.

A man in green-and-black-checked tartan trousers tucked into black Wellies turned in Iain's direction and squinted. He hopped off the curb and put both hands on the sill of the open cab window, ducking a little to smile a greeting.

"You must be Iain." The man exhibited such good-humored welcome, Iain smiled back.

"Yes, sir. Iain Connors."

"I'm Dr. Elijah Jameson. Local veterinarian and current mayor of Highland, although my tenure as leader of our fair town will soon be at an end." He stuck his hand through the window, and they proceeded to engage in an awkward shake. "When did you arrive?"

"Yesterday in the wee hours of the morning. I'm meeting Anna Maitland in a bit." Iain gestured at the door, and Dr. Jameson stepped back so Iain could exit the truck.

While Dr. Jameson was small in stature, his wiry strength was evident. His eyes twinkled and his mouth crooked into a smile when he looked up at Iain. "Well, aren't you a big boy?"

"Bigger than some, I'd say," Iain said dryly. He had spent his life as the biggest man in the room. If only size equaled confidence.

"I hope you'll have time to compete in the athletic events during the festival. You'll be surprised at the level of competition you'd face." Dr. Jameson steepled his hands and tapped his fingers together. "I'm the games manager, you know."

"Yes, Isabel mentioned that. She also mentioned your kickoff party the Friday before."

"The whisky ensures a good time." His graying eyebrows cocked over the black rim of his glasses. "I assume you and Anna will be performing the traditional opening of the games at the tasting?"

He had no idea what the traditional opening consisted of. The banging of a gong? The bleat of the bagpipes? "Erm. Of course, we will."

"Excellent. I'll make note of it. Seeing the truck, I thought for a second Izzy was home." Dr. Jameson patted the bonnet of the truck. Although a smile remained in place, a melancholy refrain weaved through his rich Southern accent. Between his clothes and his accent, it was as if Dr. Jameson wasn't sure whether he was playing William Wallace or Rhett Butler. "But I suppose Highland is no longer Izzy's home."

"Isabel speaks of Highland fondly." Iain felt the need to comfort the older man.

"We miss her sorely around here. The wedding looked lovely. Everyone in town was sharing the pictures."

"Aye. It was a lovely day." Actually, the day had been blustery with a sideways spitting rain pinging the windows and a draft whistling through the chimney in the drawing room straight up his best kilt, but the sentiment and affection between Isabel and Alasdair as they had exchanged vows had been warm and sunny.

"How's our girl feeling?"

"Poorly. She's on bed rest until she labors. She was happy to see her mum." At least, Iain had assumed her tears had been happy ones. Observing Alasdair comfort Isabel made Iain feel like he'd missed a pertinent lesson in school. Iain had sidled out of the room and tackled the less scary task of immunizing head-butting, biting, kicking sheep.

"Have time for a coffee? Or tea, if you prefer?" Dr. Jameson asked.

Iain checked his watch. "I have a quarter hour, as long as Maitland Dance Studio is nearby."

Dr. Jameson pointed down the street. "Just at the end on the left. The Brown Cow is on the way."

They walked shoulder to shoulder except when Iain gave way to let a clump of tourists by on the sidewalk. "Highland is a vibrant little village," Iain said.

"It is now. Downtown wasn't always like this, though. Thirty years ago, Highland was run-down with empty storefronts and no way to keep the young people from leaving for the bigger cities. It was rotting away from neglect and a lack of investment. Izzy's father was the one with the vision of what Highland could become. He hosted the first games at Stonehaven. It started small, but the promise of what it could be was obvious." Dr. Jameson opened the door to the Brown Cow Coffee and Creamery and gestured him to enter first.

Iain took a deep breath, the sweet scent of ice cream mingling with the richer undertones of coffee. It was heavenly. A line populated by families with kids had formed in front of the ice-cream station. Only one man stood at the coffee bar waiting for his order.

The woman behind the counter made a fancy coffee drink at one of the machines. Her messy ponytail was hot pink to complement her light pink T-shirt. She handed the drink off and shuffled to the counter to give them a gummy, wide smile.

"Hey-oh, Dr. Jameson. What can I do you for?" Her accent was different again from Dr. Jameson's and Anna's. It was coarser and more difficult to parse.

"Black coffee to go for me, Millie, thanks."

"And what about your friend here?" She flipped her ponytailed hair and gave Iain a pointed look under her lashes.

Iain was suddenly uncomfortable and not sure where to look.

"This is Iain Connors," Dr. Jameson said. "Would you prefer tea, Iain?"

"Yes, sir, a cuppa would be most welcome."

Millie inhaled with an *oh* sound. "You're one of them."

Iain tilted his head. "One of whom?"

"You know. A real live Highlander like Alasdair and Gareth." She smacked her gum and grinned at him.

"I'm Scottish, aye."

"That is so cool." She propped her elbow onto the counter and cupped her chin. Her stare had crossed from uncomfortable to awkward.

Without being able to stop himself, he touched the puckered, jagged scar with his fingers and ducked his head. Instead of saying the wrong thing, he often found it easier not to say anything at all. His method of silence wasn't foolproof, however, and had got him pegged as an unfeeling pillock more than a few times.

He wasn't unfeeling. Not in the least. He just wasn't comfortable expressing himself. His da loved him, of that there was no doubt, but he was stingy with his words. Gareth had been like an uncle, but he too wasn't known for his effusiveness. The closest thing he'd had to a mother was Mrs. Mac, and she showed love through food not words.

In short, he was an emotional knobhead, but a self-aware one at least.

"One coffee and one tea, Millie?" Dr. Jameson prodded with humor in his voice.

"Oh, right." Millie turned away to pour Dr. Jameson's coffee but cast enough looks over her shoulder, Iain worried she would overflow the cup and require medical attention. She handed the coffee over, then retrieved a to-go cup of steaming water and a basket full of individually wrapped tea bags. "Pick your poison."

"Thank you, lass." Iain snatched the first bag without looking and moved to the farthest table away to tear it open and let it steep.

"Gracious me, Millie is a character." Dr. Jameson shook his head.

"In what? A horror show? I hope I didn't scare her."

Dr. Jameson's laugh rumbled into a pensive frown. "More like a dark comedy. Her parents are ne'er-do-wells. Her brother stays out at their trailer playing video games as if it were his job. Millie's a smart girl who works hard and sees her Prince Charming in every single man who walks through the door."

Iain barked a laugh. He was no fairy-tale prince.

"I'd better get you down to Anna's studio." Dr. Jameson led the way onto the sidewalk. He leaned in as if telling a secret although his voice wasn't at a whisper. "I don't want to make Anna angry."

"Does she scare you?" Iain barely stopped himself from adding "too." Power coiled in Anna Maitland. He'd sensed it the day before but was only now able to name it.

"She's got a wicked tongue, although thankfully, she usually uses her wit for good." Dr. Jameson chuckled.

Before they made it a dozen feet down the sidewalk, a middle-aged woman in a flowing flowery caftan popped out of one of the shops and blocked their path with her arms akimbo.

"Dr. Jameson. Just the man I wanted to see. Did you get my message?" The woman didn't let him answer. "The rot is not going to fix itself. When can the city send someone out?"

"With all the building going on and the festival around the corner, it's been hard to line someone up, Loretta, but soon. I hope." Dr. Jameson shifted to include Iain. "Have you met Iain Connors? Iain, this is Loretta. The All Things Bright and Beautiful shop is hers."

Loretta turned her dark eyes on Iain as they exchanged a handshake. He had the feeling Loretta was not a person to cross. "Nice to make your acquaintance."

"You're here to help with the festival?" she asked.

"Aye."

When he said no more, Loretta turned back to Dr. Jameson. "I'll expect someone soon, Elijah. *Soon*."

Once Loretta had reentered her shop and they were several steps out of earshot, Dr. Jameson said, "The city bought up several buildings thirty odd years ago when they became vacant. Now we rent them, which means the city is responsible for exterior maintenance. Finding someone who has the skills and is available has been a royal pain in my tush as mayor."

"What's the rot encompass?"

"The outside doorframe in the back. It's not like the customers even see it."

"I could take care of it in a couple of hours." It was the sort of work Iain was used to at Cairndow. Fighting rot and the general upkeep of a castle hundreds of years old was a daily task.

"Won't you be too busy with the festival?"

Iain didn't want to admit he and Anna were at odds. "I can squeeze in a simple repair."

"I might have to come up with a creative way to pay you."

"It's fine." Iain hadn't been angling for money. Gareth was covering his room and board plus a tidy bonus for working on the festival.

"If you're sure you have the time, I'll let Loretta

know you'll be by this week to replace the frame." He and Dr. Jameson exchanged numbers, then Dr. Jameson pointed. "There's the studio. Five minutes early even. I have a skittish sheepdog showing up at the clinic any second, so I better skedaddle, but call me if you need anything. Anything at all."

After Dr. Jameson and Iain shook hands, Iain pushed into Maitland Dance Studio. The air-con washed over him like a blessed baptism. Light wood floors, white walls, and recessed lighting gave the impression of crisp elegance and serenity.

He was alone in a waiting area. One wall was devoted to selling various dance shoes from ballet to tap and costumes geared toward children. One rack exploded with different colored tutus, another with sober black, white, and nude colored leotards. Music crept through the walls. He sidled over and cracked open a door to peer through.

Chaos reigned, and in the middle of children running hither and yon stood Anna in a carbon copy of what she'd worn the day before. The rainbow-colored tutu looked much more at home in the studio than herding a wayward sheep. The "Hokey Pokey" blared over speakers set into the corners of the room. His heart wanted to join the fracas on the dance floor, and he tried to flatten himself paper thin as he slid through the door to watch Anna at work.

She spun around and clapped her hands, the different colors of tulle floating around her legs. Her hair was plaited, the thick braid hanging over her shoulder. She was smiling. He swallowed hard. He'd seen her frown and harrumph and press her lips together in disapproval, but not smile.

Anna Maitland's smile was something to behold. It crackled with energy and joy and an invitation to join her in the fun. If he had the talent of Robert Burns, he could compose an ode with the words tangling in his chest, but alas, as usual, he was left mute with the wonder.

Anna's smile hurt her cheeks. The Mommy and Me class consisted of a dozen toddlers running in all directions while their moms and a lone dad attempted to corral them into a circle for the Hokey Pokey. Normally, the antics made her laugh, but today, her focus was on the clock, where a ballerina's legs moved around the numbers in an impossible feat of flexibility.

A little girl with blond hair in pigtails tugged on Anna's rainbow-colored tutu, which retained an earthy scent from her adventures the day before. The kids didn't seem to mind. Anna scooped the girl up and propped her on a hip while they put hands in and then took them out as the song bade them do. Then, she danced the girl in a circle.

"Good job, Sophie." Anna squeezed the girl's nose and made a honking sound. Sophie giggled and squirmed. The kids made her feel like the funniest person on earth, which was a decent trade-off considering the general air of stickiness and the unmistakable waft of soiled diapers.

The "Hokey Pokey" was their finale song. Hopefully, she would have enough time to change into more professional attire for her meeting with Iain. She sent another glance toward the clock, but never made it. Her gaze got stuck on the man standing inside the door like he was tar to her Brer Rabbit. She checked him out head to toe before she could control herself.

One got used to seeing men in kilts around Highland. The Dapper Highlander was dedicated to selling them, after all, but the air conditioning wasn't strong enough for the sight of Iain Connors in a kilt. At least he had a shirt on today, otherwise she might have spontaneously combust.

He wore his utility kilt like it wasn't a special occasion. He wore it like a cowboy wore jeans. His legs between hem and socks were well-muscled, tanned, and hairy. Manly. It was the only word that fit. Actually, the word could be used to describe the rest of him as well from his broad shoulders to thick arms.

Her thoughts flitted once more to the age-old question. What was or wasn't he wearing underneath his kilt? She clutched her tutu and bit the inside of her cheek, shutting down the inappropriate wanderings of her thoughts. Why did he keep catching her in vulnerable scenarios? Bad luck and attractive men went hand in hand in her experience.

The dance studio was successful, and the festival hadn't gone off the rails as of yet. She had worked up the confidence just that morning to fill out the paperwork necessary to file for her intent to run for mayor of Highland. Of course, a bossy, intimidating, self-important man would stroll in and screw it all up. If she allowed him to. Which she wouldn't.

One of the kids tugged the back of her tutu and snapped the invisible tether between her and Iain. She turned away with a rush of relief to drop to a knee and give little Colin a hug. The parents gathered their bags in one hand and the children in the other and filed toward the door, their chatter reverberating around the room as Old MacDonald's quacking duck played them out.

Iain stood to the side like a stone sentinel, not acknowledging the curious smiles tossed his direction. His focus was entirely on her, and it was intense.

What was going on behind his stare? Was he assessing her strengths and weaknesses? Was he strategizing how to take charge of the festival? Perhaps watching her Hokey Pokey with a dozen toddlers had solidified in his mind that she wasn't capable of running the festival. Or the town.

She shook the thought clear. He didn't know of her ambition to run for mayor. No one did. But as soon as she filed her papers at city hall, word would spread throughout Highland like a virus. What would the response be?

Anna could almost hear the whispers in her ear. She wasn't old enough or good enough or smart enough. Damming her doubts behind a fake smile, she forced her shoulders back. She couldn't allow Iain to sense weakness.

She brought up the rear of the exiting parents and children, waving them out of the studio until she and Iain were alone. She cut off the music. The resulting silence was oppressive. Her mojo was off balance as if it had launched into a dozen pirouettes. Blindfolded. And drunk.

"You're early," she said as if it were an unforgivable sin.

"Promptness is generally regarded as a virtue."

She harrumphed, knowing it was ridiculous to chastise him over something she appreciated.

"I came to town, met Dr. Jameson, and we stopped for a drink." He held up the to-go cup she hadn't noticed.

"What did he allow?" she asked.

"I didn't ask his permission."

She blinked at his nonsensical response before making a small sound of realization. "Sorry, I forgot I'm speaking to a non-native. It's a way of asking what he had to say. I'm being polite. Or trying, anyway."

His brow scrunched. "Does that mean you actually want to know or don't?"

"I, uh, never mind." She waved her hand, wishing she could brush away the awkwardness. "Come into my office so we can talk."

She led the way and only realized her mistake when Iain joined her. Her office was the size of a walk-in closet because that's exactly what it had been at one time. A desk took up the bulk of the space. A laptop and a few folders graced the top. A file cabinet was jammed in one corner, which left her swivel chair on the working side of the desk and a kid-size school chair she used when a parent was late picking their child up from class on the opposite side.

She vacillated. Logic decreed that Iain wouldn't fit on the school chair. While humorous to picture, something would end up broken. Most likely the chair. Which left only one option. Anna would have to sit in the small chair and leave Iain in a position of power behind the desk.

Actually, she had another option. She could suggest neutral territory. She turned, not expecting him to be standing so close. Her nose was practically in his armpit. She sniffed. Even a hint of BO would have made him seem less formidable. Alas, his armpit smelled like fresh pine deodorant.

Anna clamped her arms tight against her body. She probably reeked after her classes this morning. Not that her armpits were as accessible as his. Why was she suddenly fixated on armpits?

"It's a little cramped in here. Have you eaten? We

could grab a sandwich over at the pub." When he didn't move or respond, she tilted her head back and took in the strong column of his throat, his trimmed beard, and the blade of his nose, before meeting his eyes. What she'd assumed was black was actually a warm, dark brown.

She blinked to clear her thoughts. It's not like she was asking him out on a date, for goodness sake. She was suggesting a business meeting. So why had nerves dried her mouth? She swallowed and darted her tongue over her lips. His gaze followed.

"Lunch?" she asked again, this time with a waver in her voice that she hated more than overcooked turnip greens.

"At a pub?" The corners of his lips sank into his cheeks as if a smile tried to break free of his restraint.

"The Dancing Jig pub. It's nothing fancy, but it's fast and has good food."

"A man has to eat."

"Okay, let me grab my purse." She turned and blew out a slow breath, bending over to retrieve her purse from the bottom drawer of her desk. It was only when she spun around and noticed his gaze had moved farther south than before that the state of her attire registered.

Resisting the urge to check what percentage of her ass cheeks was hanging out of her leotard, she said, "I need to change. Obviously."

"Yes, obviously." Red burnished Iain's skin above his beard, making the white line of his scar more pronounced. He cleared his throat and thumbed over his shoulder. "I'll wait in the front room, shall I?"

He retreated, and Anna couldn't help but stare at the way his kilt swung above the cut muscles of his calves.

Good Lord, she needed to sanitize her brain before it wallowed any deeper in dirty thoughts.

She'd been happily celibate so long, the spate of tingling feelings besetting her was a shock. An unwelcome one. Small town living meant an equally small pool of available men. Cull out the ones who were longtime friends or gay or unemployed, and she had no desire to go fishing. After her last boyfriend had left Highland for bigger and better opportunities, Anna hadn't been heartbroken. She'd been relieved. She had her own ambitions to focus on.

Cool professionalism was what would get her through the festival and a run at the mayor's office. She was doing her best to cultivate a sober, serious persona which was already difficult considering she was known more for her blue-ribbon dancing than political prowess.

She grabbed her phone and tossed a look at the door to the waiting area. It wasn't late in Scotland.

How's couch life? Anna typed before putting her phone on the corner of her desk and retrieving black slacks from a hanger in the costume closet.

Boring. I'm fat and emotionally needy and ready to get this alien out of me.

Anna chuffed a laugh. *Not long now.*

I'm scared. This was supposed to be the easy part.

No words of wisdom materialized. Settling down and having a family had never seemed part of Anna's future. She was a loner who had lots of acquaintances, but few friends. And right now, she missed her one and only true friend more than she could put into words. Tears stung as she fell back onto a platitude.

Everything is going to be fine. I'm glad Rose and Gareth can be there for you.

Me too. Has Iain arrived?

Yes. Her thumbs hovered over letters. How much—if anything—should she share with Izzy? The last thing she wanted was to worry her friend while she was already in a fragile state, physically and emotionally. Anna kept it simple. *We're having lunch today.*

You can count on him. He's a sticker.

A sticker? Anna smiled and shook her head. *The scratch-and-sniff kind?*

Heat prickled her face when she thought about leaning in to sniff his armpit. If Izzy had been there, she would have called Anna on it immediately.

Har-har. No, the kind you have no experience with.

Anna's hackles twitched. *What does that mean?*

Alasdair is here for my foot massage. TTYL.

Anna tapped her phone in her palm. What had Izzy meant? It had felt like a jab. Or knowing Izzy, more like a shove onto the path to enlightenment. Izzy had mostly kept her opinions of Anna's past boyfriends to herself, but the occasional sly comment had slipped out. It hadn't bothered Anna because the guys were temporary.

Loosening the ties of her tutu, she let it puddle around her feet and pulled on black slacks and a blue cotton blouse over her leotard. She checked her hair in a small mirror on the backside of the door, tucking escaped wisps back into her braid. Then, she shoved her feet into black ballet flats and with a moment's hesitation, sprayed herself with a citrusy body spray.

She slipped through the door into the waiting room, catching Iain unaware. He was fluffing the delicate tulle of a purple tutu and watching it float down.

"I can have one made in your size if you want a break from the kilt."

"*Magairlean.*" He spun around, and this time there was no question he was blushing. "You must have cat's paws for feet."

"What does that mean?"

"It means, I wasn't paying attention and didn't hear your approach." His face remained impassive.

"Not what I meant and you know it. Was that a Gaelic curse?"

His blush spread to the tips of his ears. "Aye, but not a proper one for a lady's ear."

"Ah, so you're a gentleman?" She was going to milk the upper hand as long as she had it.

"I try to be," he said with such earnestness, she felt almost bad for teasing him.

"If you don't tell me what that word means, I'm going to start using it with my toddlers. Get your *magairlean* over here, Tammy." Her butchered pronunciation brought a twinkle to his eyes.

"Tammy wouldn't have *magairlean*. It refers to a man's . . ." He gestured toward where a sporran might hang if he was wearing one.

"Fanny pack?"

A laugh sputtered out of him, catching her by surprise. It was deep and chesty and melodic. "Only lasses have fannies in Scotland."

"Are we speaking the same language?" She couldn't help but smile in the presence of his laugh.

"I'm not sure." His laugh petered into an awkward silence. He cleared his throat and turned to the skirt once more. "I was merely admiring the work. Difficult fabric to sew with, I imagine."

Now it was her turn to blush. It was as if they were

lobbing a hot potato of disquiet and nerves back and forth. "It's not so bad once you get used to it."

He shot her a surprised look. "You made these?"

"All the tutus and skirts. I enjoy it. I can buy leotards cheaper wholesale." She half shrugged. The tutus and skirts were priced at cost, and she'd given away more than she could count. Some of her girls wouldn't be able to dance in the recitals, march in the parades, or compete otherwise. She didn't want any girl to feel less than or left out just because her family couldn't afford fancy costumes.

His callused fingers plying the delicate fabric and satin ties were incongruous. He moved with an assured grace not common among big men, and she was reminded of Izzy's assessment. If Iain Connors was a wizard with his hands, what magic could he work on her bare skin?

No. She halted her thoughts and stamped them out before they could erupt into a wildfire not even the entire Highland volunteer fire department could contain. Redirecting her thoughts, she asked, "Do you sew?"

"Aye. Burlap, canvas, and leather these days, but I had to learn how to let the hems out of my trouser legs and mend shirts when I was a lad. That's crude work compared to this."

"Did your mother sew?" she asked.

"I . . . don't know. She was a village lass not made for the isolated life at Cairndow. She pulled a runner when I was a wee thing and never looked back. I don't remember her, but it's fine."

Damn, damn, and more damn. It wasn't fine, and Anna knew it wasn't fine, because her dad had done the same thing. She'd been old enough to remember him and the epic fights between him and her mom. Did that make the situation better or worse?

She opened her mouth, then pressed her lips back together and forced her gaze away from him. Talking about her dad was off-limits. It had been since she was ten and her mom told her never to mention his name again under her roof.

Chapter Four

The sudden change in Anna's demeanor left Iain flummoxed. A door had slammed shut—a reinforced metal one with a dozen locks—and he wandered the silence with no clue how to reestablish the tentative connection.

"Are you hungry?" he asked. Refreshments were neutral ground.

"I'm always hungry. Come on." She led the way out the door, and her defensiveness dissipated.

Or had her defenses been incinerated by the oven-like and oppressive heat? "Is it always this blasted hot in the summer?"

She tossed a smile over her shoulder. Although not as carefree and joyous as her earlier smile, it still struck him like a punch to the chest. "Usually hotter. This is a cool spell."

He prayed she was teasing him. They strolled down the sidewalk under an overhang that provided a scant amount of shade. Loretta swept out of All Things Bright and Beautiful and blocked their path like a witch demanding a sacrifice to pass.

"Anna, how lovely to see you." The woman's voice was nearly a purr, but it lacked any warmth.

"Lovely to see you as well, Loretta." All of a sudden the uber confident, intimidating Anna regressed a decade. Her shoulders hunched as she gestured toward him. "This is—"

"Iain. How nice to see you again so soon." Loretta offered Iain a hand as if he were meant to kiss it.

As he wasn't one to swear fealty, he took her hand in a brisk shake and merely nodded.

"I'm glad Anna has someone to help her with the festival. I fear it will prove to be too much on top of everything else. No one wants to see the festival suffer." Except Loretta's tone led Iain to believe she did want Anna to stumble and fall.

"I can assure you the festival was in excellent hands before I ever arrived. Now, if you'll excuse us." He put a hand on Anna's lower back, which was as stiff as a plywood board and guided her around Loretta, who hadn't moved as if unwilling to cede the field after a skirmish.

"You didn't have to do that, but I appreciate you having my back," Anna whispered as soon as they were out of earshot.

Before he could answer, she hopped down the curb and skittered across the street. He got held up by passing cars, but bounded across to join her in front of the Dancing Jig pub. Her black trousers and demure blouse seemed like a costume versus the rainbow tutu and leotard. She held the door open and gestured him inside. He narrowed his eyes, but didn't protest.

A puff of air-con welcomed him inside, and the dark wood interior made him feel right at home. The bar was a square in the middle and surrounded by tables. The semicircle of a stage was set up in the far corner with amps and microphone stands and other musical paraphernalia.

A majority of the tables were occupied, and the hum of conversation filled the room. The encounter with Loretta seemed to have nudged them out of their awkward posturing about who was in charge, at least for now.

"Y'all grab a seat. I'll be over in a jiffy to take your orders." A young girl aimed a frazzled, but chipper smile in their direction.

Anna led them to a table toward the back, where the natural light from the windows had been absorbed by the dark wood, leaving them in premature shadows that felt strangely intimate. Iain did a shuffling dance between the chair next to her and the one across the table. Considering a serrated steak knife stuck out of the flimsy-looking napkin, he chose the seat farthest away.

Anna glanced up as if surprised to see him sitting across from her. "Why does Loretta make me feel like a misbehaving five-year-old in church?"

Iain folded his arms on the table. He wasn't sure whether she was asking rhetorically or not, but he gave her question due consideration. "You grew up in Highland, yes?"

"Born down at the community hospital." She propped her elbow on the table, hunched over, and rested her chin in her palm.

"And have you known Loretta for most of your life?"

"She and Mom were good friends. I don't think she approves of the changes I've made to the studio. Like it was a betrayal of my mom."

"You see yourself through her eyes and act accordingly," he said simply.

"What does that mean?"

"The woman who stood before Loretta today is not the same one I've come to know. You're not five years old anymore." It was easy for him to say, but one step into Mrs. Mac's kitchen at Cairndow and he regressed to childhood. For him, though, he welcomed the simplicity of being mothered by the only mother he'd ever known.

"My head agrees with you, but reasoning with the five-year-old kid who lives in here"—she tapped her chest—"is impossible."

"It must be difficult dealing with people who you've known since you were young."

"I do fine with most everyone else. It's her. Loretta Edgerton."

"What sort of offensive changes have you made to the studio? Did you add a stripper pole class?"

As hoped, he coaxed a tiny smile out of her. "I can only imagine how many sermons Preacher Hopkins would aim in my direction if I did something like that. Nothing so scandalous. I updated and redecorated. Added a hip-hop class. Honestly, I think her disapproval has more to do with my personality. I'm not demure or quiet or particularly ladylike."

A chuckle snuck out of him before he could worry it might offend her, but she cast him a half smile through her lashes. "Demure, you are not," he said.

"Maybe Loretta fears I'll corrupt the young girls of Highland."

"If the young girls of Highland turn out to be anything like you, I wager you'd be doing them a favor."

She tilted her face so their gazes clashed head-on. What did she see? Most women saw a taciturn loner who qualified as a decent bed warmer for a night, never as a man with depths to plumb and appreciate. He had let himself be used in order to beat back his loneliness. Did that mean, in reality, he had used them? It was a thought he would need to examine later, preferably over a dram of whisky.

A waitress appeared and plunked down two waters. Anna ordered a club sandwich and fries, and Iain held up two fingers when the waitress raised her eyebrows at him.

"I'll have it out in a few, y'all." The woman retreated and left a trough of silence behind.

Strangely, it didn't make Iain squirm in his seat or break out into a sweat. Perhaps it was the unorthodox manner in which they'd met, but any polite barriers had been bulldozed.

"I'm sorry I snapped at you yesterday. It was the surprise of having to deal with the animals." Her shudder was exaggerated. "And also what you represent."

"What's that? An outsider?" A hint of bitterness snuck into his voice. He'd been cast as the outsider the first time he'd stepped into the village school at aged five. Cairndow had been the only place he'd ever truly fit in, but his life there had shrunk like a wool jumper in the dryer.

"No. Doubt that I can be a success on my own." Her gaze was on the table, where she traced a scar in the wood top with her finger.

He touched the scar on his face as if her touch could transmute to him. "Rose and Isabel sent me to help you."

"Because they think I can't handle planning the festival."

Underlying the general air of hurt feelings was something else. Panic? Desperation? "Isabel didn't plan the festival alone. She had her mother. Going it alone is a fool's errand."

"So I'm a fool?" Anna barked a self-depreciating laugh. "Maybe you're right."

"You're far from being a fool, but at a guess, you're stretched thin."

"I'm fine. The festival is fine. Everything is fine and under control, and I don't need your help. Except with the animals."

Their sandwiches arrived, and Iain was glad of the American portions. He was famished. The pantry and fridge at Stonehaven were bare of perishables. He took huge bites that made conversation impossible for long minutes and mulled over her adamant declaration. She was fine, was she? "Fine" was a word one used to plaster over all the nicks life doled out. It was rarely reality.

Many capable women had crossed his path over the years and earned his admiration, but he hadn't fared so well with them. He'd hung bookshelves, changed the hinges of janky doors, and leveled the legs of a kitchen table because comely lasses had asked him to. His attentions had never led to their hearts, only their appreciation.

Neither friendly nor professional, the give-and-take with Anna failed categorization. He was fascinated and wished he weren't. It would lead nowhere because they didn't share any common ground. They didn't even share the same country.

After decimating half his sandwich and making a dent in his hunger, he wiped his mouth with his napkin and leaned toward her. "I can't *not* help you. I was given a task and won't return to Cairndow as a failure."

Their gazes held for a long moment until she gave an unladylike snort. "Good lord, are all Scots as stubborn as you are?"

"I'm my own man."

Her gaze flitted over him, and his biceps clenched.

"No doubt." She picked up her sandwich but before taking a bite, said, "I'll come up with something for you to do. Are you happy?"

He wasn't sure if he was happy, but he was having bloody good fun for the first time since he could remember. They ate in silence, but their gazes kept meeting, holding, then bouncing away. After cleaning his plate, he wiped his hands on the napkin, sat back, and looked around him.

The pub had a vibe of youth and energy he hadn't expected. In fact, Highland itself buzzed with a vitality starkly opposite the tiny village outside of Cairndow. Glasgow and Edinburgh had drawn most of the young people away. It was too hard to make a living on the hardscrabble cliffs.

The village depended on Cairndow to bring in tourists, which it did during the summer months. When the weather turned harsh and forbidding, and snow made passing the roads difficult without a four-by-four, a gloom settled over the village and the people.

"What are you thinking?" Her question took him aback. Had he ever been asked for his thoughts?

"I'm contrasting Highland with the village outside Cairndow."

"How do we stack up?" Curiosity and defensiveness battled in her voice.

"Highland is alive."

"Is the village at Cairndow populated by zombies or

something?" Her dry wit made the corners of his mouth twitch.

The reality, unfortunately, wasn't a joke. "It was a thriving fishing village at one time, the trade passed down from father to son for generations, but it's cheaper to import fish nowadays. The old ways have dwindled to a few hardy souls and not many young ones. Most leave to take jobs in the bigger cities."

"Highland used to be like that." Anna pointed toward the street. "Empty storefronts, a fall in the population. Atlanta was growing by leaps and bounds and offered opportunities Highland couldn't compete with. Izzy's dad came up with the idea of the festival. The town council jumped on it and rebranded the town as Scotland in the South."

Her assessment mirrored what Dr. Jameson had said. "I hope Isabel can work the same magic at Cairndow."

"She's told me about the honey and jams." Anna poked a fry into a puddle of catsup, but didn't eat it.

"I built the hives and helped put in the greenhouse and berry bushes."

"Izzy said you were"—Anna cleared her throat—"good with your hands."

Alasdair watched a blush creep up her neck and into her cheeks with fascination. What had embarrassed her? He glanced over his shoulder to identify the instigation point, but the scene remained mundane. He shrugged.

"I can't remember a time when I wasn't puttering or building something. Da kept me with him even when I was a babe. There's a picture of me swaddled in a wheelbarrow at his side." The picture was a testament to his da's devotion, and the pang of missing him was physical and sharp. Iain rubbed his chest.

"Your dad sounds amazing." Was the wistfulness in her voice part of his imagination?

"He is a man of few words, but I never doubted his love." Iain pretended to pick at a loose string on his kilt to hide the flush of emotion pulling an embarrassing wetness to his eyes. "I left him with his hands full of Isabel's projects. He's learning how to keep bees. He grumbles at the changes, but I think he's secretly loving every minute. He's got a spring to his step I haven't seen in quite some time."

"Cairndow sounds idyllic."

"I could say the same of Highland." He turned the thought over in his head. "But no such place exists, does it? Life has its challenges anywhere, and you only pack your troubles with you wherever you go."

It was a philosophy he should heed himself. Why did he blame Cairndow for his discontent? Happiness wasn't something one found and possessed; it manifested from within. Why then couldn't he manifest it at home?

"I know you're right." She swirled her catsup into a pattern, officially playing with her food. "I left Highland after high school, but I came back."

A story lived between the two bookends. One he was sure had altered the way she viewed life in fundamental ways.

"I left Cairndow after secondary school but ended back where I started as well." Like Anna, he had been fundamentally changed by all the events encompassed in the small conjunction.

"Maybe all the songs are wrong." She finally transferred her attention from her catsup masterpiece to his face.

"What songs?"

"The ones warning you that you can't go home again. I came home, and I'm perfectly fine." There was that word again. "Fine." After seeing the real thing, he knew the lightness of her smile was fake.

She wasn't being truthful with him—maybe not even with herself—but as they'd only met the day before over a wayward sheep, he hadn't earned her truths. "I'll wager you weren't the same when you came home. You'd changed, but were lucky enough that Highland welcomed the changes."

"You are not what I expected, Iain Connors." She checked the screen on her phone. "I've got to get back to teach my next class."

He didn't have a chance to request a list of her expectations and how he had fallen short. She shoved her chair back and strode to the bar. It was only when he caught the flash of her charge card that he realized she was paying for their lunch.

"You should let me—"

The glance she gave him over her shoulder withered his words. This was a woman who was letting him know in no uncertain terms that she didn't require him in any way.

He matched her pace on the sidewalk. "We didn't discuss how to divvy up the work on the festival."

"Let me think on it, and I'll let you know when I need you. In the meantime, you can hang out at Stonehaven, take care of Ozzie and Harriet, and binge some TV shows or catch a tan or something." Anna looked both ways then trotted across the street, giving the truck who'd slowed down a wave and receiving a friendly toot in response.

Iain stayed on her heels, not willing to allow her to

escape so easily. She came to a sudden stop on the curb and whirled around on him, leaving him at street level. She was still shorter than he was.

Anna snapped her fingers in his face. "You know what would be a big help? You could water Rose's flowerpots. Ideally, they need to be done daily. Can you handle that?"

He'd built a bloody greenhouse that winter. "Which way do I turn the spigot to make wet stuff come out?"

She chose to ignore his rampant sarcasm. Her smile was brilliant, her voice sickeningly sweet. "Righty tighty. Lefty loosey. Do you need me to write that down for you?"

He answered with a glare that had sent battle-scarred men running for cover. Instead, she preened, proud of pricking his anger, and said, "I'll need to drop by in the morning to work on some stuff Izzy left on her computer for me."

"Is that fair warning for me not to water the pots naked?"

She blinked dumbly, her self-satisfied smile of a moment earlier wiped clean. Now it was his turn to hide his satisfaction at ribbing her behind a bland expression and fake acquiescence. "As you've made it clear, you don't require my help at the moment, therefore I'll cede the field."

Of course, he planned to do no such thing, but military tactics notwithstanding, there was a time to retreat and regroup, and this seemed to qualify.

He sketched a small bow, turned on his heel, and strode down the sidewalk. He'd never been one for sitting on his bum and watching the telly. Probably because his da hadn't kept a telly in the cottage.

The barn needed improvements, the stock would need

proper pens, and he'd noticed a loose hinge on the French doors leading to the patio. There was plenty he could do while he worked on Anna and prepared for their next exchange of fire. A sense of anticipation added a spring to his step and a smile to his face.

Chapter Five

The next morning, Anna parked at the front door of Stonehaven. Izzy's old truck was nowhere to be seen. It was Saturday. Had Iain taken her advice and gone sightseeing? Not having him around distracting her with his glares and growls would be a godsend. The sharp pinch of disappointment made no sense.

Nothing made sense when Iain was around. It was like he scrambled her radio signals and left her interpreting smoke signals. Yes, she found his gruff, tough demeanor attractive, and yes, he was built like a brick house, but that didn't explain the thrill she got from seeing his lips quirk into the ghost of a smile as they sparred.

Paying for their lunch had been more delicious and satisfying than the actual food. Instructing him on how to work a faucet had been even better. But then he'd countered her jab with one of his own. Her sleep had been interrupted more than once by lurid dreams in which Iain had been buck naked wielding his own personal garden hose.

Her mind had rendered an image so detailed, she was

sure Iain would be able to see it in her eyes. If he even saw the trailer of the PG version of her dreams, her only option would be to die of embarrassment. Even though the AC was still blasting from her car vents, she took a file folder from the passenger seat and fanned herself.

It was like she was sixteen years old again and driving by a crush's house. Not that she was crushing on Iain. A crush was too adolescent for what was brewing. No, she was lusting after him, which was perfectly understandable given the facts. Which were: One, she hadn't had sex in more months than she had fingers. Two, Iain had a sexy accent. And shoulders and chest and legs and hands. Three, she hadn't had sex in *months*. That bore repeating, because this crush-lust-obsession boiled down to one thing.

Anna was horny.

She would stop by Highland Drug and Dime for an economy pack of batteries for her vibrator on the way home. That would solve her problem in the long term. In the short term, she would hope Iain didn't return while she worked in Stonehaven's home office. If it became a lingering issue, she would move every file and both computers to her not-so-spacious studio office.

Anna tiptoed into the house and bypassed the Buchanans' spacious and comfortable office to take a gander out the back door. Iain wasn't watering the pots. Not that she had expected him to be naked, but a girl could dream as she had spectacularly proved the night before.

In case he'd parked out of sight and was in the shower—naked, of course—she cocked her head and listened, hearing only the ticking clock on the mantle. The house gave off solitary vibes. The layer of dust over the side table would have given Rose Buchanan fits if she could see it, but Anna didn't have time to clean. She had to tackle a slew of phone calls, confirming details or finagling deposits out of tightfisted or absentminded vendors.

She took a step backward, and as she was turning, a flash of movement outside caught her eye. Squinting, she scooched closer to the window. Had it been a deer or the wind in the trees?

It was neither. A man had emerged from the barn. Anna's blood quickened. A pair of binoculars for bird-watching lay on the dusty side table. She popped the caps from the lenses and held them up, the blur of movement coming into sharp focus.

Once again, he was bare chested. Did the man not own enough shirts? Did he not care about the health of her heart or other body parts?

Unlike their other encounters, he was unaware of her examination, and she took full advantage. His torso wasn't cut into lean muscled lines likes, magazine models', but was thick and strong in a way that spoke of hard work and not a gym. Neither was he hairless like so many men nowadays.

The tailgate of the truck stuck out from the far side of the barn. Iain strode toward it and pulled planks of wood from the bed, heaving them onto his shoulder. He wore a kilt once more, but this one was a more traditional weave of soft green and browns. His hair was damp with sweat, the dark ends curling around his ears and a lock falling over his forehead.

She adjusted the focus on his face. She catalogued a high forehead, heavy brows over long-lashed eyes, a prominent nose that was crooked at the bridge, and a dark beard framing lips that were neither thin nor fleshy.

Rather than marring his looks, his scar emphasized his ruggedness.

It was the same face she'd sat across from in the pub, yet different somehow too. His expression was unguarded. In assumed solitude, the tight rein he kept on his emotions had loosened. Iain was worried and weighed down by his thoughts, and she wondered where his mind wandered.

What had he left behind in Scotland? Did he have a wife or girlfriend urging him home? Was he merely fulfilling a favor to the Blackmoors? Uprooting and coming to the States to help with a small town festival seemed excessive. Was he running from something . . . or someone?

The thought gave her pause. She felt like she was taking something from him without his knowledge. As she was about to put the binoculars away, his gaze arrowed across the field to where she stood at the window, and the eye contact though the zoomed-in binoculars sent a jolt of energy whizzing through her body.

Muttering a curse, she slammed the binoculars down on the side the table and hid in the folds of the curtains. With her heart tap-dancing in her ear, she peeked around the curtain. He was stalking across the field.

Any hope he hadn't seen her ogling him like a horny freak died a quick death as she skip-ran to the office. Her foot caught in the hall runner, and she went down hard on her right knee. Ignoring the pain, she scrambled up and skidded on the hardwood flooring as she made the turn into the office.

Scooching behind Izzy's desk, she worked to regulate her breathing and stared unseeing at the paper she'd grabbed off the top of a stack.

The back door opened and closed, and footsteps creaked the old floors. Iain was a big man—tall and broad and muscular. She'd make all sorts of noises if he was on top of her too. A huff of frustration escaped. Iain on top of her was not an image she needed to have flashing in her head at the moment. His footsteps grew louder. She tensed and stared unblinking at the paper, her eyes burning.

"What are you working on?" Iain's rich baritone reminded Anna of dark chocolate—sweet but with a bite.

Slowly, she raised her gaze. He'd located a T-shirt in a forest-green color. She wasn't sure if she was disappointed or relieved.

"I am working on . . ." She had to look back down at the paper and scan it, ". . . a site map for the portable potties."

He propped a shoulder on the doorjamb and crossed his arms. "Titillating stuff."

Was he teasing her? Something in the way his mouth was set made her think he was. "It's a detail people only notice if things don't go well. What are you working on?"

"Nothing."

"That's a lot of wood for nothing."

One of his eyebrows rose, instantly turning his expression mocking. It was his superpower. "You *were* spying on me."

Anna shuffled papers around on the desk. "No, I wasn't. I was bird-watching, and you happened to get in the way." Not that her excuse was believable as is, but the fire creeping up her face only undermined her credibility as an amateur ornithologist.

He made a sound between a grunt and a hum, the noise dripping with disbelief. Instead of leaving her alone, he meandered farther into the office to peruse the corkboard wall covered with snapshots from festivals of years past.

"The festival looks like a ripper of a good time." He sounded serious and even admiring.

"The whole point is for people to have fun. And spend their money, of course."

He shot her a raised eyebrow over his shoulder before returning his attention to the pictures. She fiddled with a silver letter opener with a funny-looking gnome squatting under a giant mushroom. Or maybe the mushroom was normal sized, and it was the gnome that was tiny.

Iain took a photo off the board and turned slowly, glancing between it and her. Without waiting for him to ask the question hovering between them, she stood and plucked the picture out of his hands. "Yes, it's me."

In the picture, she was sixteen. It had been the first festival dance competition she'd won with a solo performance. The picture captured her mid-leap, her hair like a sunburst around her head. Much to her mother's dismay, she'd forgone the pinned fat, fake curls of many Celtic dancers, and her dance had been more innovative than traditional.

Her dress had been understated compared to the rest of the entrants'. She had merely worn a black leotard and an emerald-green, gauzy. wraparound skirt. She'd wanted to blaze her own trail and hadn't been afraid to take risks. She'd do it her way or go home empty-handed. She'd placed first.

How much of her attitude had been brash confidence and how much a rebellion against her mom's more traditional methods? She stared at the photo as if seeing a stranger and touched her face, although her expression was lost to time. Where had her confidence gone? Had time and experience worn it away like the sea to stone?

"*We twa hae run about the braes, and pou'd the gowans fine; But we've wander'd mony a weary fit, sin' auld lang syne.*" His voice was deep and sonorous and held her enthralled even though she didn't understand half of what he'd recited.

"'Auld Lang Syne.'" She parroted the recognized words.

"Aye. Robert Burns. Not his finest, in my humble opinion, but fitting for your thoughts, me thinks." His choice of words and cadence matched the old-fashioned lyrics.

"Braes are hills, but what the heck are gowans?" She took a step toward him, holding the old picture of herself over her heart.

He smiled a real smile. The first she'd seen him offer, and it was like a light flipped on inside of him. His brown eyes sparkled with unexpected charm. His teeth were white, the bottom center two overlapping. It made him seem more real to her.

"Gowans are flowers. Daisies, if you want to put a fine point on it."

She held the picture out to him. "I suppose I have wandered many weary miles since that was taken."

He tacked the picture back into the blank space it had occupied and ran a finger over her form. "You make it sound as though you're old and worn, when you are far from it."

She froze, not sure how to take his words and the sudden blast of intimacy. It wasn't the first time she'd sensed an unexpected connection between them. The first time had been when he confessed his mother's absence from his life. What could she do but ignore the push-pull?

Forcing her voice to a lightness she did not feel, she said, "If I didn't know any better, I'd think you doled out a compliment."

She sat and busied herself in the stack of papers, reaching for the cordless phone and refusing to engage any further with him.

At the sound of his retreating footsteps, she looked up, only to meet his gaze where he'd paused at the foot of the staircase. Even with the distance between them, she could sense the power of him. He was lightning and she quaked with an internal thunder. It felt melodramatic, yet fear leapt. Not fear of his physicality, but because she recognized something of herself in him. A restlessness. A desire for chaos. A need to feel out of control.

As soon as he was out of sight and she heard a door close upstairs, she dropped her head and banged it against the desk. No. This was not happening. Not right now with the festival bearing down on them like a train and her ambition to run for Highland mayor. She needed to maintain the image of upstanding businesswoman and not indulge in the kind of fling that would lead nowhere good.

The shower turned on upstairs, the trickle of water through the pipes distracting her. She stared at the ceiling for so long, her neck grew a crick. It was painfully obvious she would get no work done with Iain gallivanting around without a shirt on or reciting poetry or showering.

Anna gathered the list of numbers she needed and climbed into her oven-like car with a hint of guilt. She was leaving Iain, a stranger in a strange land (because as much as she loved Highland, it qualified as strange) to fend for himself.

If he hadn't been borderline nice earlier, she wouldn't be hesitating with her foot hovering over the gas pedal right now. Her Southern ancestors would be turning over in their graves at her lack of hospitality. Not to mention what Izzy and Rose would have to say on the matter.

No, he was a grown man who was imminently capable of taking care of himself. She made a wide turn in the graveled loop leading up to Stonehaven and headed toward the Brown Cow for a bracing cup of coffee and a table to work at, trying not to consider how a fling with Iain might leave one of them (him—never her) emotionally wrecked, but sexually (very) satisfied.

Iain spent longer than normal in the shower, maxing out the cold water tap, and pulled on a pair of jeans and a T-shirt. He shivered in the air-con as cold water droplets from his hair trailed down his back. Even in Scotland, quoting a Burns poem in casual conversation when it wasn't New Year's Eve or at a Burns Night Feast was an oddity, but he hadn't been able to help himself when the look of nostalgia crossed her delicate features, pulling her mouth into a sad pout.

The energy and verve of a young Anna had been caught in the snapshot, but still it was a pale facsimile to the woman. Looking at the picture, he sensed Anna hadn't drawn on fond memories but lost herself in the thorny brambles between then and now.

He padded downstairs and stopped in the entryway. She was gone. He knew before he pulled the drapery aside to see the graveled front driveway empty.

Now what? He'd unloaded the wood, but planned to

wait until the evening offered some respite before continuing his project in the barn. Even if he could figure out the numerous remotes, he wasn't the type to sit around and watch the telly.

Feeling unaccountably nervous, he retrieved Dr. Jameson's number and rang him up. The conversation was easier than he anticipated due to Dr. Jameson's innate friendliness, and Iain readily accepted the doctor's invitation to meet at the Scottish Lass restaurant for lunch.

Stepping into the restaurant brought another spate of nerves, and Iain scanned the crowded room for Dr. Jameson, spotting him waving from a back corner. Instead of a one-on-one meal, Iain found himself in a gathering of Highland residents, mostly over the age of sixty.

The menu was full of meat and vegetables, some familiar, some not. Iain followed Dr. Jameson's example and ordered the meatloaf along with a variety of vegetables, including fried okra. The meatloaf reminded him of a hearty Scottish pudding even though it was baked and not steamed. He decided the okra must be an acquired taste like haggis.

The talk centered heavily on the weather and how it would impact local crops and the festival.

"Too soon to say, of course, but the Farmer's Almanac calls for rough weather during festival weekend." An older man in denim overalls pulled a worn, rolled copy of a book out of his back pocket.

Dr. Jameson made a scoffing sound. "For goodness sake, Winston, that almanac is a load of bull. It was probably written by a random event generator on some computer in New York City."

Winston drew in a sharp breath then pinched his lips

together, refusing to acknowledge Dr. Jameson's opinion or presence. The tension was cut by the entrance of a man who looked to be around Iain's age. He was blond and tall and stopped at the hostess's stand to scan the crowd.

His gaze zeroed in on their group, and he weaved his way through the tables. "Sorry to interrupt, gentleman. Dr. Jameson, we need you out on the farm, if you're available."

"I'm always available. It's part of the job. What's the trouble?" Dr. Jameson wiped his mouth and stood.

"Calving difficulties, as we expected." The blond man had a tight, worried set to his mouth.

"Right-o. I've got everything I need in the truck. Holt, I want you to meet Iain Connors. Izzy and Alasdair sent him over to help out with the festival." Dr. Jameson waved a hand between the two men, and Iain half-rose to shake hands with Holt.

"Pleased to make your acquaintance," Iain murmured.

"I'm glad I ran into you. Gareth and I were talking before he left about my farm providing some of the animals for the livestock exhibition. Nothing fancy, but we've got some goats and piglets. A few chickens. Could you come by tomorrow after church so we could talk?" Holt ran his hands down the front of his jeans, obviously anxious to get Dr. Jameson back to his farm.

Iain found himself anticipating telling Anna. Providing a spark and watching her spirit come alive was becoming additive. "I'd be happy to. Already have a Highland cow and a blackfaced sheep in the barn at Stonehaven. I'm working on display pens right now."

Iain and Holt exchanged numbers, then Iain sat back down to finish his lunch, the conversation buzzing around him. While he felt no pressure to join in, he found himself making small talk about his life at Cairndow. A tap on his shoulder brought him around to face the man sitting at the table directly behind him.

"Hello. Name's Robert Bradshaw. I couldn't help but overhear. You play the guitar?" The man had floppy, light brown hair and a wide, guileless smile. A natural enthusiasm made him seem boyish, although he was pushing thirty at least.

"Aye. I'm a dab hand." In the face of such good humor, Iain found himself returning a smile. "Not much else to pass the time during the winter months."

"Do you sing?" Robert asked with a hopeful lilt.

"A fair bit." Iain enjoyed singing while he worked or in the shower.

"I don't suppose you'd like to join me for a slice of pie and a chat," Robert said.

Iain shrugged his acceptance and scooted his chair around to join Robert at his table.

A half hour later, he left the Scottish Lass with a full belly, a Highland T-shirt pressed into his hands by the waitress, and a mobile full of numbers. It seemed he'd acquired a few mates.

Stepping outside, he took a deep breath of thick air and strolled down the sidewalk. Front windows of many shops were decorated with cartoonish illustrations in greasepaint advertising the festival.

A banner was strung across the street as well, but the bottom of one end had come loose and flapped in the breeze, making it difficult to read. Two men well into middle age stood at the bottom of a streetlight and stared up at the loose ties. As Iain wasn't in any hurry to return to Stonehaven, he joined them and looked up.

"Anything I can help you blokes with?" Iain asked softly.

The closest man startled. "Howdy, young man. I didn't hear you walk up."

Iain only smiled. He'd learned at a young age how to move so as not to startle deer or pheasants. The skill had proved useful during his service. "Iain Connors. Isabel and Rose Buchanan sent me to help with the festival."

The Buchanan name opened doors like it was a magic word. The man grinned, a wad of tobacco visible in his bottom lip. "I'm Jessie Joe and this here is Jessie Mac."

The other man stuck out a roughened hand with deep creases, but didn't speak.

"He's my cuz," the first man said, thumbing over his shoulder. As if that was explanation enough, he propped his hands low on his hips and stared upward once more. "Got any ideas besides commandeering the firetruck or a utility truck with a basket? How's about a front end loader?"

Iain judged the distance and examined the light pole. It was decoratively ridged all the way to the hooked old-fashioned-looking light. "You only need it tied down?"

"That's right."

Iain toed off his trainers, peeled off his socks, and stepped forward. The cliffs had been his playground, and he'd become a proficient climber. He'd only have to climb halfway up the pole in order to reach the flapping ties. Actually securing them so it wouldn't happen again was trickier since he needed both hands, but he would give it a try. By the time he was finished, his feet ached where the narrow ridges dug into his arches. .

"What are you doing up there?" The female voice was unmistakable.

Iain looked down from his perch. Anna's face was tilted toward him, her expression a combination of shock and worry, the breeze playing with her long red hair.

"Helping Mr. Joe and Mr. Mac fix the festival banner."

Jessie Joe burst out laughing. "You here that, Anna? Mr. Joe." He rapped on the light post and stared up at Iain with a good-natured grin that seemed a characteristic like his eye color or baldness. "Jessie Joe is my given name, son. My last name is Sawyers, just like Jessie Mac's."

"I planned to call Dr. Jameson so he could authorize a truck. This looks dangerous," Anna said. Iain wasn't sure whether she was actually worried he might fall or annoyed he had inserted himself.

"Izzy sent him to help," Jessie Joe said simply.

"I know that." Impatience skipped in her voice like a throwing stone. "Come on down before you fall and crack your head open like a watermelon."

He was tempted to defy her just to see what she would do—yell at him? Pull him down?—but his feet ached. He'd gone soft. With ease, he scaled to the ground, the pavement hot enough to burn his bare feet like walking over coals.

She made a harrumphing sound. "You're not wearing a kilt today."

"A good thing too." His raised an eyebrow, a mere quirk of forehead muscles that he had inherited from his da. "Unless you were hoping to get a peak underneath."

"It never even crossed my mind." Color rushed into her face, leaving her cheeks splotchy.

With a start, he wondered if she were lying. The thought she might be at all interested in what was under his kilt left him staggered. To cover his discomfiture, he squat to slip on his socks and tie his trainers, letting his gaze trail up her shapely, toned legs as he slowly rose.

"I appreciate you helping the Sawyers, but you could have hurt yourself, Iain. I figured you'd be halfway through a binge-watch by now." Her mouth had lost its tightness, and while her lips weren't anywhere near a smile, he sensed a softening.

"I couldn't figure out the remotes. Anyway, I'm rubbish at relaxing." Once upon a time, he'd been a world-class shirker of his chores. He'd spent hours in the loft of the barn reading or daydreaming or napping. His da had boxed his ears a time or two over it, but in general, he'd indulged Iain. The military had marched and deprived and drilled any such tendencies out of him.

"Then go back to Stonehaven and practice," Anna said with a dry humor he found hard not to smile at.

Jessie Joe guffawed. "This one has red hair for a reason, boy. She's left a string of broken hearts in her wake."

Anna's shoulders shifted forward. While the old man's ribbing was good-natured, Iain caught the unintentional whiff of condescension. Instead of calling Jessie Joe to task, Anna gave them a tight smile. "If you'll excuse me, gentlemen. I have work to finish."

She shuttered her emotions behind a polite facade of Southern sweetness that wasn't natural. Fascinated with her discordant attitude, Iain followed like she was the Pied Piper.

She stopped with the door to the coffee shop open. "What are you doing?"

"I find myself in need of a cuppa. You don't mind, do you?"

A protest was ready to come to her lips when Millie

called out from the counter. "I know you weren't raised in a barn, Anna. Let the poor man in."

Anna stepped aside and gestured him to enter, but he didn't miss her muttered, "Poor man, my ass."

Iain ordered a fresh peach-infused iced tea using as few words as possible. While he waited, he studied Anna out of the corner of his eye, catching her cutting glances toward him. Her color was still high, and he wondered at the insecurity he'd got a peak at more than once.

After completing the transaction for the drink, Iain stopped at Anna's table, his hand on the back of the empty chair across from her. "May I?"

She wanted to say no. He could see her lips form the word, but she abruptly changed course. "It's a free country. You can sit where you want."

He sat across from her and made himself comfortable, stretching his legs out to the side and crossing his feet at the ankles. The chair creaked. Far from making him cower, which he was fairly certain was the intention, her laser-like gaze energized him.

He took a sip of his tea, finding the cool sweetness refreshing and delicious. It was both familiar and foreign. Exactly like Highland. He held the cup up. "I'll have to pay a steep penance to my ancestors after this."

"Over iced tea?" Anna looked up from where she was tapping something on the screen of her mobile.

"They're no doubt clawing their way out of their graves to haunt me this very moment."

"That's a fanciful if morbid thought." Anna put her mobile down, her smile a little sad, her brows drawn down over her blue eyes. "Reminds me of something Izzy would say, actually."

Iain took another long pull of tea, not missing a

scalded tongue because he couldn't wait for it cool. "You miss her."

"Of course, I do. She was my best friend."

It was interesting that Anna spoke in terms of the past. "She still is, by my reckoning."

Anna waved her hand dismissively, but her darting gaze landed anywhere except on him. "Of course she is, but things change. She's in a different country and married and about to have a kid, for goodness' sake, and I'm still here doing my thing."

"Do you not want to be here?"

"No, I do. I just want . . . more." The admission came out as if removing splinters from under her fingernails.

"You want more respect." The thought popped into his head, but instinctively, he knew he was right.

"I have respect." She sat forward and propped her crossed arms on the table. "I run a successful business, and now I'm in charge of the festival."

Was she trying to convince him or herself? "Yes. You're an impressive woman."

"You have no call to mock me." The blotches of color were back in her cheeks, and with jerky movements, she stacked papers and shoved them into a red folder.

He blinked, shocked at her reaction. She stood. Her chair scraped the floor and tipped over with a clang that silenced the buzz and brought every eye to them. She righted the chair and grabbed her mobile and the folder.

Finally, he gathered his wits enough to react and took her wrist. His fingers overlapped his thumb by a good three inches. He was aware like he'd never been before of their difference in size. Her personality was big and bold and filled the room, but she was vulnerable in ways he didn't think others noticed. It's like she had cast a glamour on the residents of Highland, but as an outsider, he could see her for what she truly was.

"I was being truthful, Anna. You are impressive."

She didn't tug out of his loose grip, and her fist uncurled, leaving her arm pliant. "You're trying to butter me up so you can . . . you can . . . What *do* you want?"

How many times had he asked himself the same question? He had arrived in Highland to escape and figure out what was next. Should he trod down the expected path or venture into the unknown? That's not the answer she would expect from him.

He let go of her, crossed his arms over his chest, and shrugged. "I want what you want. A successful festival. The question is, why won't you allow me to help more? No need to martyr yourself over something as trivial as a festival."

"Trivial?" Her gaze flicked down his body and back up as if assessing the strengths and weaknesses of an adversary. "I've dealt with men like you before. You're used to being large and in charge. You'll creep into the project until you completely take over like a cloud of noxious gas."

He stood. "I can't do anything about the large part, but I'm not here to perform a hostile takeover. I'd prefer us to form a partnership."

She slung her purse over her shoulder and clutched the file folder tight against her chest. "You don't need this like I do. I've got everything under control, so back off. In fact, why don't you go home?"

Nothing waited for him at home except days spent puttering around Cairndow with his da and working for Alasdair. Like Anna, he needed more. Not respect, but freedom. God, he was turning as melodramatic as Mel

Gibson's William Wallace in *Braveheart*. Next, he'd be painting his face blue and not showering.

"I'm not going home," he said shortly. "Anyway, who would scoop the poop and feed the beasties?"

She spun around and weaved her way to the door, throwing one last look his direction before disappearing. He expected to see scorch marks.

He regained his chair and rubbed at the condensation on his glass of tea. A piece of paper was camouflaged on the white tabletop. He flipped it over and skimmed a grid of names and numbers and occupations like potter or painter or quilter with notes in small, neat handwriting.

If he ran after her, he might be able to catch her on the sidewalk. Or . . . he could use the list as a lure. Underhanded, perhaps, but he was already anticipating their next meeting. His blood sang through his veins, and he smiled.

A throat cleared awkwardly next to him. A barrel-chested man in a kilt, sporran, and black jacket with brass buttons stood at his elbow. With thinning hair and glasses perched on the bulbous end of his nose, the man reminded Iain of Mole from *The Wind in the Willows*.

"Hello there. I'm David Timmerman."

"How do you do?" Iain said, half rising and offering a hand. "Iain Connors."

"Please, sit. I'm terribly sorry to interrupt." Mr. Timmerman took his hand in a shake and patted his shoulder with his other hand as if Iain were a beloved old friend.

"You're interrupting nothing but wandering thoughts. Please join me."

Mr. Timmerman took the seat Anna had vacated and primly sat on the edge as if loath to wrinkle his pleats. "I own the Dapper Highlander down the street."

"That explains why you're so well kitted out." Iain made a gesture toward his kilt and sporran.

Mr. Timmerman smoothed a hand over the lapel of his jacket. "Indeed. The jacket is a bit much in our summer heat, but I do find it drives sales if I maintain the full regalia during festival season. We get so much more foot traffic in the store these few weeks. The rest of the year, internet orders make up the bulk of my income."

Mr. Timmerman spoke with the formal cadence of a strict schoolteacher, and Iain found his spine straightening. Lessons from Mrs. Mac about elbows on tables flashed from his memories. He shifted his hands to his lap.

"I'm amazed so many people find the Scottish ways appealing," Iain said.

"I suppose the seeds of rebellion the Scots brought when they settled this area appeals to Americans, especially Southerners." Mr. Timmerman's slight eye roll didn't go unnoticed. "Not to mention the romance of the Celts."

"And the kilts."

"Indeed, the allure and romance of the kilt has provided me a good living. When I opened my shop, I sold men's suits, shirts, and ties. My business was drying up and flowing to the malls on the edge of Atlanta when the idea of the festival took root and Highland began to transform into what you see today." When Mr. Timmerman smiled, his eyes twinkled with a puckish charm that put Iain at ease. "I transformed with it and dug into my Scottish roots."

"I grew up wearing kilts. Except in winter, of course. Nothing appealing about a cold sea wind blowing straight up your nethers." Iain rumbled out a laugh.

"I can certainly understand that." Mr. Timmerman's broad smile turned uncertain. "Actually, I wanted to discuss kilts with you. Didn't I see you in one yesterday?"

"Aye, you did."

"Do you wear it doing chores?"

"Quite often, yes."

"I was wondering if I could get a closer look at it." Mr. Timmerman rubbed his hands together with undisguised enthusiasm. "My specialty is dress kilts. I've tried to expand into the athletic kilt market, but had little success. The men around here prefer their jeans."

"I brought several with me if you want one to pick apart and study."

They exchanged mobile numbers and arranged a meeting for the next afternoon at the Dapper Highlander. With Anna's lost page tucked into his pocket, Iain stepped lightly to the old tartan truck. If he wasn't rubbish at dancing, he might even do a little jig.

Anna might not have welcomed him with open arms, but Highland seemed to have embraced him. He wasn't sure if he had the skill to win her over, but he was determined to try.

Chapter Six

Anna stomped up the rickety metal stairs to her apartment above the dance studio, slipped inside, and threw the double bolt behind her as if she had anything to worry about in Highland. The door was narrow, short, and like Goldilocks, exactly right for her. The apartment itself wasn't as great a fit. A realtor would call it cozy; cramped was more accurate.

Her mom's sudden decision to sell her childhood home and move to Florida had left Anna floundering for a place to live. While she could have rented an apartment in one of the new developments outside of town, she didn't want to waste the money. Most of the time, she didn't regret her choice.

Most of the time. Now was not that time. She flipped on the inadequate window AC unit. It would freeze up before it got the apartment cooled, but roasting at eighty was better than roasting at a hundred.

Anna stripped off her shorts and T-shirt and went to the fridge in her bra and panties for a glass of ice water.

She needed to cool down in more ways than one after her confrontation with Iain.

He'd actually asked her if she'd been disappointed he wasn't wearing a kilt so she could get a peek. Of all the outrageous suggestions. Of course, she'd said no. Hopefully, emphatically enough to drown out the yes her body had chanted like a pagan. What was wrong with her? Her first reaction had been to pout at the sight of his legs encased in well-worn denim.

She threw herself back on her couch and tried not to move until the room had cooled enough so that lifting her cell phone to her ear didn't cause a sweat to break out. Fifteen minutes passed.

Fifteen minutes she should have been using to mentally tick through her checklist of items to get done. Instead, she used the time to imagine Iain in progressively less pieces of clothing.

Anna rubbed the heels of her hands against her eyes as if that would grind the inappropriate fantasies to dust. What *did* he wear under his kilt? The question was becoming her obsession.

Her phone dinged with an incoming text. She read it and groaned. The Bluegrass Jacobites, a local Celtic band, were putting on an exhibition at the Dancing Jig pub during the week leading up to the festival and had asked her to dance to a handful of songs. Practice was scheduled for that evening at the studio.

She would never have agreed if Robert wasn't the de facto leader. In school, he'd been the unpopular, but brilliant nerd. She'd been the cheerleader who was failing math. He'd tutored her to a B, and if it had been a typical teen movie, they would have fallen in love and lived happily ever after. Instead, she'd been the first person he'd confessed his homosexuality to, and she had made sure none of the jocks or jerks had bullied him when he finally came out to the world their senior year.

Normally, she would enjoy dancing with the band. Even though she spent her days in the dance studio, teaching wasn't the same as doing, and she missed the high of performing in front of a crowd. At the moment, though, it was just another commitment to add to her overflowing bucket.

It was more important than ever that she get some items ticked off her to-do list. She riffled through the papers in her folder for the list of vendors to contact. Nothing. She went through each paper more carefully, but the most important sheet hadn't miraculously appeared.

Had she even had it to begin with? Yes, she remembered staring at the phone numbers as Iain had walked over with his tea. She'd been in such a hurry to escape Iain's magnetic presence, she'd probably dropped it.

Best case scenario, some Good Samaritan had turned it in and she could trot down to the Brown Cow and collect it. Worst case scenario, she would be forced to venture to Stonehaven to print another copy.

A lukewarm shower restored her. Unable to face the thought of using a hairdryer, she twisted her damp hair and clipped it into a messy updo and dressed in a fresh cotton skirt and T-shirt. She left the window unit on low and walked back to the Brown Cow, entering as if an ambush waited, but the table she'd shared with Iain was empty of both man and paper. Neither Millie nor the teenager manning the ice-cream station had the document either.

Moving slowly so as not to work up a sweat, she made

her way back to the studio and her car. Izzy and Rose had wanted her to make any changes to the copy that was on their computer at Stonehaven, and Anna understood why. It was too easy to mistakenly consolidate or over-write the original.

There was nothing to be done except return to Stone-haven and pray that Iain was still out and about making new friends. She crept along the lane leading to the big house as if she could sneak up in her car. No sign of Izzy's old truck, but it could be lurking on the other side of the barn like earlier. No matter, she would be in and out like a ninja.

She stopped outside the office door. The air conditioning chugged out refreshing air, but a warm breeze fluttered her skirt around her legs. Had Iain gone off and left a door open? Making her way toward the back, a whistled tune halted her at the corner into the living room with its floor-to-ceiling windows and French doors leading to the back. One of the doors was open, and Iain was standing in the breech working on the hinge with a screwdriver.

He was back in a kilt and black boots, socks shrug-ging toward the tops. This one was made of a light-weight fabric of green and tan, the pleats fluttering with the breeze. No doubt it was cooler than a pair of jeans and infinitely sexier. His green T-shirt was branded with the Highland logo—THE HEART OF THE HIGHLANDS IN THE BLUE RIDGE. He was looking more and more like a native.

The whistling turned into words sung a cappella in a soul-quivering baritone. Like a transfusion, his voice entered her bloodstream, inspiring an aching melancholy in her chest. She closed her eyes and was transported to a high cliff in Scotland with the wind blowing and facing an endless, empty sea.

> *"Had we never loved so kindly,*
> *Had we never loved so blindly,*
> *Never met-or never parted-*
> *We would ne'er been broken-hearted."*

Maybe it was the fact she hadn't been sleeping well. Or the fact she was frazzled at the length of her to-do list. But tears burned her eyes and she swallowed to contain them. She had to remain cool and collected if she was going to succeed.

The air stirred around her and the silence registered. She popped her eyes open and met Iain's gaze. He stood at the corner, his brows and mouth drawn into a serious, pensive expression.

"Are you all right there, Anna, my lass?"

She blinked rapidly and forced a smile to her face, but she could feel her cheeks folding like a house of cards. "What were you were singing?"

"'Ae Fond Kiss.' Another classic by Burns," he said.

"Wow. You are a serious Burns groupie."

The farthest corners of his lips twitched. It wasn't much, but it was enough to settle her emotions back where they belonged—hiding under her outward facade of cool sarcasm and lighthearted tease. Not even Izzy knew about the deep still waters where her insecurities lived like the Loch Ness Monster. Sightings were rare, but devastating.

"Burns was an amazing storyteller and translator of the human heart," he said.

She gaped at his pronouncement. On first meeting,

Iain hadn't struck her as being philosophical. He seemed to be a practical man concerned only with the tangible. Did he too have deep waters to explore? While she was intensely curious, she didn't have time to mount an expedition.

"Why are all his songs so dang depressing?" She forced a tease into her voice, and only realized she'd hit a nerve when his face shuttered. She bit her lip to keep from apologizing.

"Why are you here?" he asked.

"I misplaced something."

Without answering, he stalked to a side table in the entry and held a familiar piece of paper in her direction. She took it and stared down at the names and numbers until they blurred like a Rorschach drawing. "Thanks and . . ."

Her words stalled and before she could recover, he said, "Use the office. I won't interfere. I've got my own work outside. Ta-ta."

She waited until the back door closed before moving into the office like a sleepwalker and dropping into Izzy's chair behind the desk. She had successfully pushed Iain away. Why didn't she feel more elated?

Her phone dinged an incoming text. It was Izzy. *How's the partnership going? Not shockingly, Alasdair isn't getting info from Iain.*

How the baby-growing business is going is the more important question, Anna fired back.

Good news is the baby is welcome to make an arrival any time now. She is officially baked.

That's great! I'm actually sitting at your desk right now to make calls to vendors.

Did Loretta pay yet?

What do you think?

Ugh.

I'm going to shake her down this week. We might end up on TV. I'll send you the video if I'm not in prison.

Har-har. Has Iain been a big help?

Anna's stomach squirmed. Izzy's questions felt like a pop quiz. *He's working with the animals.* Not a lie, but no way could Anna keep zigging around Izzy's questions. She'd just have to zag then. *Picked out any names?*

I put my foot down on Mathilda. Alasdair nixed Briony. What do you think of Annie? She was a kickass Blackmoor ancestor.

I'm all about kickass names with a backstory. Plus I can pretend I inspired her name.

Izzy sent a smiley face. *Make sure Iain isn't eating every meal by himself, would you? He's too much of a loner.*

You're worrying like he's at summer camp. He's a grown man. Was he ever. Prying questions scrolled. Did he have a girlfriend? What was he like when his guard was down? How did he get his scar? Anna's thumbs hovered over the letters. Any one of the questions would put Izzy on the scent. Instead, she typed. *Gotta go and rustle up some deposits.*

Good luck and thank U!

Anna sent a thumbs-up and dove into the calls. Handling teenaged girls had taught her how hard she could push and prod to get the desired results in the dance studio. The same principle applied. She was alternately sweet and tough with the vendors until they had all promised to get their deposit in. Loretta was the last one on the list and the one Anna dreaded the most. It felt like a skirmish in the larger war.

Izzy's earlier request irritated her like she sat on chair made of sweetgum balls. Iain was all alone and had no friends in Highland. Loner or not, he was sure to get lonely rattling around Stonehaven all by himself. Especially if he didn't know how to work the TV. She smiled thinking of him fumbling with the numerous remotes and hitting random buttons.

The least she could do was offer to keep him company at dinner for a night. The decision alleviated a portion of the guilt she carried. She stepped onto the back patio, but there was no sign of him. She spent a few minutes watering the flowers and listening.

A crow called mournfully in the distance, probably complaining about the heat. A hammering sound punched through the humid air and made her jump. It emanated from the barn. She turned the water off, nerves jangling in her chest for no reason whatsoever, considering asking him to dinner was not a date but a mission of mercy.

The tartan truck had been backed halfway into the barn, the bed laden with another load of wood. With the slight breeze ruffling his kilt, Iain measured a long piece and pulled a pencil from behind his ear to make a mark. Sweat dampened his hair, and it looked like he'd run his hands through it as he worked, leaving it charmingly disheveled.

"Hi," she said dumbly.

He shot her the briefest of glances before returning his focus to his project. After slipping on a pair of clear safety glasses, he hefted the wood to a buzz saw, stepped on a pedal to start the jagged blade, and guided the wood. Shavings burst like confetti from the cut, and the noise precluded conversation.

Anna supposed she deserved his silence. To cover the tension, she picked her way to where Ozzie the sheep was shut into a stall, happily munching on hay. She rubbed the soft wool between her ears. An ominous rumble barked from her chest. Anna snatched her hand away and stepped out of reach of any errant teeth.

Ignoring her, Iain rubbed his thumb over the cut he'd made as if checking the smoothness.

She attempted another overture. "I finished my calls."

He gave her a nod, but didn't reply.

"It's almost dinnertime."

He checked the chunky manly watch on his wrist and made a grunting sound which Anna counted as an improvement.

"Are you hungry, big guy?" Was that a softening around his jaw?

"I can always eat." His full attention was on the length of wood in his hands.

"Are you interested in eating now?" When he said nothing, heat flared across her chest and up the back of her neck. Maybe he hadn't understood. "With me, I mean."

Finally, he looked up at her and stared for a long, embarrassing moment as if tallying up her good and bad points. She knew which column was longer. Then, he pulled out his tape measure and pulled another length of wood closer. "Can't. I have plans."

"Plans? With who?" Had that sounded as shrill and accusatory to him as it had to her? "I mean, it's great you've made a friend in Highland."

Her brain searched for possibilities like a robber tossing a room. Who was he having dinner with? Millie? She was cute and obviously enamored of him. A dozen other women scrolled through her mind. A single, good-looking man was chum in the water in a small town. Or maybe it was a nonromantic date. Did Dr. Jameson want to grill Iain on all things Scotland?

When Iain didn't throw her the merest scrap of a bone, Anna said, "As it happens, I've got plans too."

Iain cut her a look through his lashes before making a pencil mark on the wood. "Why did you ask me out if you already had plans?"

"*Ask you out?* Don't be ridiculous." A huff of disbelief popped out. "You make it sound like I was asking you out on a date. Which I wasn't."

"Did you want to discuss the festival, then?" He straightened and crossed his arms over his chest. "What can I help you with?"

She swayed a little on her feet, worn down but with a packed evening of dance practice. Why not offload some tasks to him? He gave the impression of being capable and reliable, but she'd been burned too many times by putting her trust in someone else. Even her mom had turned flighty and left Anna basically homeless.

"Nothing." She added a shake of her head, not sure which one of them she was trying to convince. "I've got everything under control."

Again his attention shifted back to his work. "All right then, I'll see you around."

"Sure. See you around." She took a step backward and then another, but it was like fighting against a giant rubber band, which was crazy considering this was the perfect outcome. She could even tell Izzy that she'd made an overture, but he'd turned her down.

He measured and made a mark on the wood. "By the way, there's nothing to be feared of. Ozzie is gentle."

She stopped short. "What?"

"You can pet Ozzie. Harriet too. They enjoy carrots and apples if you're in the mind to bring them a treat."

"I'm not good with animals," she said.

"Did you not have a pet growing up?"

"Not even a fish. Mom said they were too much trouble and prone to wandering off. Dogs and cats, not fish, obviously." Anna had been desperate for a dog when she was in elementary school, but she'd soon come around to her mom's way of thinking.

He cocked his head and examined her thoughtfully. "That's a shame."

"I suppose you had all sorts of pets."

"Aye. Sometimes they were my only friends." Although his voice was steady and matter-of-fact, the statement hollowed an ache in her chest.

"I thought you and Alasdair were besties growing up," she said.

"We were mates, aye, but he only came to Cairndow for visits. Summers, holidays. He wasn't in school with me." He lay a fresh piece of wood over two sawhorses, his hands deft with the measuring tape.

"School was difficult for you." While she'd meant to pose it as a question, the answer hid poorly in his stoic expression.

He paused in his work for a moment before continuing to measure and mark. "I imagine school was easy for someone like you."

School *had* been easy, minus her struggles in math. She'd been a cheerleader with no shortage of boys and girls in her social circle. "School was easy. It was everything else that was hard."

The hours spent at the studio with the strain of her mom's expectations had been like dancing on broken glass, leaving her psyche battered and bleeding. Although she didn't elaborate, understanding bound them, and she took a step toward him without thinking.

No. She forced herself to stop. She couldn't get attached. Iain would end up being too much trouble and prone to wandering just like the dog she'd craved as a child. Soon enough, he would wander all the way back to Scotland. In the interest of self-preservation, she turned on her heel and walked away. With him out of sight, retreat became easier, even though her lungs remained tight.

Returning to her loft without a dinner companion, she made herself a BLT on white bread and ate it while watching reruns of a favorite sitcom to cheer herself up. It didn't work. Like a hawk on the wing, her subconscious circled Iain. Who was he with? Was it business or a date?

A date. It was none of her business. Iain wasn't even her type. Typically, she dated artsy guys who understood the energy involved in the creation of something, whether it was intangible like a dance or concrete like a painting. Iain measured and hammered and built utilitarian shapes meant to fence.

She flopped to her back and closed her eyes. She would allow regret to swamp her for a minute and no more. She had to get ready to practice with the Bluegrass Jacobites.

Opening the accordion-style door of her closet, she rooted around for her tartan bustier and a floaty green wrap skirt to match. It was sexy, but not too sexy, and progressive enough for a pub performance. This would be the first year in more than a decade she wouldn't be competing in the Highland dance competitions during the festival. Not only was it a conflict of interest, but her hands would be full, organizing her dance troupes on top of keeping everything else running smoothly. Anyway, it was time for the torch to be passed along to someone like Keisha or Gabby.

All the little things she couldn't anticipate going wrong during the festival worried her. She'd had a nightmare earlier in the week about the portable potties never arriving, forcing everyone to squat in the woods. The first call she'd made upon waking was to confirm the date, time, and number of potties with the company. What else was she missing?

Barefoot, she skipped down the outside stairs and let herself in the back door of the studio. After unlocking the front door for the Jacobites, she went to the costume closet to sort through dresses for her dance classes. All her Celtic dance students would march in the parade while the older girls would also compete at the festival. The studio always took home several ribbons, which she displayed in a row along the perimeter of the wall above the doorframes and mirrors.

Her mind drifted to Gabby and her ghosting act. Another problem she needed to tackle, and soon. A cluster of male voices drifted from the waiting room. She slapped a smile on her face to cover her tiredness and turned, the words of welcome withering at the sight of a dark head inches taller than the rest.

"Iain!" His name popped out of her mouth and echoed, stifling conversation for a few heartbeats.

He met her gaze with an inscrutable stare, although seriously, everything about him was inscrutable. He'd cleaned up and was in a different kilt and T-shirt from his work in the barn.

Robert came forward to give her a hug, lifting her off her feet to whisper in her ear. "Based on your drool, you're partial to our Scottish man of mystery, eh?"

"I'm not drooling; I'm surprised." Anna slapped him on the arm until he released her.

Robert set her on the floor and moved toward the storage closet, keeping his head close. "I found out the hard way that he's unfortunately straight."

"I can't believe you were brave enough to give it a shot."

"I calculated my chances beforehand, and they were on par with winning the lottery, but I figured I can't score unless I take a shot." Although his smile was wry, disappointment lingered. "He let me down quite nicely after he got over his surprise at getting propositioned by a man."

"When did you two meet?" Anna asked.

"At lunch the other day. I was eavesdropping, of course, and heard him say he played guitar. We've been short one since January." Robert helped Anna pull folding chairs for the members of the band from behind the frothy skirts of the costumes. "He met the other boys tonight over some warm-up drinks at the pub, and everyone seems to get along fine."

The rush of relief had her murmuring, "So he wasn't meeting a woman."

"Were you worried, honey?" Robert was the only one who got away with calling her honey.

"Of course I wasn't. We're not . . . together or anything. I barely know him. He can do whatever he wants."

"*Whoever*, you mean." Robert's laugh was like the crack of a whip. Before she could come up with a snappy retort, he clapped his hands as the leader of the merry band of Jacobites.

Anna sidled over to Iain. He'd slid his chair apart from the rest of the men and was fiddling with the pegs of a guitar. "Why didn't you tell me where you were going?" she whispered between teeth clenched in the semblance of a smile.

"You didn't ask, and I had no idea you would be dancing until tonight." He strummed a sweet-sounding chord then folded his arms over the body of the guitar. "As I recall, you're the one who urged me to keep busy with anything but the festival. Are you taking issue with my presence?"

"No, of course not." Any other answer would make her seem like a shrew. Anyway, a warm happiness had sprouted at the sight of him. Especially since she knew he hadn't met another woman. "It's no big deal."

The tremor weakening her knees told a different story, but luckily it didn't have a say.

The members of the Bluegrass Jacobites unpacked. Two fiddles, a banjo, an upright bass, and two guitars counting Iain's. The bass player could also play a mean tin whistle.

Robert tapped his bow on the neck of his fiddle and everyone quieted. "Are you ready, Anna?"

Moving toward Iain, she stared into his dark brown, unfathomable eyes. Oh God, she'd be dancing for him. No, not *for* him—this wasn't a strip club—but in front of him. Great, now she couldn't get the film reel of giving him a lap dance out of her head. While he could be distant and gruff, he exuded an intensity that drew her as if he'd cast a spell over her.

"Anna?" Robert hip-bumped her.

"What?" She swung around and blinked at Robert.

"I asked if you were ready." Robert's eyes narrowed as if reading her mind was part of his vision test. She needed to put distance between her and everyone.

"Hang on. I need to lace on my shoes. Why don't you guys do a warm-up song?" After her dancing shoes were on, she met her eyes in one of the mirrors and whispered, "You are going to be fine. Don't let a man distract you."

Giving herself a bracing nod, she hiked the tartan bustier up another inch. It would be her luck to have a wardrobe malfunction. Izzy would have thought the entire situation was hilarious, of course.

Robert counted off a rhythm, and the twin fiddles began their mournful call. It was "Coming Through the Rye," another Robert Burns creation, but with a twangy twist of bluegrass. Iain was so traditionally Scottish, she watched his reaction, but he merely closed his eyes and smiled before his rich voice cut through with a grounding confidence that spoke of deep familiarity and love of the material no matter what form it took.

Anna couldn't take her eyes off Iain. Yes, he'd kicked her libido like stirring up a hornet's nest, but it wasn't the physical holding her mesmerized. He embodied something that felt just out of reach for her. Purity and passion and commitment. Something she had lost years ago. Tears came to her eyes, and she blinked, not sure whether to blame the music or the man.

The last note from the fiddles echoed through the studio, reverberating in her chest. A few beats of silence followed before the men erupted into chatter. She wanted to yell at everyone to shush as if they were in church, but she remained still and silent.

Iain didn't join in with the others. Instead, he turned to snare her in his gaze. Anna couldn't look away. Communication between them seemed to be taking place on a subconscious level. Was she sending Mayday signals? Because she was a drowning woman.

She took a step toward him. Then another. She wasn't sure what would have happened if she'd reached him. She would never find out, because Robert chose that moment to throw his arm around her shoulders and guide her to stand in front of the players.

"Let's see what you've got, honey."

Anna had choreographed new dance steps to an old Scottish folk song, "Loch Lomond." It was a sad song, even keeping to its traditional Scottish arrangement. Bluegrass only added another layer of melancholy. After all, the Scots who'd immigrated to America and settled in the Blue Ridge Mountains had brought their music. The mountains had proved fertile ground and while new branches of music emerged, the roots were recognizable.

Again, Robert's fiddle led the way into the music. Anna briefly closed her eyes, feeling the floor beneath her feet, grounding her in the notes. At her cue, she opened her eyes and stepped into the dance. Her internal organs rearranged themselves when Iain's baritone and Robert's tenor melded in harmony as if they were the two soldiers in the song traveling back to Scotland together, one alive, one dead.

She tried not to look at Iain, but her eyes never strayed from him for long, and eventually, she stopped fighting the compulsion. She could sense his approval and admiration. Admiration coming from a man wasn't unusual, but it didn't feel sexual. Or, at least, not wholly sexual.

It wasn't until the song ended and the men erupted into high fives that she snapped out of her semi-trance. She didn't want or need anyone's approval or admiration. A vicious little voice cracked with laughter in her head at the lie. Hadn't she been desperate for her mom's benediction? Would she forever seek to fill the void?

She ground out the questions as if they were roaches, but like all infestations of doubt, there were too many to silence.

"That was amazing!" Robert paced in front of the group. "How long did you say you'd be in Highland, Iain?"

"At least through the festival. Maybe longer."

Longer? The word spurred her heart faster. What would keep him in Highland after the festival?

They practiced another song she would accompany them on, then the band launched into half a dozen more she would not dance to. The long day was turning into a marathon, and a headache brewed behind her eyes. She rubbed her forehead.

Iain tapped his fist against the wood of the guitar, drawing everyone's attention, including hers. "It's time to head out and let Anna get some rest, blokes."

Some good-natured grumbling commenced, but Iain herded them toward the front door like a giant sheepdog. Anna flipped all but the storage room light off and was halfway through lugging the folding chairs to stack inside when Iain rejoined her, taking the chairs away from her and finishing the job.

"Thanks," she mumbled.

The music had left her feeling vulnerable. While they hadn't hashed out the tension between them through words, the day's encounters had confused her and left her wanting to know more about him.

He squinted at something behind her, and she glanced over her shoulder to see the two of them in the mirror standing in shadows almost like their reflections existed in a different realm.

"You're a bang-up dancer," he said softly. "Not that I expected anything less, considering the way you walk."

Anna shifted on her feet, not away from him like a smart, sane person, but putting them a few inches closer. "How do I walk?"

While his lips only tipped a little at the corner, his dark eyes twinkled. "Not like a mortal woman."

"I'm not sure if I should primly thank you or punch you in the face. Are you trying to say that I walk like the undead?"

A laugh burst from him. Unlike his smiles, the sound was uncontained and laced with a wildness that drew Anna ever closer. "It was an attempt at a compliment. Unfortunately, I wasn't gifted a silver tongue when it comes to the fairer sex."

Anna stared nonplussed at him for a few heartbeats, which wasn't actually that long considering how fast hers was beating right now. "If we're doling out compliments, I have to say you are a very talented musician. Have you ever sung professionally?"

"Singing isn't a proper job." The shock at the suggestion wasn't feigned.

"Tell that to Elton John."

"I'm no Elton. Whilst I enjoy music, I don't care for being on a stage and having people looking at me. Not like you do."

"You think I enjoy having people watch me perform?" It wasn't genteel to admit she more than enjoyed being on stage. She gloried in it.

"Aye." Before she could mount a half-hearted argument, he added, "And there's not a bloody thing wrong with reveling in the attention when you possess your kind of talent."

"There are some who would say it isn't ladylike." Her mother had berated her preening high spirits after her performances.

Iain cocked his head, his brows drawn low, his gaze like a scalpel. "Doesn't performing go hand in hand with choosing dancing as a profession?"

"Yes. And no." Anna rubbed her arms, goose bumps rising in the cool of the AC now that she wasn't moving.

"Once again, I must admit I don't understand."

"My mom taught me a dancer on stage should give themselves over to the music during a performance, which the audience then enjoys. A dancer shouldn't take the audience's admiration as fuel. It's like you and your music. You as much admitted that you'd rather sing to yourself than for an audience, whereas I'm the opposite."

"I see," he said, but Anna knew he didn't really see. "But I still call your theory poppycock. Speaking of Elton, performers feed on the crowd. Haven't you been to a rock concert?"

"Nothing bigger than the small clubs on the Lower East Side."

"Lower East Side of what?" Iain asked.

"New York City." She'd forgotten about the gulf of the ocean between their experiences. Iain was Scotland personified. Central casting would have picked him out of a lineup for a tourism ad. She could picture him standing on a craggy cliff with a castle in the background, his kilt whipping around his legs, and playing a mournful tune on a set of bagpipes. "Do you play the pipes?"

"I could bleat out 'Mary Had a Little Lamb' at one time, but it's been years. When did you live in New York City?"

She brought her hand up to her neck, feeling the need to shield herself. "Right after high school graduation. Is this your first time away from Scotland?"

His jaw worked and his gaze slide to the floor. "I was in the army for five years. Got out last fall. What took you to New York City?"

"Chasing a stupid dream. Where were you deployed?"

"Afghanistan. Why do you think your dream was stupid?"

"Because I was a total and complete failure." Their conversational game of hot potato had turned scalding. "I'm tired and need to lock up."

Instead of acting like his feelings were hurt, or arguing, he merely inclined his head and turned to retrieve his guitar case. He paused in the doorway leading to the waiting room and glanced over his shoulder. Their eyes met. Even over the distance and through the shadows, the look on his face stilled her breathing. She waited for something momentous to occur. A lightning strike or a thunder clap or the laws of space and time to be broken.

He merely walked away as if nothing at all unusual had occurred. She should have paid more attention in science class. Could a person be drawn to another on a molecular level? He was the positive force, which made her the negative one. That sounded about right.

She locked up the studio and climbed the metal stairs

to the loft. Only the hum of the AC unit filled the silence, and she beat back a feeling that hadn't plagued her in a long time—loneliness. Not for sex, but for companionship. While she missed Izzy like crazy, it wasn't her best friend she pictured next to her on the couch watching TV and eating junk food. It was a Highlander with complicated eyes and a habit of muscling past her defenses.

Chapter Seven

Anna parked behind Dr. Jameson at the Piersons' farm. Her church clothes—knee-length skirt, white eyelet blouse, and sandals—were fine for handling most festival business, but Holt's farm had landmines in the form of cow patties scattered about.

She was here for two reasons. One was to pick up a sponsor check from Holt's daddy to purchase ribbons for the farm animal judging. The second was because according to Dr. Jameson, Iain was at the farm. She told herself she needed to keep tabs on his activities as they related to the festival, but in reality, she just wanted an excuse to see him. Which she would refuse to admit to anyone, even if tortured.

She and Dr. Jameson made small talk on the stroll to a big red barn that could have starred in a children's book. Farther down the lane sat a modern brick building which housed the milking machines, or so Dr. Jameson informed her. A trio of gray storage tanks stood like turrets on one side.

Various outbuildings dotted the surrounding fields.

On top of the hill overlooking the operation stood a craftsman-style farmhouse where Anna assumed Holt still lived with his parents. Not that she was one to throw stones, considering she'd still be at home if her mom hadn't sold the house from under her.

Anna took a deep breath. Cut grass mingled with the earthy scents of animals under the hot sun. Not a single cloud marred the sapphire blue of the sky. The lowing of cows in the fields serenaded them. It was oddly peaceful and loosened the anxious knot in her stomach.

They stepped into the shadowy barn, and Anna pushed her sunglasses to the top of her head and blinked to get her bearings. She hadn't had cause to visit the Piersons since high school. She remembered a party Holt had thrown in the barn one Saturday night when his parents had been gone. She'd picked hay out of her hair all the next day.

Holt and Iain stood at the door to a stall. Iain was in jeans and a dark blue T-shirt. He turned his head to watch her approach, his expression not reflecting welcome or resentment. She had no idea how he felt about her showing up in his domain. Or for that matter, how he felt about her at all.

Holt shifted to lean back against the stall door, tipping the brim of his ball cap up, propping his elbows behind him, and hooking the heel of his mud-caked boot on the lower metal rail. His blondish hair was sweaty and curled around the bottom edge of the cap. He was nice, hardworking, and good looking in an all-American way that had never interested Anna.

"Well, looky here. I wasn't expecting Jane Goodall to make an appearance." He winked. The tease in Holt's voice was good natured and spoke of their decades' long connection.

Anna stuck out her tongue at Holt. "For your information, I've formed an attachment to the sheep and cow out at Stonehaven, Ozzie and Harriet. See, we're even on a first-name basis."

Holt slapped Iain's shoulder with the back of his hand, then pointed to Anna. "I remember a girl who screamed and stampeded for the door when a piglet got loose in the gym during the 4-H demo in high school. Who was that again?"

A flush heated her face, and she fought the urge to shut Holt up with a jab to his crotch. "That is a total exaggeration. It was barely a holler, and a swift jog doesn't qualify as a stampede. Anyway, that pig was possessed and ran straight toward me. I swear, it wanted to rip my throat out."

Holt shot Iain an amused look. "It was the cutest piglet you've ever seen. A total Wilbur."

Anna had read *Charlotte's Web* in the third grade and cried her eyes out, hating the way it had made her feel. Not sad as much as jealous. Anna suspected her mother wouldn't have sacrificed half as much as Charlotte had for Wilbur.

Normally, she could give as good as she got, but with Iain standing there beside Holt, she couldn't come up with a single snappy comeback.

"I don't know. I've seen some wee piglets with scary teeth that might make me run in the other direction too," Iain said. Even though she knew he was lying—he would never run from danger—she appreciated his effort at dousing her humiliation.

Dr. Jameson cleared his throat. "You want to get one of your boys in here to help me, Holt?"

An open black case with syringes lined up like a science experiment gone bad lay on a hay bale. Anna stood on her tiptoes and peeked into the small pen. A cow and two babies milled about.

"You've got me for help today. I'm short a couple of men." Holt worked on the latch to the gate and tossed a smile over his shoulder. "I'm having to get my hands dirtier than usual."

"Are those immunizations?" Anna stared at the long needles and shuddered.

"Yep, plus the doc needs to check out our mama—it was a difficult birthing—and one of the calves needs to be hand-fed a bottle."

"Why?" Anna asked. One of the calves was bleating.

"The mama refuses to let the smallest calf feed," Holt said.

"So it will get a baby bottle?"

"Yep. A big-ass baby bottle." Holt stepped into the pen. Iain followed. "I can cull the rejected babe out."

The cow shied away from the men, and the two calves followed. One latched onto a teat and nursed, but when the smaller of the two calves approached, the mother nipped at the calf to drive her away.

A well of empathy floated a lump into her throat. "Why won't the mother let both nurse? Is there not enough milk?"

"Twins aren't terribly common for a reason. They're hard on a mother. Nature bends toward survival, and it's easier for the mother to survive with one calf versus two." Dr. Jameson stood next to her.

"She'll let her calf starve and die?" Anna asked.

"In order for the calf she perceives as being stronger to live." Dr. Jameson's matter-of fact voice transmitted an acceptance, even an admiration, of nature's methods.

Anna, on the other hand, felt sick to her stomach.

"The bleating is starting to grate on my nerves," Holt said. "Let's get it set up in a different stall."

Iain put a loose halter on the calf and pulled it out of the stall. Its cries grew more strident and desperate the farther away it got from its mother. Dr. Jameson gave the calf its injections, and Iain scooped the calf up under the belly with both arms. It squirmed as if aware it was to become an outcast. Anna followed Iain into a smaller stall with a pile of hay in one corner.

Iain set the calf down, its hooves scrambling on the dirt floor. He spoke in a low soothing voice, the nonsense words calming the calf. Anna stepped closer, realizing he wasn't speaking nonsense, but in Gaelic. He'd done the same with Ozzie.

"Stay with it while I get a bottle, lass." Iain motioned her over, and she found herself following his orders without balking. He held out the halter and she took it, even though her last experience minding animals had turned into a pansy massacre.

Iain returned in less than a minute with a comically large bottle of milk. "Would you like to do the honors?"

The calf batted its big brown cow eyes at her. Its lashes were feathery and long. "I can try. You won't leave me, will you?"

Iain crouched next to her and rubbed the calf behind the ears. Meeting Anna's gaze, he said, "Of course not."

She dangled the bottle over the calf's mouth. After three failed attempts, the calf latched onto the nipple and sucked as if it were starving, which she guessed it was. Anna's back started to ache, and she eased to her knees on the dirt-and-hay-covered floor.

"I came from church, or I would have dressed more

appropriately. Not that I imagined I would be feeding a baby cow today." She let out a little laugh.

Regular attendance at church had been a simple step to take when she decided to run for mayor of Highland. Old rumors lived on like they were on life support, whereas good deeds died like mayflies. Surprisingly, though, she'd come to enjoy Preacher Hopkins's sermons. They were less fire and brimstone and more peace and wisdom, which were two things she scrambled for on a regular basis.

The calf swung around and leaned her rump against Anna, the warm, furry body comforting in way she'd never experienced. As the calf gulped milk, Anna petted its flank, at first tentatively, then with more confidence.

The bottle emptied, and Anna set it aside. The calf wobbled as if drunk and leaned farther into Anna. She sat on the ground and tucked her legs to the side. The calf flopped down, laid its head in Anna's lap, and rolled its eyes to look up at her as if she were its savior and not some random woman with a bottle. Anna smiled down at it.

"Is it a boy or a girl?" Anna asked.

"Female. She's a bonny little thing, isn't she?" Iain asked, basically reading Anna's thoughts.

"I can't believe her mama abandoned her," Anna said softly. "Animals can be cruel."

"Humans can be just as bad."

Anna looked up at him, but he was focused on the calf, stroking her foreleg, his fingers gazing Anna's shin. Had his touch been an accident or on purpose? A zing raced up her body, but it was more than physical. "You're thinking about your own mother, aren't you?"

His eyes met hers in a brief flare of acknowledgment of their odd connection. "Aye."

"Have you ever tried to find her?"

He gave a slight shake of his head.

"Weren't you curious?"

"Of course, I was, but Da shied away from my questions, and I could tell talking about her hurt him. When I was a child, I dreamed of her coming home, but I had no desire to go out into the world and find her. I couldn't imagine ever leaving Cairndow, then."

Anna stroked the calf, her fur soft and springy. "My dad left when I was young too, but not so young I don't remember him."

"Did you try to find him?"

"Yes, I found him." Her lips didn't move with her whisper. She hadn't told anyone, not even Izzy about her search.

"Were you satisfied or disappointed?"

That was a question she still couldn't answer. "He was living in New York City in a dump of an apartment. He'd left us to become an actor. By the time I showed up, his dream was not merely dead but decomposed."

"Was he happy to see you?"

"Maybe? But he wasn't so happy when he figured out I had no money."

"Did you come home, then?"

"I should have, but my dream was still alive and kicking. I was young and invincible." She barked a sarcastic laugh. "I thought I was special."

"You are special."

Anna's harrumph was as dry as the desert. "Not by Broadway standards. It took me a while, but I finally gave up."

"Did you pack regrets to bring home with you?"

"Bitterness maybe, but no regrets." Anna shrugged. "Mom was upset I left in the first place and infuriated I made contact with Dad. A decade later and she still hasn't forgiven me. She thinks I rejected her and Highland."

"But she gave her studio to you, so she must have gotten over it."

"Gave? No. She made me pay for it." Anna paid good money for the studio, but she also paid with a thousand tiny cuts over her childhood.

Iain's hand bumped hers, but when she tried to pull away, he covered her hand with his and squeezed. Caught between the solid warmth of his hand and the soft fur of the calf, Anna could feel the physical lessening of the tension across her shoulders. Maybe she should get a furry animal for stress relief. Or a big strong Highlander. She had a feeling which would be more trouble.

The door to the stall rattled open, and Anna snatched her hand from between Iain and the calf as if caught in the cookie jar. Holt shuffled inside, wiping his hands on a work towel. "How'd the little tyke take to the bottle?"

"Gobbled up the milk. What happens now?" Anna was loath to disturb the sleepy calf even though her legs were joining it in sleep.

"I'll have one of the boys hand-feed her until she weans. A pain in the ass, to be honest, but at least they were both female."

"What happens when they aren't?"

"If it's a set of male-female twins, the female is sterile, which means no milk. And we're in the business of milk, so . . ." Holt made a leading gesture.

Anna instinctively clutched the calf closer, her voice

dropping to a whisper as if the calf might understand. "You'd *kill* her?"

Holt pretended to clutch his pearls. "Oh, I'm sorry. Did I miss your crusade into vegetarianism?"

Anna gave him a scathing look, which left Holt unfazed. She couldn't even offer an argument. She loved a good burger.

Holt smiled and sent a wink in her direction. "Don't worry, your calf is in safe hands with me. Come on, Jane Goodall, let's check out the animals Mom has offered for the festival."

She didn't particularly want to leave the little calf, but she'd never hear the end of it from Holt if she balked. Easing from underneath the calf's head, she took the hand Iain offered, and he hauled her to her feet. She shook her half-asleep, tingly legs out, keeping ahold of his hand until feeling returned and she was sure she wouldn't face-plant.

"Maybe I could drop by and feed her again?" Anna kept her voice as casual as possible, falling back into an old habit to mask how deep her feelings could cut, but even as she asked, she knew she had no time to spare for the calf.

"Whatever," Holt said indifferently.

Stealing a last glance at the calf, Anna brushed the dirt and hay from her skirt as Holt led them out into the beating sun toward a smaller enclosure with a roof but no walls. Iain and Holt entered into a conversation about feed and other challenges dealing with animals.

Anna wandered over to the chicken coop that took up one corner and watched a gloriously plumed white chicken peck the ground. Giving a sow and her piglets a wide berth, Anna instead went to where three small goats cavorted. They bumped heads and one fell over like they were performing a Three Stooges comedy routine.

Even as Iain participated in the discussion, Anna sensed his regard like the blip of a radar signal verifying her position, and stole a glance over her shoulder to catch him in the act. When their gazes met, he gave her a nearly imperceptible nod.

"What do you think of Mom's goats?" Holt called out.

"They're funny," Anna said. "I like them."

"Mom's got a wild hair to start goat yoga. Don't tell her I said so, but they *are* pretty cute, and that's not a word I use often." Holt shook his head even as he smiled. Raising cattle was a business, and Holt had never been one to ooh and aah over animals. "She'd be willing to lend them as part of the demo."

"I sure the kiddies would enjoy watching them," Iain said. "I'll have the holding pens ready by the end of the next week."

"Sounds good. I'd be happy to load them up and drop them off when you give me the green light." Holt checked his watch. "Now, if you'll excuse me, I've chores to tackle."

Iain and Holt exchanged a brisk handshake, and with a feeling like she'd been demoted, she inserted her hand between them. Holt hesitated, but shook her hand with a bemused smile. Understandable, considering Holt had been prone to snap her bra strap in sixth grade. Of course, she'd grabbed the back of his underwear and yanked more than a time or two.

He pointed at Anna. "By the way, Dad's got your check up at the house if you want to stop by before you head out. He also got the UGA extension agent to agree to judge the youth husbandry competition."

"That's great news all around. Thanks, Holt."

Holt waved two fingers over his head as he struck out toward the milking barn.

Anna was loath to break the camaraderie she and Iain had established. The goats continued to romp and play. "Are you going to be able to construct enough pens for the animals? And what about all the kids who are bringing their bunnies and chickens and—Lord help me— piglets for the husbandry competition? The barn simply isn't big enough, and we can't put them under the sun."

"This blasted heat. Isabel tried to warn me." Iain rubbed his nape, exposing a tan line where his T-shirt lay.

Anna lifted the edge of his shirtsleeve to see a similar demarcation. "You're going to be a genuine redneck by the time the festival rolls around."

"Is having a red neck good or bad?"

Generally, the term was bestowed derisively with connotations of ignorance, but many wore it with pride along with a strong work ethic. The latter seemed to apply to Iain. "In your case, it would be a good thing."

A smile took over his face, banishing shadows that crept closer when he thought no one was looking. "Was that a compliment?"

"Maybe, but don't get a big head to go with your red neck. Now, what about the pens?"

"The only viable option is to outfit the barn for the large animals, and to construct shaded pens for bunnies and the like in the pines. The festivalgoers will funnel through the middle of the barn leading to the pens on either side until they exit to the field." He made a clicking sound with his tongue, and as if it were a universal language, all three goats trotted toward his outstretched hand for a scratch.

"That plan will bring people close to the main house, which is off-limits."

"Stonehaven proper will remain off-limits, although we may have to post extra security in the area to keep the rabble from looking for air-con or a washroom."

"You're sure you can get the work done in time?" It seemed daunting. The look he shot her was so disdainful of her doubt, she couldn't help a chuckle. "Sorry I asked. I guess you have plenty of time since you don't veg out in front of a TV."

"We didn't have a telly growing up." Iain's shrug didn't give the impression he felt at all deprived while Anna couldn't imagine life without *Friends* reruns.

"Not even up at the castle?"

"Gareth had one in his study, but it was rarely on. Da keeps the radio on after supper in the cottage."

"What kind of music does he like?" She gathered each new factoid like crumbs to a starving woman.

"Classical mostly, although he liked Tom Jones and his ilk. Lots of BBC news reports. Weather alerts if things looked tetchy outside, which was most of the time in winter."

The picture of a stone cottage with smoke from a fire puffing from the chimney standing on a hill blanketed in snow was picturesque. *But.* There were so many buts that outweighed her initial impression. He was solid and dependable but possessed the voice of a dreamer. He loved his father and had been loved back, but he understood loneliness. He'd lived it.

When she didn't say anything, he cocked his head. "I feel like you're getting ready to pass judgment on me."

She pasted on a light smile. "No judgment. I'm just surprised local girls weren't crawling all over Cairndow in pursuit."

Surprise lightened his face even though he gave no hint of a smile. "First you go and ask me out to dinner, then you insinuate I might not be a total Barney. Be careful or I might think you like me a wee bit."

Apparently, spontaneous combustion was really a thing. Anna only wished she hadn't verified the phenomenon in front of Iain. She needed a fan. And more deodorant. "What? I was just trying to be nice and offer some Southern hospitality. I don't *like* you. Geez. That's crazy insane. It's bonkers. Why would you say that? Why would you even *think* it?"

His face shuttered like a gale force wind blew through the barn. "I was merely . . . Never mind. I have work to do." He turned on his heel and stalked away.

What babbling nonsense had come out of her mouth? Iain was serious and tough, but he had feelings that could be hurt. Worst of all, she'd lied. Unable to make her feet move in his direction, she stood there and went down in flames.

Did a bigger idiot exist? Based on Iain's current levels of embarrassment, he assumed not. Why had he tried to flirt with Anna? There wasn't anything between them beyond the forced connection of the festival. His hopeful, desperate imagination had played a horrible joke on him. Of course, she didn't like him like *that*.

Next time he saw her, he'd pretend the conversation hadn't taken place, and in the meantime, he really did have work to do. Making his way back to the tartan truck, he only looked over his shoulder once to see her walking to the main house to talk to Holt's da.

He had every confidence she possessed the charm

to finagle whatever she needed from Mr. Pierson and pointed the truck back toward Highland, where he had an appointment with a rotted door.

He parked in the back of All Things Bright and Beautiful and knocked on the door, performing a visual assessment of the rot. When there was no answer, he let himself in, dodged around the piles of inventory yet to go out on the floor, and found Loretta sitting behind the counter tending a customer. "You go ahead and get started, Iain. I can't thank you enough for being so prompt."

Smiling, he nodded to Loretta. The store was crammed full of crafts and knickknacks, mostly Scottish themed. It was his nightmare of a store, but several people browsed the overcrowded shelves.

Iain didn't dillydally, but got straight to work prying out the rotten wood from the frame and commenced his measurements. He was methodical to avoid mistakes. His da had been frugal, and whether through heredity or example, Iain was the same. Whatever scraps of wood Iain had left over went toward new projects or toward his whittlings.

His whittlings were sometimes whimsical creatures from his imagination or from books. Sometimes they were instruments like utensils or picture frames that were both useful and decorative. For him, they were better than meditation or yoga or whatever people used these days to relax. The small projects had kept him sane during deployments. Maybe that's why he'd been so keyed up lately. He hadn't had time to whittle. His rising frustration had nothing to do with a red-haired lass who tormented his dreams.

The bell over the front door rang often enough that Iain

had stopped paying it any mind, but as soon as he heard the familiar, honeyed voice of Anna, he stilled, the measurement he'd tasked himself to remember forgotten.

On soft feet, he made his way to the curtain partitioning the storage area from the store and peeked around the side. The two women faced off, their profiles to Iain.

Anna's smile was friendly, but tension resided in the set of her jaw. "I'm here to collect your deposit for the festival."

Loretta's smile was more genuine in that it was the mere baring of her teeth, yet her voice was sweet enough to give him a toothache. "I'm not quite ready to pay. Given that this is your first year involved in the planning, maybe you don't understand that Rose has always allowed local businesses extra time."

"What I understand is that I have deposits to make as well, and if I don't get them paid on time, then the festival won't have enough food trucks or portable potties or stage equipment." Anna squared her shoulders. "Anyway, I've given you extra time. I need your deposit if you want to reserve your space."

"How about you pencil me into my usual spot, and I'll get you a check by the end of the week." It was not framed as a question, but a statement. Without giving Anna a chance to agree or disagree, Loretta floated over to help a customer who had waved to get her attention.

Anna let her head drop back and rubbed the bridge of her nose. She looked worn down. All the more reason for him to step in and step up. If only she weren't determined to go it alone. Iain had avoided the last three calls from Gareth and Alasdair, not sure how to describe the situation.

He'd underestimated how enmeshed Anna was in the

complex ecosystem of Highland and how valuable her capabilities were. Still, he had handled smaller events on the grounds of Cairndow and could certainly help beyond mucking out the stables and building fencing.

Anna heaved a sigh and retreated in defeat. He could scarcely believe it if he didn't see it happen.

It took another two hours to complete the reframing, but he was happy with the results and so was Loretta if her smiles—warm and wide this time—and effusive thanks were to be believed.

"This is top-notch, quality work, young man." Loretta ran her hand along the nearly invisible joint.

"Thank you." He loaded the tools in the bed of the truck.

"Have you done any renovation work?"

"A bit." Besides his stint in Glasgow working for a housing contractor, he'd done plenty of renovation work at Cairndow.

"Do you mind if I pass your name along?"

"I certainly don't mind, but I'm not sure how much time I'll have to take on projects with the festival fast approaching." He wiped his forehead with a work rag he kept tucked into his waistband.

"I understand." A wistful look passed over her face, softening the harsh lines around her mouth. "My husband passed a decade ago now, and I have several lady friends who are in the same predicament. It would be awfully nice to know someone trustworthy who could help us with various projects around the house."

"I'll be glad to help where I can." When she turned away, he took a chance. "About the festival. Could I collect your deposit? It would save Anna a trip down and make things easier for me."

She regarded him a moment then jerked her head in a follow-me gesture. He obeyed. From behind the counter in the store, she pulled out a sealed envelope with her name and FESTIVAL DEPOSIT written across the front.

"Here." She held it out.

He looked from her to the envelope and back again. Why in blazes had the woman not simply given the deposit to Anna earlier? He decided it was best not to question his luck, tucked the envelope into his pocket, and left after thanking her.

He thought about dropping by the studio and giving Anna the deposit, but opted to leave it on the desk at Stonehaven. Would she perceive his success as a help or an intrusion? After their awkward last parting, he wasn't willing to find out.

Chapter Eight

The next evening after teaching at the studio all day, Anna timed her arrival at Stonehaven with the efficiency of a spy mission. She softly closed her car door and tip-toed across the pea gravel to the front door. The sound of power tools came from the barn. As expected, Iain was taking advantage of the cooling air.

An envelope sat on top of the closed laptop. Loretta's name slashed across the white. Anna pushed the corner of the envelope with one finger. Nothing happened. Not that she was expecting a booby trap or anything. She opened the seal and a check dropped out. A check dated three days ago.

Unless Loretta was into breaking and entering, she must have given it to Iain. A power play. She and Loretta were in the first round of a title fight, with the mayoral contest the fifth and final round.

At least Anna had the money. She had other things to worry about at the moment. She opened Izzy's laptop, but the screen remained dark. The charging cord was on the floor. She picked it up and stared at it as if it had betrayed her before plugging it in. She could have sworn she'd left it charging the day before. Just one more inconvenience. Her head had felt stuffed with cotton all day. Allergies were annoying. Add in her regrets over her last conversation with Iain, and she was officially in a pissy mood.

Finally, the screen flickered on as the computer booted up. She clicked on the festival folder and scanned the file names for the current year's vendor spreadsheet. She'd put in a couple of hours on calls and notes over the weekend and had highlighted where to pick up today. She resorted the files by save date. The most recent file was twelve months old. She resorted by name and then file type. No sign of her updated file, even though she was sure she had clicked save after making her notes.

Could she recreate the spreadsheet from the prior year's information and memory? Not with the same level of detail. Who had she called? Could she remember them all? She jotted down a half dozen she could remember, but her brain was as shaky as her hands.

Another thought jolted her up from the chair. Had Iain sabotaged her? Had he unplugged the charger? Her wobbly logic fell into a patch of doubts. Was he really the sort of man who would delete a file out of spite? No, he wasn't. Iain wasn't immature and neither was he dishonorable.

But it's possible he knew what had happened. Maybe he'd been on the laptop and accidentally deleted the file. Anna sidled toward the barn. A nail gun pierced the relative silence with sharp *thunk*s. She stepped inside and shuffled across sawdust toward where Iain worked in the back of the barn.

A portable fan whirred and stirred the air against her bare legs. With the front and back doors open, the cross breeze made it almost pleasant.

As she drew closer, Iain turned toward her and pushed a pair of clear safety glasses to the top of his head, the nail gun pointing to the ground. Not that she was worried he might threaten her with it.

"What?" he asked brusquely.

"I . . . You . . ." Sentences refused to knit themselves together. His white T-shirt stuck to him with patches of sweat. His army-green utility kilt was one she'd seen before, but this time tools were tucked into pockets and loops along the hips and hem she hadn't noticed before. It looked actually useful and not worn merely to jump-start her libido.

"What do you need, Anna?" No note of welcome colored his flat tone, but his one rebellious eyebrow was quirked up in a way that transmitted mockery.

"How do you do that?" she asked.

He set the nail gun aside without taking his gaze off her. "Do what?"

"Lift one eyebrow. Were you born like that or did you practice in the mirror?"

"Winters at Cairndow could be dull, but not so dull I would stare at myself all day."

"I wish I could do it." She tried to raise one eyebrow but could feel both pop up. "It's like a superpower."

"And would you use the power for good or evil?" His voice had lost its edge.

"While I would like to say good, I'd probably go with evil. Or like Robin Hood. I would help those less fortunate stand up to the powerful." How on earth had her panic devolved into such a silly conversation?

"Do you face injustice on a regular basis?" He leaned back against the wall and crossed his arms over his chest and his feet at the ankles. The position put his biceps and calves on attractive display.

She forced her gaze up his body to his face, and once again, she met his sardonic eyebrow. "You're doing it again."

The eyebrow twitched, then toppled to line up with his other, normal eyebrow. "Sorry, can't help it. I can't imagine anyone would be brave enough to bully you."

"I was called carrot-head plenty as a kid, but it never bothered me. I like carrots."

"Me too." They shared a smile.

How had he managed to sidetrack her so easily? She cleared her throat and winced. The soreness had dogged her all day even after taking allergy medicine. "Were you on the laptop earlier? Like to check your email or something? It wasn't charging when I got here."

"Haven't touched it. Maybe you forgot to plug it in last time you were here." He pushed off the wall, not sounding like a man who had accidently deleted a file.

If it wasn't him, then it was 100 percent her fault. "I'm missing a file. The file that I worked on over the weekend."

"Why would I would delete your work?" He had every right to sound aggrieved. "Do you think I'm that much of a bastard?"

"No! Of course not." She gripped the back of her hair. "It may not look like it, but I'm panicking on the inside. This file is critical, and if I can't find it, then the entire festival might fail and everyone will think I'm incompetent and can't be trusted with anything important."

"That's rather . . ." What was he going to say? Stupid?

Paranoid? ". . . dramatic. I'm sure the file has been stored on the laptop. Probably in a temp folder."

"A temp folder?" she parroted dumbly. Computers were not her thing. The basics she could handle, but when things went wrong, she got lost.

"Do you want me to look at it?"

"Why are you being so nice?"

"Would you rather I was a foul git?"

As she had no idea what a "foul git" was, she bumbled out a chuckle. "As long as you aren't an axe murderer."

"How did you find out?" he whispered and took a ground-swallowing step toward her, his brows low over his eyes and his mouth tight. He reached for a wooden handle leaning against the wall and swung up the tool, the silver blade glinting in a narrow shaft of sunlight sneaking through the slats. It was a mother-flipping axe.

With her mind wading through molasses and unable to make logical connections, she startled backward, her pained throat ready to release a scream no one except Ozzie and Harriet would hear. Neither were likely to come to her rescue. She bumped her hip against a saw-horse. She lurched to catch her balance, but the layer of sawdust didn't provide stable footing and she went down on her butt, the fall hard and ignominious.

"God's blood, are you hurt?" The axe clanked to the floor as Iain squatted next to her.

Her lower arm was numb from a bang her funny bone took, but she was mostly fine. "Except for the near heart attack you gave me."

"It was a joke. Did you really think I would hurt you?" First, she accused him of sabotaging the laptop and now this. Even though the streak of fear had been quick to dissipate, she couldn't deny its existence.

She didn't mean to make a habit of hurting his feelings, and she wanted to make amends, but she was having a hard time focusing on a heartfelt apology when she finally had an answer to the universal question.

She knew what a Scotsman wore under his kilt.

Actually, she didn't have the definitive answer to what *every* Scot wore under their kilt, but she knew what Iain wore. Absolutely *nothing*. Not that she saw nothing. Unless her eyes were playing tricks on her, what was underneath was . . . substantial.

She should look away. Instead, her eyes felt grainy because they refused to even blink. The noises stumbling out of her were part appreciation and part embarrassment. "You're showing."

"I'm what?"

"I can see your . . ." She cupped her hand and gestured toward him. "You know, your *junk*."

He leapt to his feet and smoothed his kilt down like a debutante of old after giving a peek at her ankles. He mumbled something in Gaelic before asking, "Why were you looking?"

"I couldn't help it." Her voice had morphed into a hoarse squeak. Heat rushed through her body. Not the kind that appreciated his ample offering to womanhood, but the mortified kind. "It was in my face. Well, not literally, but you know what I mean."

Even behind the camouflage of his beard, a blush raged. It was entirely endearing.

"Just so you know, I don't usually . . ." He gestured with his hands. "But it was so blasted hot and the breeze felt— Never mind."

Did she want to know how the breeze felt? Yes, she

did, but she wasn't stupid or brave enough to ask. "I can imagine."

Why had she offered that? Now she really was imagining. Had it felt like a woman's breath right before she took him in her mouth? Or maybe right after she'd licked up the length of him. Her brain was careening down a dark path of scenarios she might have to revisit that night in the privacy of her bed.

He offered a hand, and she slipped hers into his. Once again, she felt dwarfed by his size and strength, but no fear colored the moment.

He didn't release her hand. "Do I truly scare you, Anna?"

The seriousness of his expression stilled the joke ready to spring out of her mouth. The question peeled back a bandage on a wound he'd carried for a long time, if she had to guess. Instead of a trite answer, she offered what was owed—honesty.

"You can be gruff and intimidating, but no, I'm not scared of you." His mouth lost a measure of its tightness, and she couldn't stop herself from adding, "Unless you're coming at me with an axe. Not cool."

"Sorry."

"I'll forgive you if you forgive me for thinking even for a millisecond you did something to the computer. I know you're not that kind of man."

He squeezed her hand. "All is forgiven. Would you like some help locating your wayward spreadsheet?"

"Yes, please."

He let go of her hand, and she hid her disappointment by falling a couple of steps behind him on the way to the house. The swing of his pleats hypnotized her, and she alternated between wishing for the wind to bless her with another peek and silently berating her wayward libido. It had been tossing and turning since Iain had come to town, but it had officially emerged from hibernation. The timing couldn't be worse.

In the office, she attempted a brisk, professional tone as she used the mouse to open the folder the file should have occupied. He stood behind her, braced a hand on the desk, and peered over her shoulder.

"You've been saving regularly?" he asked.

"Of course. I'm not a doofus." Anna glanced up where he loomed over her.

"I assume that's similar to a dobber."

"We need a Southern-Scottish translator." She smiled and even though his focus was on the computer screen, the corner of his mouth she could see tipped up.

"We seem to rub along fairly well now we understand each other better."

"Rub along well? Is that a euphemism?"

He barked a laugh. "No. Why don't you let me drive?"

They exchanged places, and she paced behind the chair. "My file is probably floating around cyberspace as a disconnected series of zeros and ones."

He merely grunted as he clicked through various folders and entered search strings in the box.

"You're good at this," Anna said, trying and failing to keep the surprise from her voice.

He clicked through more layers of files. "I used computers quite a bit in the service, but not much since. I spent the last lambing season in a little stone cottage all alone with no internet."

"How long is lambing season?"

"The bulk of the births happen in six weeks."

"You spent a month and a half alone except for sheep as company?" She tried to imagine the silences. Would it be peaceful or torturous?

"More like four months. In fact, Alasdair had to come find me when it seemed the baby was not going to co-operate with the timing of the festival."

"You must have hated to leave your fortress of solitude."

"I didn't say that." He turned and graced her with the rise of his haughty eyebrow.

With her brain taking a nap, she smoothed over the sleek dark eyebrow with her thumb. "That thing is out of control, Highlander."

For a moment he appeared nonplussed, but then a slow smile tilted his lips and crinkled his eyes. "Is this it?"

Is this it? It seemed like a philosophical question for the ages. Is this a beginning or an ending or something else entirely? "Is this what?"

"Your file?" He pointed at the screen, and she transferred her focus with difficulty.

She blinked. Sweet relief soothed her acute anxiety. "Thank you, sweet baby Jesus, yes! Where was it?"

"In a temp folder. Apparently, you downloaded it from somewhere and never changed the default file folder when you saved."

He stood and put her in mind of a tree. Nothing exotic like a gingko or a Japanese maple, but a sturdy, dependable oak. A tree that weathered storms without a fuss. She understood the compulsion to become a tree hugger.

"You really saved my bacon. Thanks." She forced a lightness she didn't feel into her voice. In fact, her body and mind felt weighed down.

"Americans are obsessed with their pork products, aren't they?"

"Yes, because it's delish. Have you ever had a BLT with a fresh-picked tomato and still-sizzling bacon?"

"I can't say I have."

She realized her question sounded suspiciously like an invitation. "Uh, well, you should get one before you leave to go home."

A crease formed between his eyes. "I'll make sure I do."

She spotted the envelope from Loretta on the desk and waved it in front of him. "What do you know about this?"

"Loretta asked me to pass it along to you."

"When?" she asked.

"I replaced a rotting doorframe in her shop. I believe it was after you talked to her about it." His gaze danced around the room, never quite meeting hers.

"I thought for sure I was going to have to hit her up again. I wonder what brought around the change of heart."

His answer was a shrug. "Can I help you with anything else?"

"Naw. I'm good. Are you good?" Why had she asked him that?

"I'll get back to my work, then, lass."

"Lass" was basically Scottish-speak for "girl," and if anyone else had called her "girl," she would have cut them with her tongue. Why then did a tiny thrill zip through her when Iain called her "lass"? It made no sense. It was a Scottish double standard.

"Okay. Thanks again."

He nodded and walked out, the front door snicking shut. Anna slumped in the chair, looking not at the spreadsheet she'd been so desperate to find, but the empty doorway of the office, feeling as if she was still missing something vital.

Chapter Nine

The next day, all of Anna's nerve endings vibrated like she'd plugged into an electrical source. Even her skin was supersensitive, her T-shirt more like a Brillo Pad than cotton. Her stomach felt like it was hosting a battle of the bands. Her mind struggled through a bog, thoughts falling away to be lost in black water, and her usual high energy dipped to an all-time low. Had she even gotten four hours of sleep the night before?

A solid night's sleep tonight would put her to rights. She checked her watch. She still had her class of high schoolers to teach, costumes to fit, and festival work to organize. But then, she would definitely get a great—okay, decent—night's sleep and feel back to her normal self in the morning.

Her class flew by as they were polishing their routines for the competition. Gabby was once more a no-show, and worries about one of her star pupils piled onto the heap of others. The fitting went poorly as her fingers were clumsier than usual, and after poking the same girl twice, she dismissed them, promising to finish after their next practice.

After locking up the studio, she waffled at the foot of the stairs to her loft. It was almost eight and the sun was setting. She hadn't eaten since grabbing a granola bar at lunch, yet her stomach wasn't grinding itself into dust for food. Her throat had worsened overnight and through the day. Georgia pollen was no joke.

Before she could crawl into her soft bed, she had one more piece of business to attend to. The printers needed the map of the festival grounds for the pamphlet, and she needed to add the barn and the planned pens to last year's map. As she didn't have the necessary program on her laptop, she would have to head to Stonehaven and work in the office. Once it was sent off, she could collapse and sleep without guilt.

Iain would be taking advantage of the cooling evening to work on the enclosures, so she wouldn't even have to worry about a six-foot-something distraction. She hadn't been able to stop thinking about him and blamed him for her poor rest. Sure enough, when she pulled in to the front of Stonehaven, Iain stepped out of the barn, wearing another one of his utility kilts and no shirt, wiping his forehead on a small towel.

She slid out of the car, her knees shaking so badly, they were almost knocking together. If this was how her body had started reacting seeing him from a distance, what would happen up close? Would her ovaries explode?

He gave her a little wave, which she returned then pointed toward the front door and sought the safety of the house. She flipped the light on in the office, squinting when the brightness made her head hurt. Had Iain put a supercharged bulb in?

Once she sat in the cushioned office chair, her shoulders slumped and her spine curved as if her bones had turned to taffy. She slapped her cheeks to regain focus and fired up the computer, pulling up last year's map with no trouble. The animal exhibition needed to be added as did the extra portable potty station Anna had booked. It was geared toward families and included a diaper changing station.

She squinted against the bright light and found her clumsiness had carried over to the mouse. Maybe a power nap would clear her head and get her back on track. Ten minutes max. She put her head down and closed her eyes.

Iain stepped quietly down the stairs, which was difficult considering their age and his size. The wood creaked with every step. He ducked his head before reaching the bottom and peered into the office. Anna hadn't moved since his return to the house. Her head was tucked into her crossed arms like a bird against a storm. He'd thought for sure she would have woken by the time he had finished showering.

What now? He propped a shoulder against the door-jamb of the office and considered his options. Leave her or wake her? Her red hair was braided, but pieces stuck out at all different angles. The lass was running herself ragged. While the enclosures were a big undertaking, he had time to help her, especially during the hot afternoons when he took a break.

He could only imagine the crick in her neck if she spent much more time slumped over the desk. Barefoot, he shuffled to her and put his hand on her shoulder for a slight shake. Heat radiated through her thin cotton T-shirt and ignited a different worry than mere exhaustion.

"Anna, lass. Wake up." He shook her shoulder more vigorously.

As if she'd entered a dimension with a different set of laws defining space and time, she lifted her head and blinked at him in slow motion. No recognition registered in her blue eyes. She looked drunk or dazed or . . . feverish.

He touched the back of his hand to her forehead. Definitely too hot. Now he knew the problem, he could solve it. Medicine and water and somewhere to lay down.

"How about we head to the couch?" Although he framed it as a suggestion, he scooped under her arms and helped her to stand.

She was a wet noodle, her forehead landing on his chest as her weight pitched into him. He picked her up in a cradle hold, carried her to the overstuffed couch in the living area, and laid her down gently. Her eyes were closed, and he wasn't sure if she was awake or asleep or passed out.

He ran his hand over her forehead, pushing her disheveled hair back in a motion that was more caress than she'd be comfortable with if she were awake. She'd made herself perfectly clear at the farm; she wasn't interested or attracted to him in any way. The memory still had the power to sting, but the discomfort would fade like all the other rejections he'd received over the years. And it felt as if they'd smoothed things over the day before. Minus the accidental peep show. Heat flushed through him as if he were sick too, but with embarrassment.

He merely looked at her for a long moment, not sure where the boundaries lay. While they weren't friends, it felt like they had moved beyond being enemies. He was in no-man's-land.

He foraged through the kitchen for fever reducers, finally locating a cache of first aid supplies in a cupboard by the stove. Setting the bottle and a glass of water on the coffee table, he dropped to his knees next to Anna. Her cheeks were rosy, but underneath she was pale. Her delicateness was usually camouflaged by the strength of her personality.

Once more, he resorted to shaking her shoulder. When her eyes blinked open, he said matter-of-factly, "You're sick, Anna."

Her gaze sharpened, if not to its normal stiletto deadliness at least to rusty pen knife levels, but her voice was weak and hoarse sounding. "That's a terrible thing to say."

"It's not terrible, merely a fact."

"I can't help it." Her bottom lip trembled as a wave of emotion broke through her usual strong facade.

"I know you can't," he said gently, not sure why she was getting emotional or what to do to stop it. Did they make a medicine for that?

"It's all your fault." She poked him weakly in the chest with a finger.

Was she delusional from the raging fever? "I didn't make you sick, lass."

"Yes, you did. You showed up, looking like you do, and planted all sorts of sick, perverted thoughts in my head. It's totally your fault."

Perverted thoughts? He rubbed his forehead. Was he the one who was feverish and delusional? "What sort of perverted thoughts?"

She reached out and grabbed the side of his kilt. "I can't stop thinking about yesterday. I could barely sleep, and when I did, I dreamed about you. Not that it was the first time."

His lungs were tight and his breathing shallow. All

sorts of questions rampaged through him like, What did she dream of? And how was he involved? All that stuttered out was a simple "Wh-what?"

She barked a laugh he had become familiar with. It teetered between true humor and sarcasm. "Oh please, like you don't know."

He was at a loss how to respond because he truly didn't know. He had stepped out of the shower and into an alternate universe. Or, more likely, she was hallucinating. "Here. Take these."

He helped to prop her up on the pillows and shook two pills into one of her hands and pressed the water into her other. She swallowed and grimaced. "My throat hurts."

At least, she was making sense again. "The medicine will help," he said.

"I'm so tired."

"You've been working hard and not taking care of yourself. When's the last time you ate?"

Her eyes grew unfocused. "I had a granola bar for lunch, I think. Or was that for dinner last night? I don't remember."

"Wait here," he said stupidly. As if she had the strength to up and leave. Although, if anyone would try to escape his help and drive herself home, it would be Anna. He retreated to the kitchen to find something she could eat, finally settling on some yogurt with fresh blueberries.

He resumed his position on his knees next to the couch and handed over the bowl. The first scoop barely made it to her mouth, her hand shook so badly.

He took the bowl from her and fed her one small bite at a time, ignoring her initial protests. She stared into his eyes like a lost sailor searching for a beacon. When the bowl was half-empty, she pushed the next bite away, her hand clasping his wrist and not letting go even when he put the bowl down.

"How do you feel?" He lay his hand against her forehead and let the backs of his fingers slide to her cheek in a moment of weakness. Her skin was soft and not quite as blazing hot as it had been.

"A little better?" She lilted what should have been a statement into a question, which meant she still felt like shite.

He pulled a soft fleece blanket from the back of the couch and tucked it around her.

"I don't want to be a bother. I should go home." She struggled to sit up, but he pressed her back down by the shoulders. It took hardly any effort.

"You're no bother. I can't in good conscience allow you to drive home to an empty house with no one to care for you."

He had no idea what he said that triggered her, but suddenly she was blinking tears away and her chin was wobbling at the precipice of a cry.

"I don't even live in a house. I live all alone in a cramped apartment above the studio. You're right, I'm pathetic."

"I said no such thing! You're not pathetic; you're lovely."

"You should throw me outside and lock the door. Let Bigfoot take me to his lair and gnaw on my bones." Her melodramatic tone had him fighting a smile, but any amusement vanished when tears trickled down her temples into her hair and her face scrunched.

"Oh, no. Don't fash yourself, lass. Please." When the crying jag only intensified, he panicked, patted the top of her head, and murmured, "There, there."

She sat up, wrapped her arms around him, and buried her face in his shoulder. Her hands clutched at his back, her nails scraping through his T-shirt. It felt like she wanted to crawl inside of him to steal something of vital importance.

His breathing turned ragged as he allowed himself to react instinctively. He held her close, rubbing her back with one hand and massaging her nape with the other. Despite the medicine, he could register her fever.

The tears seemed interminable, but the longer they fell, the looser her body grew in his arms as if her cry was a release valve. When finally she lifted her head, he was ready with tissues. She blew her nose and rubbed at eyes nearly swollen shut.

She flopped backward on the couch. "I look terrible."

There was no way around the fact she was an ugly crier.

Iain cleared his throat. He might not be suave like Alasdair, but he knew well enough not to agree with *that*. "Well . . . you look a wee bit like your head got trapped in a sack with a hive of bees."

A laugh-sob erupted from her throat.

He cupped her jaw and ran a thumb along her cheek, his skin callused, hers soft. "I'm sorry. No more crying. Please."

She nuzzled into his touch and closed her eyes. The vulnerability surprised him. No, it *shocked* him. Anna was tough and confident. She didn't need anyone and made sure everyone understood she needed no one. Was that true, though? He'd seen flashes of longing in her face, but he wasn't intuitive enough to interpret what she longed for.

Her breathing evened out, and he tucked the blanket

tighter around her legs. What she needed more than anything was sleep. If she was no better in the morning, he would insist she visit a physician. When he shifted to rise, she surprised him once more by grabbing his hand and threading their fingers.

"I'm sorry," she whispered.

"Nothing to be sorry for."

"I need to tell you something very important." Still her eyes didn't open. He grunted his readiness to hear what she had to say, and he was relieved to see her lips tip into the smallest of smiles. "I love Robert Burns, and I love that you love him. I only teased you about him to get a rise out of you."

He huffed a laugh, wondering at the way her brain worked, and brushed her hair back from her hot forehead. "Do you realize how close I was to calling you out at dawn to fight for Rabbie's honor?"

She rewarded him with another small smile and blinked her eyes open. "You have a sexy voice, Iain. Will you sing me a song?"

It would take a man of herculean strength to deny such a request from her. And, he was discovering she was his weakness. He went with classic Burns, singing it low and slow.

"My love is like a red, red rose
That's newly sprung in June.
My love is like the melody
That's sweetly played in tune.
How fair art thou, my bonnie lass,
So deep in love am I;
And I will love thee still, my dear,
Till all the seas gang dry."

As he sang the next verse, he considered the state of his love life. "Dry" about summed it up. Or perhaps "barren" was more apt. By the time he finished, she was asleep, her fingers slack between his. He extricated himself and tucked her arm under the blanket.

Pacing in front of the windows, he threw glances toward the couch every few seconds. He didn't even consider his bed upstairs as an option. If she awoke during the night, he needed to be close. Worry kept him on edge.

The moon was high when he finally pulled a leather armchair close to the couch and settled in with a book. After reading the same page three times, he put the book down, stretched his legs out, and did what he really wanted to do. He watched her sleep. Hopefully, not in a creepy way.

Her face was flushed, and except for her puffy eyes, the evidence from her crying jag had faded. Her mouth was slightly parted, and she'd shifted to her side, her hand under her chin. At some point, he dozed off but was awakened by her restless moan. Her fever had soared. Iain dosed her with medicine, but she was unable to take more than a few swallows of water.

Holding her throat, she said, "My throat is lined with broken glass."

"Might be streptococcus. You need to see a physician tomorrow." He sat on the edge of the couch, his fingers itching to offer a small comfort.

She shivered and curled closer to put her head in his lap, her cheek against the top of his thigh and her arm slung loosely around his waist. "I'm so cold."

He hesitated only a moment before stretching out beside her on the couch and tucking her into his body.

While she might feel cold, the fever had turned her into a space heater.

"I don't want to get you sick." Her protest was muffled where her face was pressed into the side of his neck, her lips tickling his sensitive skin. Her legs twined with his and her hands slipped under his shirt to press against the bare skin of his back. Now he was the one who shivered as a different sort of fever raged.

Chapter Ten

Without opening her eyes, Anna could discern it was no longer dark. Summer light danced beyond her. Trouble was, she wasn't sure she could even open her eyes. They felt gritty and dried shut. She swallowed and winced. If possible, her throat was worse than it had been the night before. A hot tea with honey would put her back to rights.

She tried to roll to her back, but she was on a couch, not in her bed. Memories crept into her consciousness like thieves. She had been at Stonehaven working when exhaustion had swept over her. Iain had been kind and wonderful, and she'd repaid him by crying all over him. And not a cute cry. A snotty one. She vaguely remembered wiping her nose on his T-shirt.

Pulling a pillow over her face, she wondered if she could smother herself with it. What other mortifications had she brought upon herself? A recollection of him singing her to sleep bobbed to the surface like a life buoy. He really did have a panty-meltingly sexy voice.

With any luck, he wasn't around to see her bed head because she had work to do. She hadn't finished the map, and it was due today. She had classes to teach, things to do, people to see.

But before she could do any of that, she had to open her eyes. The effort it took to blink did not bode well for her plans to work on the computer and then drive home. The brightness of the white ceiling hurt her eyes, and the birds tweeting outside made her head throb.

A couple of aspirin would fix things. She lifted her head and the room spun. Okay, fixing things wasn't happening. Merely functioning would be a stretch. Her eyes stung with the desire to cry, but she was so parched, nothing materialized.

"Ah, you're awake." Iain's unmistakable voice rumbled from somewhere on the other side of the room.

He came into view, looming over her, his hands propped on the back of the couch. She should have been annoyed or embarrassed at her display of weakness in front of him, but she didn't have the energy. He might not be her friend, but he'd taken care of her the night before without complaining or making her feel even worse.

"Morning." The single word took three tries to get out of her shredded throat.

"I would ask how you're feeling, but I'm not daft or blind."

Her laugh stuttered to a stop before it could get started. She gasped and grabbed her throat. "Hurts."

"Aye. I figured as much." He checked his watch. Was he itching to get her out of his hair? She couldn't blame him.

Grabbing the arm of the couch, she hauled herself to sitting and then heaved herself to standing, her knees wobbly. "I'll go."

"I called this morning and made you an appointment with a physician. It's in a half hour. That's how it works here, right?"

"How did you know which doctor?"

"Google. I called a couple before I found the right one."

She formed an *O* with her lips, but didn't speak. She wasn't sure what to say. He was so dang capable. She might have stomped her feet in annoyance if she weren't so grateful.

He held out a glass of water and shook two pills into her palm. "Take these. They'll help until we can get something stronger prescribed."

She did as he instructed without any arguments, even though the pills felt like jagged rocks bumping down her throat.

"Do you need the loo?" he asked.

She nodded, and he helped her stand. She couldn't locate enough strength or pride not to take his arm and let him guide her to the downstairs powder room. When it appeared he was ready to squeeze into the small half bath with her, she shooed him away. "I can handle it from here, I think."

"Call if you need me." He backed to the far wall, crossed his arms over his chest, then dropped his hands to his side, looking like he wasn't quite sure what to do with himself.

His jeans had been worn soft and fit every slope and bulge of his body. Not that she could blame them. Even deathly ill, she could commiserate with the urge to fit herself close to him. She shut the door before the sight of him made her any more light-headed.

Catching sight of herself in the mirror, she let out a gasping yelp. Her hair was like a haystack blown over by the Big, Bad Wolf. Her pallor wasn't a porcelain white, but a sickly greenish-yellow against the flowered wallpaper. And, it tasted like something had died in her mouth.

First, she peed. Then, she washed her hands and face. The color the scrubbing imparted faded fast. Finding a mini tube of toothpaste in one of the drawers, she finger-brushed her teeth and made herself gag. Everything felt hypersensitive, and she didn't need a thermometer to tell her the aspirin hadn't made a dent in her fever yet.

Her clothes were wrinkled, and she felt stale, as if she'd been through some fever-sweat cycles during the night. She stared at herself in the mirror and patted her cheeks. Iain was seeing her at her worst. While she tried to work up proper horror, she really just wanted to feel better.

She opened the door and scraped her shoulder against the frame on her totter out into the hall. "How do I look?" she joked.

He gripped the back of her neck and the support was so welcome, she let her head rest in his grasp. His thumb stroked her jaw, and she closed her eyes. She should pull away from him and maintain a safe distance. She'd learned not to rely on anyone. Not her mother, not any of her boyfriends, not even Izzy.

"You look like shite, Anna." The sympathy in his rumbly brogue took any of the sting out of the words.

"I appreciate your honesty." And, strangely enough, she did. Iain didn't seem like the type to sugarcoat or feed a person what they wanted to hear. He was a man of hard truths, but truths nonetheless.

"Your appointment," he said.

"Yep. Where are my keys?" She tried to remember if she'd brought her purse in or left her keys on the desk in the office.

"I'm driving you."

"But I can—"

"Lass, don't be stubborn, you can barely walk. You'd be a danger to yourself and anyone else on the road. I'm driving." His voice brooked no argument. Not that she really wanted to make one. She meekly followed him outside to where Izzy's old pickup was parked close to the front door. Had he moved it so she wouldn't have to walk so far?

He opened the passenger side door as if it were a date. The seats were warm from the sun, and as the warmth seeped into her fever-chilled body, she closed her eyes and turned boneless.

A hard arm pressed against her torso and her eyes popped open. His head was close. So close, she could see his dark hair wasn't one color, but made of many shades. This was what happened when she let herself get close. Things got complicated and interesting. She wanted to sift her fingers through the strands and study each one. She raised her hand—

He pulled the seat belt across her body, snapping it into place and snapping her out of her reverie. The fever was planting foolish thoughts. The jouncing trip to town left her feeling vaguely nauseous, and she sank lower in the seat and took deep breaths.

"You're not going to toss your biscuits, are you?"

"My appetite is nonexistent at the moment."

His laugh was like hot chocolate on a cold day or being covered in wriggling puppies or a BLT made with sun-warmed freshly picked tomatoes. In other words, it made her feel good and might qualify as one of her favorite things.

"Tossing your biscuits means throwing up."

"Oh." She smiled despite the roil of her stomach. "No, I think my biscuits will remain untossed."

"Good. I wouldn't want to explain to Isabel how her truck became a biohazard when I get back."

Her smile flipped upside down. It was a good reminder he was leaving and she shouldn't get attached. "I'll be fine," she said defiantly, not sure if she was talking about getting over her sickness or the reality of him eventually leaving.

She helped him navigate his way through downtown Highland, where the summer bustle was in full swing. The number of tourists would explode as the festival drew closer. Iain parked in front of a plain cement block building a mile out of town.

She'd gone to Highland Family Practice since she was a kid, but couldn't recall the last time she'd been in. As a small business owner, her healthcare insurance was costly, and she had adopted a "this too shall pass" mentality. But she would sign over her first-born child—if she ever had one—to feel better.

Iain rounded the cab and opened her door. When she tried to get out, it was like the weight of the universe pressed her back down.

"Seat belt," he said shortly.

"Huh?"

He reached across her again and freed her from the pressing weight. She exhaled. "Thanks. My brain is spinning its wheels and getting nowhere."

Inside, they shared a waiting room with people of all ages. A coughing toddler and an eighty-something-year-old lady twirling a cane between her knees were called back.

Finally, Mrs. Pettigrew, the nurse practitioner, stuck her head out of the door to the exam rooms and called Anna's name. Iain rose with her, but she waved him off. If she was getting naked in front of him, it wouldn't be like this. The vision rampaged through her along with another chill.

She shuffled toward the door, where Mrs. Pettigrew tutted. "Come on back. I haven't seen you at the office for years. You look like death warmed over."

"Gee, thanks. Isn't it bad form to be joking about death in a doctor's office?" she asked.

"It should reassure you. If I thought you were really at death's door, I wouldn't crack a joke. Let's get you in a room before you fall over on me." A comforting hand between her shoulder blades guided Anna into a small exam room.

Mrs. Pettigrew possessed a soft motherliness that appealed to some base instinct Anna carried from childhood. Her mom was all angles and bones. With an ample bosom and arms made for dispensing hugs, Mrs. Pettigrew was the glue of the medical practice. She was also a staunch volunteer during the festival and headed up the library's used book sale that coincided with the annual parade. It funded literacy projects around the county.

Mrs. Pettigrew closed the door, and Anna lay on the paper-lined table. "My throat feels like I ate broken glass, and I'm pretty sure I have a fever."

Mrs. Pettigrew took her temperature and blood

pressure then clicked on a mini flashlight and looked in her mouth. "You do have a fever, and I would guess you have strep throat, but we'll work up a culture to verify."

"That's what Iain thinks too."

Mrs. Pettigrew's eyes sparked with an unholy interest. "Is Iain the sexy snack out in the lobby waiting for your return with bated breath?"

"Gross exaggeration, but yes."

"You're right. He's not a snack, he's a three-course meal. Do tell me all about him."

"He's Scottish and—" Anna gagged as Mrs. Pettigrew swabbed her throat, then resumed, "Izzy is getting ready to pop, and of course, Rose wanted to be there, so they sent Iain over to help with the festival."

"And what's going on between the two of you?"

"Nothing. Why would you think there was something going on?" Defensiveness crept into her voice. Had Mrs. Pettigrew picked up on Anna's internal thoughts? The swirl of emotions Iain inspired were conflicting.

Mrs. Pettigrew's gaze sharpened. "If I wasn't sure before, I am now. You're red as a radish. It's not every man who will accompany a woman to the doctor when she's sick, especially looking like you do right now. Danny Tinkle made his wife drive herself to the hospital when she was in labor with their third because he was on the seventeenth hole and wanted to finish."

"You're telling tall tales." Anna wanted to laugh, but even more, she wanted to curl up on the paper and take a nap.

"I swear on a Bible." Mrs. Pettigrew shook a small canister. "That didn't take long. It's positive." Mrs. Pettigrew picked up a tablet and tapped on the screen. "By the time you get to the Drug and Dime, they should have your script ready."

"How long until I feel human again?"

"Once we get you started on antibiotics, it won't take long, but it will be twenty-four hours before you aren't contagious." Mrs. Pettigrew wagged her finger at Anna. "So no sampling the three-course meal waiting on you."

Anna sputtered as she followed Mrs. Pettigrew to the checkout desk. A young girl tapped on the computer and informed her a bill would be in the mail. Anna couldn't even bring herself to worry about how much it might cost.

She stumbled into the waiting area. Iain stood, and a wave of emotion threatened to swamp her. It's not like she had expected him to bolt, but on the other hand, neither would she have been surprised to find him gone.

She walked up to him and croaked, "Diagnosis: strep throat. You were right. Do you mind running me by the Drug and Dime to pick up my antibiotics?"

"Of course I don't, ye silly woman." His brogue grew thicker when he was teasing her.

Iain loaded her back into the old truck. He rolled down his window and cocked his elbow out, the wind ruffling his hair. Anna lolled her head on the back of the bench seat and allowed herself to stare at him.

In profile with his scar front and center and his beard obscuring any softness, he was even tougher looking than usual. And he was tough when it came to how hard he could work, but he wasn't mean. Her fingers itched to explore the old wound. How had it happened? Was it a knife fight in a dark alley? Had he been injured while deployed? She wanted to know everything.

He cruised down Main Street, taking the first available parking spot, which was in front of Loretta's All Things Bright and Beautiful shop. The Drug and Dime was across the street and farther down.

"You stay here while I pick up the medication." Iain had the door open before she could argue. Not that she wanted to. The pharmacy felt like a grueling uphill hike away.

She leaned over and grabbed his arm before he could close the door. "Wait. Don't forget my birthday."

"Do you want me to get you a prezzie from the pharmacy? Lip balm? Tissues?"

She fell prone on the seat, giggling. His face came over hers, upside down, his grin looking like a frown. Without thinking, she touched his cheek with the scar. His mouth drew into a neutral line, and she snatched her hand back and tucked it under her chin.

"You need to tell the pharmacist my birthday to get the medicine." She rattled off her birthday.

He cocked his head. "The day after Christmas? That's bad luck."

"Yeah, it was the worst as a kid. When is your birthday?"

"April fifth."

Another fact about him she ferreted away like a squirrel with a nut. "That's a nice time of year. Spring. Rebirth."

"I'll be back in a jiff." He backed out of the cab and closed the door.

Anna lay across the bench seat until it grew hard to breathe in the heat. She hauled herself to sitting and opened the passenger window using the old-style crank.

A breeze skidded off the foothills of the Blue Ridge and offered a measure of relief.

What did she need to get done today? Her mental to-do list was scarily blank.

A knock on the door of the truck jolted her out of a semi-doze. Loretta stood at her window, looking in at her with hard eyes. Dealing with Loretta required a pep talk in the mirror and the *Rocky* theme music, neither of which she had on hand.

"Hi, Loretta. Thanks for the deposit."

"Thank Iain. He really is quite something."

Was there a hidden meaning behind the offhanded compliment? Anna decided to take the woman at face value. "He is very handy."

Loretta's eyes narrowed as they seemed to search for chinks in her armor. Usually, Anna met fire with fire, but the chills racking her body were not helping her confidence.

"I filed first thing this morning." There was no mistaking the statement as anything other than a challenge. It was the first day the city offices accepted intent to run forms from mayoral candidates.

"Good for you," Anna said blandly, unable to muster even a spark of enthusiasm. She wasn't surprised, of course. Loretta had been salivating for a run at Highland's mayor even before Dr. Jameson won. She had been biding her time, ready to pounce on the opportunity. What Loretta hadn't counted on was Anna wanting it too.

Anna wasn't a power junkie. She genuinely loved Highland, which was ironic considering she'd escaped as soon as possible after graduation, but after things hadn't worked out in New York, Highland had welcomed her home and lifted her up. She was proud of her little town and wanted it to thrive and grow.

Anna didn't doubt that Loretta loved Highland too. It was their visions that clashed. Anna wanted to press forward with plans to expand the summer festival into a Highland Christmas celebration. She had an entire digital folder full of ideas she could sell to the city council if she was elected. Loretta, on the other hand, was content with the way things were and wanted them to stay that way. While familiarity might breed contempt, it also provided comfort.

"I figured you'd be waiting for them to unlock the front door. Have you changed your mind?" Loretta asked with a leading edge.

"I haven't actually. In case you weren't aware, I've been rather busy planning the festival."

"How is the festival coming along? Will it suffer without Rose and Izzy's leadership?"

"I've got things well in hand, thank you very much." Anna cleared her throat, then winced at the pain.

"By the way, I expect my usual booth. I hope the Buchanans left you with a detailed setup."

"They did, but things will be shifted around a bit because of the husbandry display and competition."

Loretta wrinkled her nose. "I hope the smell doesn't put people off from spending their money on food."

"Change is invigorating and offers opportunities for better things." God, she sounded like a motivational poster.

"Not every change is positive. That's a lesson only age and wisdom will impart. The voters will understand."

Anna harrumphed. "I would make—*will* make—an excellent mayor."

"I'm sure you will. In twenty years. For now, you should allow more seasoned adults to make decisions that will impact every resident of Highland for years to come. No one wants to see their taxes increase. That's a fact."

Anna tucked her hair behind her ear, wanting to close the window and her eyes against Loretta and the outside world. She didn't, of course.

"But a penny tax would—"

"No one wants a tax increase, girl, and that's that." Loretta's voice had risen and attracted the curious glances from the tourists walking along the sidewalk. Her gaze pinned Anna to the seat like mounting a butterfly.

Would it warrant a Sunday sermon if she told Loretta to go to hell? Politely, of course. Before Anna could weigh the pros and cons, a deep voice broke their stare down.

"You all right, Anna?" Iain placed a hand on the open window frame and angled himself to face Loretta.

"Did you get them?" Anna's only thought was getting the miracle of antibiotics into her system.

Iain held up the pharmacy bag, shook it, and waggled his eyebrows. Loretta took a step backward, her eyes huge and darting between them. Anna could practically see the hamster wheel spinning in her head. Oh God, what did Loretta think was in the bag? Lube and condoms?

Anna tried to work up some embarrassment, but all she wanted to do was laugh. She only stopped herself because it would hurt her throat.

"How is the door, Ms. Loretta? If it's sticking, I can adjust it," Iain said.

"It's perfect. Have you thought any more about taking on more work?" She smoothed the graying hair at her neck and favored Iain with a coquettish smile that charmed the American Legion bunch.

"I've been busy, but I'll let you know if I have time. If you'll excuse us, we have things that can't wait another minute." Once more Iain shook the pharmacy bag.

Loretta quickstepped to stand in the door of her shop and watched until they drove off. Anna retrieved the medicine and the bottle of iced tea Iain had kindly provided, popped a pill, and forced it down.

Then, she laughed weakly before grabbing her throat. "You know she thinks we're going to boink like rabbits. In the light of day, no less. The scandal."

He brake-checked and shot an incredulous glance over at her. "What in blazes are you talking about?"

"I'm talking about you and your cute little eyebrow waggle as you shook the bag and informed her we had things to do that couldn't wait."

"Getting you feeling better can't wait."

"My guess is Loretta thinks you can't wait to rip my clothes off and take wild advantage of me." The antibiotics couldn't be working yet. Nevertheless, she felt lighter. Hope was a powerful drug.

"Would it be taking wild advantage of you?" He raised a single eyebrow and shot her another look.

A look that could only be interpreted as evocative. But evocative of what? Did he want to take wild advantage of her? Not that any overture he made would be taking advantage of her. If anything of that ilk occurred, it would be mutual. More than mutual. In fact, she might be the one taking wild advantage of him. Every spare moment, her brain revisited the incident in the barn. The question of what was under his kilt warranted further investigation.

Unfortunately, the sounds coming out of her mouth did not emerge as words. She was speechless. It might be a first. He didn't backtrack or make excuses for his leading question, he merely drove on, waiting and silent.

Their arrival at Stonehaven broke the deadlock. She swayed out front, unsure. Her car was there, so she could drive herself home and curl up in her own bed. But work awaited her in the office. Maybe she could close her eyes for a few minutes on the couch and then make some calls.

Iain put a hand on her lower back and guided her up the steps and inside the house. "You're going to lay down in one of the spare rooms upstairs."

"I can't."

"Why not?"

"I have classes to teach." She swayed on her feet.

"Not only are you physically unable to teach, you are also contagious. You must cancel." He spoke gently but firmly. "Tell me what to do."

She wanted to argue, but he was right. She walked Iain through how to post the cancellation on social media and send a mass email to her students and their parents. "I've got to get the map done too."

"What map?"

"The festival grounds. It has to go to the printer today." She only made it one step toward the office before he had her shoulders.

"I'm fully capable of handling the map and anything else that comes up. I'll let you approve the changes before I send it." His face went in and out of focus with each of her blinks. Did she have a choice?

While she rested on the couch, he had the map done

faster than she could have. After getting her okay, he emailed it, then guided her up the stairs.

"I should go home. You have work to do, and I'm imposing."

"No, you'll be making things easier on me. If you went back to your flat, then I would have to leave Stonehaven and my work to periodically deliver soup and make sure you're taking your medicine. Here, I only have to walk up the stairs. It would be very selfish of you to insist on going home."

His reasoning was weak at best. She was an adult who could take care of herself. After all, she'd been doing it for years and years and years.

And yet . . . and yet, warm fuzzy feelings wrapped her like a favorite blanket. "Okay."

"Really?" His surprise made a laugh sneak out of her.

"Am I that tough of a nut?" Now that the decision had been made, she couldn't crawl into bed fast enough. "By the way, what is your favorite nut?"

Anna made for Izzy's old room. It had been cleared of most of her personal items. Only the ghost of her friend remained. A ghost was better than nothing.

"I'm partial to walnuts in my Christmas pudding."

Anna burrowed under the covers and made a gagging sound. "That sounds gross."

"It's delicious."

"Have you had a pecan pie? I'll make you one. I bet I could make pecans your favorite nut." She sighed and closed her eyes, sleep claiming her like a curtain slowly falling on a stage.

Somewhere near or maybe far, she swore she heard him say, "I've changed my mind. You're my favorite nut," before she fell asleep.

By the afternoon, her fever had dropped enough to make her aware of her gross hair and stickiness. She staggered into the bathroom, stepped under a warm spray, and scrubbed the fever sweats away. Izzy had left an assortment of shampoos and conditioners, and she took her time cleaning up.

After she dried off, she borrowed a T-shirt and yoga pants from Izzy's dresser and climbed back in bed, exhausted. Had she even slept this much as a baby? According to her mom, Anna never slept and had tortured her mom all night as an infant. Forever a disappointment.

She was dimly aware of Iain checking on her and making her take aspirin and antibiotics with glassfuls of water. As the sun touched the line of trees outside, he reappeared with one of Rose's flowery aprons tied around his waist.

She laughed. Her throat twinged like all the broken glass had been glued back together. Sore, but manageable. "Cute look."

He fumbled with the apron ties. "I forgot I still had it on. Dinner is ready if you've got an appetite."

Her stomach rumbled to life at his offer. "What's on the menu?"

"Beef stew. I should warn you, I'm rubbish in the kitchen."

She swung her feet over the side of the bed and waited until her head stopped swimming to stand. While she wouldn't be dancing any jigs, she felt stronger than she had that afternoon. "Anything sounds good as long as I don't end up back at the doctor with food poisoning."

He hovered next to her, but didn't take her arm or hand on the way down the stairs, the barrier that had been lowered while she was sick was back in place.

He doled out two bowls of stew and pulled a crusty, store-bought loaf of bread out of the oven, setting everything on the kitchen table. The two places he'd set were next to each other, and she slid into the nearest chair.

She inhaled the rich aroma of beef and broth and red wine. "It smells divine. If this is your idea of rubbish, I'd be perfectly content eating out of your trash can."

He froze with a spoonful halfway to his mouth to laugh and shake his head. "You make me laugh."

"I'm going to take that as a compliment and not that I'm a joke." She smiled to take any sting out of her tease and ate her first bite of his stew, heaping compliments on him.

They made small talk between bites. She sopped up the dregs with a hunk of bread and might have licked the bowl if he hadn't been there. He doled out her next dose of medicine and she meekly took the pills.

"Do you want to go back to bed?" he asked.

It had been months since she'd shared dinner with anyone. It was . . . nice, and she didn't want to go back to bed. Alone. "How about I introduce to the brain-rotting pleasure of American TV?"

Even though she knew he had work waiting in the barn, he nodded. "You get the telly on while I feed the beasties."

By the time he returned, smelling of sunshine and hay, she had one of her favorite sitcoms cued up and was cuddled under a multicolored afghan. His rusty laugh was gratifying. By the second episode, she'd stretched out on the couch, her eyes heavy. His hand covered her foot, his thumb rubbing circles on the arch.

The homey comfortableness of the moment was foreign.

Tension flowed out of her and left her in a dreamy state. She wanted to stay awake, but couldn't. The next thing she knew, she was in his arms, being carried up the stairs and tucked into bed.

Chapter Eleven

With the antibiotics kicking bacteria butt in her body, Anna spent the next two days playing catch-up. She had so many balls in the air, she could have joined the circus. Actually, some days she felt like she was in a circus. Or in a farce. Or maybe in a tragedy. She wasn't sure how the story would end.

The festival was one piece. Then there was her bid for mayor, the worrisome situation with Gabby hanging like a dark cloud over her, and last but far from least, Iain. He was her biggest worry of all, because she felt in danger from him in a multitude of ways.

Iain had shattered the label of "domineering male" she'd assigned him early on. He was in turns intimidating, gruff, steady, helpful, and sweet. His complicated nature was fascinating to her. Were all men more complicated than Anna had given them credit for?

She pondered the theory a few minutes, but dismissed it. Had to. Because if she went all the way back in her history and applied the theory to patient zero, her father, then assumptions she'd built her life on would rot and collapse. Her father was a "selfish deserter." It *was* simple. Maybe she just hadn't found the appropriate label she could slap on Iain.

Anna opened the studio and went about getting ready for the morning's classes. The toddler class was its usual brand of chaos and hilarity. After the little gremlins had all been handed off to their parents and caregivers, she changed the music and performed more serious stretches. Her high school girls were next, and as she wouldn't be competing for first place in the dancing, she wanted one of her girls to take the ribbon.

Keisha was the first through the door. She excelled at all forms of dancing, but had focused on Celtic dancing the past six months. The raw, modern energy she brought to the traditional dances was infectious. Anna wasn't sure how the judges would react, but the crowd would eat it up.

"Hey, Keisha. Listen, I called Gabby, but she wasn't exactly Miss Sunshine. Maybe she really is sick." Anna noted the girl's unusual seriousness.

Keisha gave a snort. "You really think that?"

"No, but my only other option is to talk to her dad. And he's scary. You know if he could, he'd ban dancing across the county à la *Footloose*."

Keisha barked a laugh. "You and me would lead the dance revolution, wouldn't we?"

Anna held up her hand for a high five. "Hell yes, we would."

Keisha slapped her hand and backed away as other girls streamed through the door and began stretching. "You better watch the potty mouth when you go talk to her dad, though, for reals."

Anna laughed and clapped her hands to get the class's

attention. The hour and a half sped by with the impending performance at the festival looming. When practice was over, Anna fit the remaining costumes on the girls, then retreated to her postage-stamp-sized office as the chatter faded through the doors.

Now that Anna was alone, she opened the top desk drawer and pulled out the completed form declaring her candidacy for Highland mayor. It was time to turn it in. The paper trembled in her fingers. The point of no return. Would Anna be taken seriously or laughed out of city hall? Would anyone vote for her with Loretta running too?

After doing a quick change into streetwear, she was on the sidewalk in the sweltering noonday sun. The Highland city offices were located at the far end of Main Street in an old, white-columned house surrounded by blooming crepe myrtle trees. It was picture-postcard perfect.

She passed the Brown Cow, but didn't stop for her usual pick-me-up coffee. Caffeine would make her nervous jitters even worse. The jangle of the door sounded behind her, but she stayed focused on her destination. Iain fell into step next to her, his khaki utility kilt swinging over mud-spattered work boots.

"May I beg a word, Anna?" His voice was oddly formal considering their recent interactions had consisted of him playing nursemaid and binge-watching TV together.

"Cattywampus."

His mouth opened then closed, and he blinked at her before shaking his head. "Pardon?"

"You begged for a word, and I gave you a word. It means 'off-kilter.'"

"Cattywampus." Said with his burr, the word took on a new life. "I like it. The Scottish have a multitude of funny words."

"Like what?" The city offices grew closer with every step, and she was pathetically grateful to have Iain as a distraction.

"Bahoochie."

A smile tipped her lips despite her nerves. "Can you use it in a sentence?"

"'Get yer bahoochie out the bed, laddie!' I heard that one almost every morning from my da."

"Your backside?"

"Exactly." His smile was nostalgic and full of love for a person and place that seemed long gone, but she knew still existed.

The brick storefronts of downtown ended with a line of trees, signaling the start of old houses that had mostly been converted into doctors' offices or law firms with family homes peppered in between. As Highland grew, Anna anticipated most of the private homes would slowly be converted into business spaces, although some of the old guard of Highland opposed the idea of losing any more homes along the thoroughfare.

It was sad to think of the family history mortared between bricks and hammered in the planks being lost to the bustle of progress, but the change would bring revenue which could be reinvested in Highland's current citizens. Anna envisioned a special loan program for new businesses or the town could even host a competition to award funds to the most promising start-ups.

"Where are we going?" Iain asked.

"City offices." She pointed toward the wooden sign

hanging in the front of the house. "I need to turn a form in."

"Has it got something to do with the festival?" He peered toward the paper she held, and instead of acting casual, she whipped it behind her back as if he were trying to cheat off her.

"It's a personal matter." She kept her voice cool, hoping he'd get the hint to leave well enough alone.

He didn't. "Has it got something to do with the studio? Are you in financial straits?"

"The studio is doing well." She ground to a halt and stared up at him. No breeze rustled the branches overhead, so even though it was shady, they were like Hansel and Gretel shoved into a witch's oven. Haltingly, she said, "If you must know, Dr. Jameson is retiring, and I'm going to run for mayor of Highland."

She braced herself for shock or, even worse, laughter. Neither emerged. He merely nodded. "I understand now."

"Understand what?"

"The animosity between you and Loretta. She's threatened by you."

"By me? I'm the young, wild, upstart with no experience. She's got the advantage."

Iain smoothed his beard and tilted his head to study her with his usual intensity. It had stopped rattling her, and she'd come to appreciate his ability to focus. "Does she? You're well-liked, quick-witted, stubborn, and full of ideas."

She refused to admit how much his assessment bolstered her confidence. "How do you know I'm full of ideas?" she asked.

He raised his errant eyebrow. "Aren't you?"

Anna harrumphed. "I've got a few percolating, but I'm not sure if the general population will appreciate them. Loretta especially. She can be so close-minded and old-fashioned."

Iain shrugged. "She's lost control over certain aspects of life—like getting older with still unfulfilled dreams—and therefore needs to seize the reins of control over the parts of her life she can. Plus, I think she's lonely. Her husband has been gone a long time now, hasn't he?"

"Have you been reading psychology books in your spare time?" Once again, she was being confronted with the knowledge that people could be more complicated than the mask they presented to the world at large.

He gave a half-shouldered shrug. "Something I sensed."

Something niggled her memory. Hadn't Loretta mentioned sending other work Iain's way? "Are you going to start hiring yourself out?"

"Word got around that I have certain skills."

"That makes you sound like the James Bond of home improvement."

"The best James Bond was Scottish so . . . almost samsies?"

How could she not smile at the irreverence she never would have guessed at a week ago? Then, she remembered why she was standing under the oak trees with him and sobered up quickly. She waved the paper between them. "Once I turn in my intent to run, my candidacy becomes public record."

"Which means everyone will know."

"Exactly." She gnawed on her bottom lip. "I need

to knock the festival out of the park. If anything goes wrong, like overflowing potties or food poisoning or thunderstorms, then no one will vote for me."

"That seems a bit extreme. No one would blame you for an act of God."

"Yes, they will. They'll say I didn't pray sincerely enough." It was going to be difficult to get the older, more conservative population to buy into her progressive ideas for the town. She couldn't hand them an excuse to dismiss her.

"If they can't see what I see, then they don't deserve you leading them." More confidence resonated from his words than she'd felt in a long time. Even more startling was his sincerity. He wasn't feeding her a platitude like most people might have done.

"You've known me days when most of Highland has known me years."

"Perhaps that's why I can see you clearly. No history exists to cloud the present." He gestured down the sidewalk. "Would you like me to accompany you?"

She shouldn't want him. She should want to march inside and hand in her letter of intent standing on her own.

"Yes, please," she said softly, waiting for a rush of defeat. It didn't come.

Iain gestured for her to lead the way.

And she did with a springier step than she'd left the studio with. She didn't feel weaker because of his support; she felt boosted. It was unfamiliar, but not unpleasant.

It was the work of minutes to turn in her letter of intent. Baxter Dixon retrieved his reading glasses from his bald head, smoothed his callused brown hand over the letter, and smiled. "I was hoping the scuttlebutt was true. Glad to see you running, Miss Maitland. What will your platform include?"

It seemed the town gossips hadn't waited for Anna to make things official. Loretta had no doubt been on the phone campaigning already.

"I've got lots of plans, Mr. Baxter. I want to expand upon the festival and start a new tradition at Christmas. A Very Scottish Christmas." She waved her hand as if highlighting a banner.

Iain stepped forward. "What a wonderful idea. The possibilities are endless. Does Highland host a Burns Night celebration?"

Mr. Baxter tapped his lips with a finger. "I remember Dr. Jameson hosting one many years ago. I'm Baxter Dixon, by the way."

"Geez, I'm not normally so rude," Anna said. "Mr. Baxter, this is Iain Connors. He's from Cairndow, like Gareth."

"Yes, indeed, I've heard all about you, Mr. Connors." While the sentiment came off slightly stalkerish—*welcome to a small town*—Mr. Baxter's smile was friendly. "What were you saying about Burns Night?"

"It's traditionally held in January, but I see no reason why you couldn't host one around Christmastime. It's a grand time with traditional Scottish songs and food."

Anna picked up the idea and ran. "It could be a street festival. What if we closed down Main Street for a day to cars and allowed only foot traffic? Food trucks could set up and the businesses in town could showcase their stock. Roving singers. What a great idea."

Iain grinned. "You don't have to sound so shocked. I've helped plan a multitude of celebrations and events on the grounds at Cairndow. Gareth was always looking at ways to divert tourists to the castle. Cairndow is not exactly on the path well-taken."

"Do you think the town will support the idea if I'm elected?" She tensed, waiting for Mr. Baxter's assessment. His opinion meant more than one random man's thoughts. He was a deacon of his church and a well-respected elder of the community. If he approved, then others would agree.

"No doubt, it would be a boost to the economy, plus it sounds fun." His smile was wide and warm and offered much-needed encouragement. "A nice combination of the old ways and new traditions and a draw for families and young people alike."

Anna controlled her urge to fist pump. Instead, she exchanged goodbyes, shook his hand, squared her shoulders, and strode out with confidence, Iain at her side. Once they were back on the sidewalk, she couldn't keep herself contained a moment longer and performed a little jig, ending on a jaunty heel-click.

"That went way better than I expected. The Burns Night idea was genius, by the way. I've heard of it, of course, but I'm not sure what it is exactly."

"Basically, a giant party celebrating Robert Burns. Traditional Scottish food is paired with certain Burns songs. Everyone is expected to sing along."

"I assume there's whisky involved."

"Without a doubt." He snapped his fingers. "The whisky tasting."

"What about it?"

"Dr. Jameson said something about opening the festival. I told him you and I would handle it."

Anna stumbled over a root that had buckled the sidewalk. "You volunteered us to dance in front of everyone at the whisky tasting?"

His brows drew low. "No I didn't."

"The whisky tasting opens with the hosts performing the St. Bernard's Waltz. Izzy's parents started the tradition decades ago."

"I assumed we'd make an announcement or cut a ribbon."

"Do you know the St. Bernard's Waltz?"

"Of course I don't," he said incredulously.

"It is a traditional Scottish dance, Iain. Not so farfetched. I thought you Scots might have something similar to our cotillions."

He sighed and looked heavenward. "What the devil are cotillions?"

"Young boys and girls meet for several weeks to learn etiquette and social graces. Things like holding a chair out for a lady or not to put your elbows on the table or which utensil to use when. And *dancing*. I happen to teach that part."

He looked dumbfounded. "You're telling me lads sign up willingly for this torture?"

The T-word had been bandied about by more than one boy over the years. "It depends on your definition of 'willing.'"

"Mayhap, you should ask one of your former cotillion students to open the games with you."

"No way. Even the thought is icky."

"You'll have to come up with some other plan, because I can't dance."

"Everyone can dance." A qualifier slipped out. "Of course, not everyone can dance well."

He groaned.

"And why do I have to come up with another plan? You're the one who got yourself into this mess in the first place. I should leave you to find another partner." She poked him in the chest.

He caught her hand and tangled their fingers. "Don't abandon me, lass. If you can teach some lad with spots all over his face, surely you can whip me into shape."

"You're lucky I'm an excellent dance teacher." Why was she breathless? It probably had something to do with the pollen count or her recent bout with strep throat. She resumed their walk, slower now as she contemplated what it would take to whip him into shape. "The only time I have available will be the evenings. Can you meet me at the studio at eight? We'll see how things go and can meet every night until the tasting if necessary."

"*Every night?*" The dread in his voice wasn't encouraging.

"Yep. I have to represent the studio well. If I can't teach one actual Scotsman a traditional Scottish dance, then why would Highland seek my tutelage for their sons and daughters?" Of course, she was being a tad overdramatic. It wasn't like the parents of Highland had much choice, but now the idea had been planted, the sick part of her that loved torment *wanted* to spend every night in Iain's company. *In his arms.*

"Next time I'll ask to read the fine print before I agree to anything."

"You'll survive. I can't guarantee you'll survive with your dignity intact, though." While she was feeling confident, she should tackle another dreaded task. She'd ride out and talk to Gabby and her dad.

She squared her shoulders and took a deep breath.

"What is it now?"

"Nothing. Everything is fine."

"I'm beginning to think we have very different definitions of the word 'fine.' You look like you are being forced down the plank at sword point."

"No. That would be more like this." She grimaced and acted like she was biting all ten fingernails at the same time. "Or this." She opened her mouth in a soundless scream and put the back of her hand on her forehead in an old-fashioned parody of a swoon.

Iain did not look amused. He crossed his arms and planted himself in front of her on the sidewalk. When she tried to go around him, he shifted one way and then the other to match her evasions.

"Our dance lesson doesn't start until tonight, Highlander." Her joke garnered a tiny smile, but he didn't move. She tossed up her hands. "If you must know, I have a student who is an excellent dancer, but her father is strict and doesn't approve of her dancing in front of crowds even though she could win a ribbon this year. Maybe even Lass of the Games."

"Doesn't her dad have a say in what she does? Why are you inserting yourself in their business?"

Anna performed a faux pearl-clutch. "Are you insinuating that I'm a busybody?"

"'Busy' is not the word I would pick to describe your body." Was that sexual innuendo hiding behind the tease in his voice?

"What word would you pick?" She immediately regretted her question and held her hand up. "Don't answer that. This is not the time or place."

"What will going to talk to your student's da accomplish?"

"It's what Gabby wants. To dance, I mean."

"She told you this and asked you to intervene on her behalf?"

"Not in so many words." Anna hoped her strained phone conversation with Gabby was a fluke. "But Gabby's talented. She deserves to be up on that stage."

"So, your plan is to inform her da that he's a bad parent if he doesn't allow her to compete?"

"Of course not. I'm going to tell him how gifted his daughter is and explain how much she loves to dance."

"You're going by yourself?"

"Yes, by myself. What could possibly happen?"

"As I don't know the bloke, I can't predict his reaction. I'm coming with you." Iain looked like a man no one would want to meet in a dark alley. No one who had pissed him off anyway.

Anna didn't buy into the alpha male stereotype. She had successfully taken care of herself all her life without a Y chromosome in the vicinity. "I can handle Gabby's dad. I'm a big girl."

His gaze dropped to her feet and meandered back up to her face. She knew exactly what he was thinking. "Not muscly big like you, but I've got a big mouth that can jaw with the best of them."

"Jaw?"

"Talk trash. Rubbish. Whatever you Scots call smack talk." She waved his confusion away, hopped off the sidewalk, and into the street to bypass his bulk. "I can handle myself. Don't worry."

He fell into step beside her, obviously not buying what she was selling. She shot him an assessing side-eye glance. He might actually prove useful if she needed backup. If Iain wanted to play knight-errant, who was she to deny him? "If you're going to be stubborn about it, you can come, but you have to wait in the car."

When he looked like he was ready to mount a protest, Anna held up her hand. "That's the deal. Take it or leave me to get my business done."

His jaw twitched even as he gave a brusque nod.

She led the way to her VW Bug and opened the passenger door and gestured him in. He stood in the opening and stared.

"I'll never cram myself in that bloody tin can." He pointed down the street. "The truck's right there."

"I'm not showing up sweaty. It would put me at a disadvantage."

"The windows lower."

"Then I'd show up sweaty and windblown. Not happening." She circled around her car and slipped behind the wheel.

Teasing Iain was too much fun. How determined was he to play her protector? She cranked the engine and revved the gas pedal to add some urgency to his decision.

"Are you my wingman or not?" She dipped her head to meet his gaze.

"The devil take it!" He mumbled in Gaelic as he levered himself into the seat, first one leg, then the other, all while adjusting his kilt so as not to flash her or any passersby. His head touched the roof, and his knees were forced wide and brushed the dash. He was wedged in so tight, he wasn't going anywhere, but he struggled to snap the seat belt into place anyway.

She pressed her lips together to stem her laughter and

pulled out onto the road. The glare he aimed in her direction would have melted her spine if she didn't know his tough demeanor hid something sweeter and more vulnerable than he cared to admit or even recognize.

"You'll have to translate all that for me. I'm ready for another lesson," she said lightly.

"What I said is inappropriate."

"Excellent. It's always handy to know some curses in another language. And Gaelic curses would be totally on brand for me."

He ignored her and stared out the window, his arms crossed over his chest. She turned down a narrow two-lane country road, the shoulders crumbling and the lines fading. On one side were dense woods and on the other stretched a field dotted with a few lazily munching cattle.

Against the rise of a foothill stood a two-story farmhouse. A hundred years ago, it had been grand, but time had laid a heavy hand along the sagging eaves.

She turned onto the drive, narrower by half than the road. Her little car jounced in a hole. Iain's head smacked the roof. He let out an *oof* and sent a glare in her direction.

"Sorry. The Bug is not an off-roader." She slowed to a crawl. The rocking motion wasn't doing her stomach any favors either. It had been a nervy day already with the trip to the city offices, and her confidence was leaking out into the ruts.

"What's your plan of attack?" Iain asked.

She clutched the steering wheel tighter to keep from being slung back and forth. "My plan is to use logic and appeal to his love for his daughter. I'm sure he wants her to be happy, and dancing makes her happy."

"If it were so simple, you would not be on your way to talk to him."

Iain had a point. She pulled up to the front of the house. From a distance, the house had appeared slightly derelict, but closer up, someone was doing their best on upkeep. White paint shone on the clapboards and the windows sparkled. The bushes were trimmed and yellow, and purple petunias lined the walkway to the front porch. The house was undergoing a genteel aging.

She rolled the windows down and turned the car off. "This shouldn't take long, but if you get hot, you can restart the car."

"Stay on the porch where I can see you," he said.

"This isn't a special ops situation. I'll be fine."

He stared at her without a change in his hardened expression. She heaved a put-upon sigh that would have made the teenagers she taught proud. "Okay, *fine*. I doubt he's going to invite me in for a cookie anyway."

She slipped out of the car, smoothed down her blouse, and climbed the stairs, casting one last glance back at Iain, glad he was there even if she wasn't going to admit it aloud.

She rapped on the metal screen door and waited. Footsteps sounded on the other side and she pasted on a smile. The person that came into focus wasn't Mr. Donaldson, but Gabby.

"Miss Maitland." Surprise brightened her voice, but otherwise she looked wan, her hair messy and pulled back into a low ponytail. She wore a baggy T-shirt and a sweatpants. "What are you doing here?"

Anna didn't like being called Miss Maitland. It put her mind of their spinster physical education teacher in middle school who tried to teach them sex ed, but couldn't say the word "nipple." Anna had convinced most of the girls in her senior level dance classes to call her by her first name, but Gabby had never been comfortable with the familiarity.

"You've missed a week of rehearsals right before the festival. I'm worried about you."

Gabby's initial pleasure dove into moroseness. "Dad doesn't want me performing onstage. That leaves marching in the parade, which I don't need to practice for."

"Is your dad here? Maybe I can change his mind about letting you compete."

She cast a furtive look over her shoulder and dropped her voice. "That's really nice of you, but it won't do any good. When Dad makes up his mind, that's that."

"But you love dancing, don't you, Gabby?" Even though Anna had interpreted the emotion Gabby infused her dances with as love, maybe it was something else entirely.

"Of course, I love it. Dancing is the only time I can be myself. But I love Dad too." The firm line of Gabby's mouth contradicted the tears glimmering in her eyes.

"Gabby! Who's that out front?" a male voice called from somewhere in the depths of the house. Footsteps creaked the boards, and a man came into view over Gabby's shoulder.

Mr. Donaldson wasn't a big man, but he exuded a competency and energy common among men and women who worked the land from dawn until dusk. She imagined he didn't often sit and relax, and if he did, he would find himself asleep within minutes.

"Hello, Mr. Donaldson. It's Anna Maitland. How are

you doing?" She put on her best "I'm an excellent role model" smile.

"Busy. Harvest is fast approaching."

"I've heard it'll be a good year."

He grunted. "Looks that way right now, but anything can happen before we get the crops in."

She'd put the grooves in his forehead and the crinkles at the corner of his eyes and mouth down to being in the sun, but now she could see worry had done its part to carve them. She understood the stress of owning a small business. Farming added extra pressures.

Success or failure depended largely on how hard she worked, but a farmer wasn't necessarily rewarded for twelve-hour days. They were subject to the tempest of weather, made even more unpredictable because of climate change. The summers were hotter, the storms fiercer, and it would only get more difficult.

"I'll hope nothing happens before harvest, then." She cleared her throat. "I'm actually here because I was hoping to talk to you about Gabby competing in the festival."

Mr. Donaldson never took his steely eyes off Anna when he said, "Get on inside and finish your chores while your teacher and I talk."

"Yes, sir." Gabby retreated and Anna was sorry to see her go. Gabby was the oil that kept the conversation running smooth.

Mr. Donaldson stepped outside and let the screen door bang shut behind him. Anna backed up until her butt hit one of the square columns at the edge of the steps. A glance over her shoulder showed Iain's arm crooked out the window, and Anna took a deep breath, buoyed by his presence.

"I know you want her to dance up on that stage and compete for Lass of the Games," Mr. Donaldson said.

"Gabby and Keisha are the two most talented dancers in my class. On their best day, they're better than I ever was. Either one could win Lass of the Games. I'd like to see Gabby have that chance."

"I don't want Gabby up in front of all those people flaunting herself." His voice was sandpaper against her nerves.

"Celtic dancing is about control and grace and elegance."

"But you teach other classes, don't you?"

"Of course. Ballet, popular dance, even ballroom for the cotillion kids."

"Popular dance." He infused derision into the words. "Our church doesn't condone such, and Gabby will no longer participate. It sexualizes those young girls."

Mr. Donaldson attended a small, fundamentalist church on the outskirts of town. While Anna had never stepped inside his church, she'd bet the pew he warmed every Sunday was uncushioned and that the preacher always went long.

But she also couldn't entirely deny his accusation. Her hip-hop class did involve the occasional booty shake.

"You attend the festival every year, Mr. Donaldson. You know Celtic dancing doesn't sexualize the dancer." She could sense no softening of his stance and slipped her phone out of her pocket for a final, last-ditch effort. "I'll show you the outfits the girls will be wearing. They are demure and very pretty."

She pulled up the picture and found the one of Keisha modeling the dress. While there were similarities among Irish and Scottish dancing, the costumes marked

a stark difference. The short, flouncy Irish skirts and
fake bouncing curls weren't a part of Scottish dancing.
A knee-length skirt and white blouse with a plaid worn
over one shoulder was more common.

Mr. Donaldson made a throaty noise she couldn't
interpret. "It's suitable, I suppose."

"You'll consider letting Gabby compete? Not only is
she talented, but she loves it so much. How can you take
dance away from her?"

She said the one thing Iain had warned her not to say,
and she regretted the words as soon as they were out of
her mouth.

Like a spark striking coal, Mr. Donaldson's anger
flared. "Who are you to come to my house and insinuate
I don't love my daughter?"

It's not what she'd said or meant, but now was not the
time to argue. Now was the time to retreat. She backed
down the steps while Mr. Donaldson advanced. Ancient
instincts of self-preservation told her not to turn her back
on a perceived threat.

"I didn't mean to imply you don't love Gabby, sir. Not
at all. All I meant was that she loves to dance and she's
good at it. I want her to be happy." Anna shuffled another
step backward and bumped into something big and hard.

She felt behind her and her hand landed on the leather
clasps of Iain's kilt. She hung on and sucked in a deep
breath of humid air scented with cows and grass and . . .
Iain. It was as calming as it was heady.

Mr. Donaldson stopped halfway down the steps, leaving him looming over them both. "And I don't want her
to be happy? I'm not sure you're a good influence on
Gabby or on any of the girls in this town for that matter.
I could make things mighty difficult for you."

"What is that supposed to mean?" She tightened her hold on Iain.

The man didn't speak again, but turned and disappeared inside his house, leaving her and Iain baking in the sun. A cow by the fence watched them and chewed on grass.

"Come on, lass." Iain took her by the shoulders and steered her to the driver's side.

She climbed in and cranked the engine. With the windows down, the cool air barely made a dent in the heat. As soon as Iain crammed himself back inside, she hit the gas and spun out on the loose gravel of the driveway, but eased up immediately. That kind of reckless behavior would not earn her good marks with Mr. Donaldson.

"That went well," she said with maximum sarcasm.

"I—"

"Don't say 'I told you so' unless you want me to dump you on the side of the road."

He cleared his throat. "If you'd allow me to continue, I was going to say that I think you handled it as well as could be expected, but he is her da and makes the rules for his family."

"But he's wrong."

"In your opinion, not his. It's up to Gabby to either change his mind or find the strength to defy him."

"She won't defy him."

"Then she's not meant to compete this year," he said simply.

The fact he was right only upset her more. "What you're saying is I should keep my big fat nose out of their business."

"I wouldn't call your nose big or fat. It's more like

a blade." He cut his hand through the air for emphasis. "But yes."

She wasn't sure if he intended the assessment as an insult or compliment. "A blade will cut you, so watch out, Highlander. Haven't you seen the movie?"

He looked out the passenger window, but not before she noted the start of a smile. "Ah yes, the movie where they cast the actual Scotsman as a Spaniard. Poor Sean Connery."

"Is he your favorite James Bond?"

"Are there others? I wouldn't know." His voice was deadpan.

She fought a smile and the feeling the man didn't realize how appealing and sexy she found his dry humor. He was eccentric in a rather wonderful way. The wind whipped her hair around her shoulders. It would be a snarled mess, but she left the windows down, reminded of simpler times driving the backroads in high school with her cheerleader friends, laughing and talking about nothing and everything.

After she'd come home from New York, her old friends had moved on to college or gotten married, and her relationships with them had shifted into the shallowness of acquaintances. While she was happy for their successes, she'd not attempted to rekindle deep friendships. She had changed for better or worse. She'd never been able to decide which.

Her reminiscing reminded her that she owed Izzy a call. She pulled behind the tartan truck on Main Street to let him out. "I'll see you tonight for our lesson."

His answering grunt could have been an affirmative or a negative.

"You're not going to stand me up, are you?" she called as he levered himself up and out, giving her a flash of a well-muscled thigh.

He didn't afford her with an answer, but he didn't have to. He would be there.

Chapter Twelve

As soon as Anna stepped into her apartment above the studio after her afternoon classes, she stripped off her clothes on the short walk to the shower. The lukewarm water refreshed her and gave her a jolt of energy to tackle the rest of the day and evening tasks, including teaching Iain to dance.

She toweled off, but before dressing, stood in front of the window AC unit and let the cool air rush over her until goose bumps rose on her arms. While she was literally chilling out, she shot Izzy a text, asking how she was feeling, but it was late in Scotland and Anna didn't expect an answer until morning.

A ring cut through the hum of the AC, and she fumbled her phone. It was a video call request from Izzy. Surprise kickstarted her heart. Had something happened?

She tapped the button and her voice barked with worry. "What's wrong?"

Izzy slapped a hand over her eyes. "You crazy woman.

You're naked. Please tell me you didn't answer in the middle of *you know*?"

"Hang on." Anna put the phone facedown on her bed and pulled on panties, shorts, and a tank top. Picking the phone back up, she smiled at her best friend. "Sorry for the peep show. I just got out of the shower. I haven't had *you know* in quite some time. Unfortunately. It's late there. Is everything okay?"

"I'm bloated and miserable, but yes, I'm okay. I had to pee and couldn't go back to sleep. The timing of your text was perfect."

Anna curled up against the pillows on the bed and smiled into the phone. "God, it's good to see you."

Izzy's hair was loose and longer than it had been last summer, but glossy and full. Despite her complaints, the fullness of her face suited her. Her cheeks were rosy and her eyes snapped with bored, unspent energy in spite of the late hour.

"Even though I saw *too* much for a hot second, I concur," Izzy said.

Anna laughed. "My place is an oven, and I'm the foil-wrapped potato baking."

"It's cool enough here for a jacket. What a change in circumstances from last year." Izzy shook her head, but there was a smile on her face. Last summer, Izzy had been planning the festival with her mom. She'd been single and restless and untrusting. Alasdair had come into her life like a bolt of lightning and changed everything.

"Any signs the joyous event is imminent?" Anna asked.

"Check out my cankles." Izzy aimed the phone at her feet. They were swollen.

"That can't be good."

"It's not. That's why I'm calling." Izzy's eyes filled with tears. "I'm scheduled for a C-section."

"When?"

"Day after tomorrow. We're leaving for Glasgow in the morning." Fear trembled Izzy's voice.

"Everything is going to be fine." Anna forced what she hoped was a reassuring smile, but her lips were quivery.

"It's not what I planned."

"Girl. You didn't plan on meeting a hot Scot, being whisked to a remote castle, getting knocked up, or having a shotgun wedding. None of the good stuff is ever planned."

Izzy choked back a sob, and Anna filled the gap. "Doctors perform thousands of C-sections every day, and if I know Alasdair, he is taking you to the best hospital in Scotland. Plus, you have Gareth and Rose there and me and Iain here to handle things. All you have to do is trust everything will be fine because it will be."

Izzy nodded and sniffed. It wasn't often she let her emotions have free rein. "You're right. You're always right."

"Hell yes, I am. I'm going to need for you to make a campaign video telling the residents of Highland." Anna waggled her eyebrows.

"You did it!" As Anna had hoped, the change in topic staunched the anxiety over the impending birth.

Anna relayed her interactions with Loretta and the filing of her paperwork. "That's not all. Your boy Iain volunteered to open the festival at the whisky tasting."

Izzy was treading and no longer drowning in her emotions. "I've never seen him dance."

"Exactly. He thought opening the festival involved cutting a ribbon."

"What are you going to do?" Izzy covered her mouth, but a smile played there.

Anna infused her words with mock outrage. "I'm the best darn-tooting dance teacher in town. You don't think I can teach one measly Highlander to dance?"

Izzy's laugh was lower and sounded more like the old her. "If you can teach me, you can teach anyone. You're his partner, I assume."

"Of course." The decisiveness in Anna's voice made Izzy perk up.

"I wasn't sure, considering your not-so-enthusiastic feelings about him being there to help." Izzy gave Anna an admonishing look that made her squirm. She thought she'd done a better job hiding her ambivalence from Izzy.

"I thought maybe you and Rose didn't have confidence in me." On such a small screen, it was difficult to avoid Izzy's eyes.

"Of course we did—*do*—but you have a business to run on top of everything else, especially with Gareth pulling the trigger on the animal exhibition."

"I'll admit, even with all the legwork Rose and Gareth did before they left for Scotland, it's a lot. I'm terrified I'm going to forget something important."

"Portable potties. Ample parking. Food trucks. Music. As long as you have those, you'll be fine." Izzy let her head loll against the back of the couch. "This is the first games I'll miss. I'm sad."

"I'll send lots of pictures and videos," Anna said.

"You'd better." Izzy yawned. "I should go before

Alasdair figures out where I am and drags me back to bed."

"Take care and tell your mom to text or call when the baby arrives. No matter what time."

They exchanged goodbyes, and after Anna disconnected, she lay on the bed and stared at the blank white ceiling. Izzy would have more to worry about than the festival in a couple of days, which was as it should be. Anna closed her eyes and said a little prayer even though she wasn't sure she even believed in a God who took notice.

A knock brought her out of her reverie. She opened the door to find Iain casting a long shadow. He wore one of his more traditional kilts in a plaid pattern of hunting colors like a more organized version of Southern camouflage. His wavy dark hair was slightly damp and finger-combed. His scent was fresh from the shower.

"Sorry, I'm early." He shifted, the metal staircase creaking under his weight. "I'm a bit nervous."

The admission surprised her. Iain was big and capable and had seen and survived more hostile environments than a dance floor.

"It's a dance, not a battle."

His eyes narrowed on hers, and she wanted to stuff the offhand remark back in her mouth. She swallowed and forced a smile.

His gaze left hers, but her relief was short-lived as it meandered down her body, taking in her tank top and worn-thin cotton shorts. This was her everyday sleep attire—her sexy stuff was moldering in the back of her drawer—but by the hungry, predatory look on his face, he didn't care.

Her toes curled and she tipped her face up, waiting for . . . what?

"Are you going to invite me in?" he asked.

Yes. The word reverberated in her head, but when she moved her lips, her mouth felt stuffed with cotton balls. Her first thought hadn't been about letting him inside her apartment, but dragging him to her bed and allowing him entrance to a much more intimate space.

He tilted his head and looked at her like she was having a relapse of strep throat. She shuffled backward and waved him inside. He had to duck his head to clear the low doorjamb. Once inside, he was like an oversize action figure forced into a dollhouse.

He swept his gaze around the room, and she did the same, seeing things from his perspective. The mini-kitchen, where she cooked the simplest of meals. The bathroom with her wet towel crumpled on the floor. The short red couch and flat-screen TV where she vegged out. Her bedroom, where the queen-size bed and dresser took up almost the entire space. She'd decorated it in an eclectic splash of colors that put her in mind of summer flowers.

"It's not much, but—"

"It's cute. Unique. It suits you." His focus returned to her and left her flustered.

Was that a compliment? She thought it might be. "Thanks."

He migrated to a group of pictures she'd tacked to a cork board. At one time, she'd planned to frame them, but as the years rolled by, the accomplishments seemed less important.

He touched a picture of her mid-leap, her dark red

hair haloing around her, a grin on her face. "You are gifted."

She wasn't sure how gifted she was, but she did feel lucky. She loved to dance, and even though she wasn't making a living dancing like she'd hoped—on Broadway or in a professional dance troupe—she was making a living doing what she loved. How many people could say that?

"Thanks. I don't know where I'd be without dance. I guess I should thank my mom for that. It's why I'm fighting so hard for Gabby. Mr. Donaldson thinks dance is about shaking your ass and attracting the male gaze, but that's not why I enjoy performing. It's about eliciting an emotion and making the difficult look effortless. Dance teaches discipline and instills self-confidence. Show me one teenage girl who doesn't need more confidence." She turned her head to find him staring at her and not the pictures.

"And *that's* the argument you should have made to Gabby's da today."

Dammit. Instead of insinuating he didn't love his daughter enough, she should have outlined the intangible benefits of dance. "You're right," she whispered.

He cleared his throat and cocked his head closer. "I'm sorry, what? I must have misheard."

She playfully shoved his arm. "You are right and I was wrong. Are you happy?"

He considered her flippant question with a seriousness she hadn't intended, his finger tracing his scar into his beard in a manner she guessed was unconscious. "Happier than I've been in a long while, strangely enough."

"Why is that strange?"

"Because it's so unexpected."

A lump clogged her throat, but she managed to choke out, "Highland is special."

"Very special." His eyes crinkled in a way she found undeniably appealing, and she found herself leaning closer to him.

Jerking herself back, she thumbed over her shoulder toward the bedroom. "Let me change right quick."

Dressed in her uniform of a black leotard and simple wraparound skirt, she grabbed her Scottish dancing shoes and peeked through the narrow crack in her bedroom door. Iain was sitting on the couch, with his back to her. He rolled his shoulders and stretched his neck to one side and then the other.

Her confidence grew inverse to his nerves. She plopped on the couch next to him to lace on her dancing shoes. "I talked to Izzy right before you got here, by the way."

"It's late there. Is something amiss?"

"Little Annie Blackmoor will be making her debut soon." Anna filled him in on the conversation.

"Isabel and Alasdair have brought a vigor back to Cairndow. A child will wake the land and bring much happiness. She'll be the eventual Countess of Cairndow. It's right she should take Annie's name." The whimsical nature of Iain's declaration took her by surprise, but perhaps it shouldn't have. His spirit seemed age-old. A keeper of Cairndow's secrets and bound to the old place as much as Gareth and Alasdair were.

"Do you miss your dad and your sheep?" She let out a sound of impatience with herself. "Not that your dad is on the same emotional plane as a flock of sheep. I didn't mean to imply you miss them in an inappropriate way."

His laugh rumbled. "I never got *that* lonely or desperate, but yes, I miss Da. Are you ready to humiliate me?"

"I would never humiliate you." She rose when he did and moved to the door. "Just torture you a bit."

The metal staircase shuddered under their combined weight. He stopped at the bottom to examine where the staircase bolted into the brick. "You need more anchor points."

"I rarely have six-foot-plus jacked men traipsing up to pay me a call." She unlocked the back door of the studio and flipped the lights on. "In fact, you're the first."

She continued on to her office to sync her phone to the wireless speakers. When she turned, she flinched to find him blocking the doorway. "For a big guy, you sure can sneak up on a girl."

"Learned to be quiet hunting and fishing at Cairndow. Serving only reaffirmed the lessons." He took a step toward her, cutting the space nearly in half. "Why don't you have a bloke?"

"You mean a boyfriend?"

He grunted his assent.

"I've had *blokes*. Just not for a while. The last one . . ." She leaned back on her desk, looked up at Iain, and shrugged. "He left town."

"Like your da."

"Nothing like my dad. I was ready for this guy to move on. He left because our relationship was going nowhere." She didn't add that none of her relationships had gone anywhere important.

"I see."

What did he see? Was it good, bad, or pathetic? She was voting for the latter.

Before she could ask, he retreated. "How do we start?"

Thrown off her mojo—which she pictured as a multicolored unicorn who liked to curse—she fumbled with her playlist and accidently hit an Usher song. A dirty, sexy song about tangled sheets and sweaty bodies.

Her body flushed. The sugared beat actually suited her plan to teach him the steps at a slower pace than the actual dance. Her heart matched the pulse of the bass. She faced him and invaded his personal space, putting her left hand on his shoulder and holding her other hand up for him to take in a classic waltz position. He took her hand in his and clasped her waist with the other, stiff and unyielding.

"The St. Bernard's Waltz is a bit different than a traditional waltz although it is in three-quarter time." She demonstrated the first counts of steps, which were fairly simple, yet he still stumbled. She shook his shoulders. "Loosen up. You're as hard and stiff as a piece of wood."

Red flared on his neck, but if she had to put her finger on his mood, he wasn't embarrassed as much as fighting a burst of laughter.

"This is serious, Iain. We have to dance in front of the town, and I can't become a laughing stock right before I make a run at mayor."

He cleared his throat and tamped down some of the twinkling in his eyes. "My apologies."

"You're having problems because you're getting inside your own head and losing the rhythm."

"I can't lose what I never possessed."

"I call BS. You can play the guitar and sing."

"That's different. I don't have to think about playing. It just happens. My arms and legs are on a delay when I try to dance."

Attempting to teach Iain a formal dance before he had relaxed and found the beat was doomed to fail. "Let's go for something a little less structured."

"What do you mean?" Suspicion darkened his voice.

She grabbed his hips and tried to force him to sway with her, but he was rooted to the floor like a tree. "You must have spent some nights in clubs getting your groove on."

"I've been known to hold up a wall or two in my time."

"*Please*. Girls had to have been all over you." Her gesture encompassed him head to toe.

"Not so much. Seeing me in a dark corner generally inspired fear in the lasses."

"Are you serious?" She didn't expect an answer to her incredulous, knee-jerk question, because she could see he was serious. Even more, she could see it bothered him, and she understood why. His natural state wasn't an aggressor, but a protector.

He raised both eyebrows at her this time. "I scare you, don't I?"

She made a pishing sound. "When we first met, I was cautious in the way any woman alone with a strange man might be, but that was before I got to know you. Now, demonstrate please." She nudged him toward the wall. "Stand like you would have in a club or pub or whatever."

With a small shake of his head, he did as she asked. Crossing his arms over his chest and propping a shoulder against the wall between the two massive mirrors, he let his face fall into a grimace.

"I get it now. You have resting bouncer face. You look like you're ready to toss someone on their butt."

His shock quickly morphed into a smile. "I didn't know that was a thing."

"It is now."

"What sort of face do you have?"

"I have resting 'bless your heart' face." At his quizzical look, she said, "'Bless your heart' is a backhanded way of telling someone, 'you're an idiot but a harmless one.' See?" She graced him with a sample of her sarcastic face and was gratified to earn a rumbly laugh.

The song looped on repeat. Anna sashayed toward him and gave him her sultriest look from under her lashes. "I saw you from across the room. Wanna dance, Highlander?"

He didn't immediately answer. She pulled his arms apart and drew him toward her.

"I don't know." His voice was barely audible.

What did he not know? What they were doing? How he was feeling? She wanted to tell him to join the club. Instead, she whispered back, "You don't have to know. You just have to feel."

This was simply a dance. For Anna, though, a dance was an emotional experience. She couldn't dance and not be vulnerable. Which made dancing with him dangerous. She didn't heed the warning and wrapped her arms around his neck, her fingers finding their way into his hair.

One of his hands slid to the middle of her back, his thumb grazing the bare skin exposed by the low scoop of her leotard. The other gripped her hip and scooted her even closer, so their feet notched together naturally.

Their size difference was emphasized. The top of her head barely reached his shoulder, and his hands branded her with their strength. But there was a gentleness in his touch as if he were handling something breakable.

She raised her face to his and shook her hair over her shoulders. He bowed over enough to rub his bristly jaw against her temple. And then lower until his hot breath near her ear sent an aroused shiver through her.

"Is this okay?"

She hummed and closed her eyes. Okay? It was incredible.

"Am I on the beat?" His lips skimmed the shell of her ear.

What was he talking about? She pulled away only enough to see his face, their noses brushing. He had extraordinary eyes. Like rich dark chocolate with caramel sparking from his irises. He wasn't a sexy snack, but a big, scrumptious dessert.

"Oh, the music." She blinked to refocus and said incredulously, "We're dancing."

"Aye. That we are." His rumbly brogue did something to her insides doctors would never be able to explain through science.

Her heart ached and bled and tried to claw its way out of her chest. Her bones melted. Her hips tipped into him and her back arched. The flannel of his kilt was soft on her inner thighs. He shifted and drew her up on her tiptoes. Their faces were close.

Anna wanted more. She had never been shy about taking what she wanted, but it felt different with Iain. *She* felt different. With a hesitancy unlike her, she brushed her lips across his in the lightest of touches before retreating and staring into his eyes.

Time passed. Enough to prepare herself for rejection. Was it hours or milliseconds?

With a suddenness that was shocking, his mouth came down on hers with none of her tentativeness. His kiss was hungry and demanded appeasement at the same time he offered satisfaction.

She rocked higher on her toes and tightened her grip in his hair, needing to get closer. With a growl, he grasped her bottom with both hands and pressed her against the wall between the mirrors. Her feet were off the ground and her only source of stability was Iain himself. She was stuck between a wall and a very hard man.

She pulled his bottom lip between her teeth and was rewarded with a chesty rumble. Oh, she'd come to enjoy his grunts and grumbles and groans. They communicated more than most men's polite, superficial words.

"Is this your way of loosening me up, lass?" His lips never lost contact with her skin.

"Is it working?"

She could feel his laugh all the way to her toes. "Actually, I'm as hard and stiff as a piece of wood."

Her earlier assessment of him flooded back, and she understood now what he'd found amusing. Instead of feeling embarrassed she hadn't been in on the joke earlier, she kissed him again with her lips curled into a smile.

She was putty against him, and if he'd asked nicely (or even not-so-nicely), she would have taken him to her bed. Instead, he acted like kissing her was the culmination of his need. She didn't know how long she'd been locked between him and the wall, but eventually, his arms loosened, and she slid down like goo, her feet back on solid ground, but her world was officially rocked. She was both satiated and frustrated.

"What are you doing?" she asked breathily.

"Leaving." The word held a finality that brought reality crashing down.

Why was she shocked? Thank God, she had only made out with him. She gave herself a mental "bless your heart," because she was an idiot.

"Yeah, of course. This was a mistake. Merely a product of the music. Damn Usher's sexy beats."

A door closed on Iain's expression. "A mistake."

Had that been a statement or a question? His brogue made it difficult to tell. "So we agree." She put the slightest of lilt onto the end, making her own intentions questionable.

He didn't deign to clarify.

"Next time, we'll stick to bagpipes and the waltz." She grabbed her phone and silenced the music. The vacuum of sound sucked out any remaining sexual vibes. "Let's call it a night, shall we?"

"Aye. That's probably for the best."

Probably? Why had he thrown in a qualifier? She didn't have the energy to suss out his intentions, and she didn't have the time for a relationship even if it was only about sex. Tomorrow, she had classes to teach plus calls to make, and in the back of her mind lurked worry over Izzy and the birth of her goddaughter.

"When is our next lesson? Tomorrow evening?" he asked.

"I don't know. I'm busy. I'll be in touch." A phrase that should have encompassed hands or lips inserted a distance she wasn't sure they could overcome. Had a kiss ruined newly found accord?

He stood another moment before nodding brusquely

and turning to go. She didn't stop him, even though her hands twitched to grab the folds of his kilt and pull him to the floor with her. The door banged shut.

It is for the best. She cursed the platitude and whoever wrote it, because what was for the best made her feel like the worst.

Chapter Thirteen

Two days, but more importantly, two nights had passed without even a sighting of Anna. She'd become as elusive as the Lock Ness Monster, and he'd become as obsessed as a Nessie watcher. Iain channeled his frustration into his work. The pens for the husbandry exhibit were almost done. He worked now on organizing the barn and making a welcoming, walkable path for the visitors who would descend on Stonehaven.

Along with the work for the festival, he'd been contacted by a half dozen Highland residents for small jobs—various pieces of furniture, a wheelchair ramp, a fancy chicken coop. The list was growing, and Iain wasn't sure he could finish the projects before the festival, which would mean turning them down or staying on in Highland for a bit after the festival, which would leave his da upset.

While he had nothing pressing drawing him back to Scotland, he had nothing to keep him in Highland either. Soon, Rose and Gareth would return to Stonehaven, and he would be expected to vacate the guest room.

He'd received word from his da that Annie Blackmoor had entered the world squalling with a full head of black hair and the Blackmoor gray eyes. Isabel and Annie had come through the surgery with the highest of marks while Alasdair had almost passed out. Iain had already sent his congratulations to Alasdair along with a fair amount of teasing. Alasdair had floored him by calling to ask him to be Annie's godfather. Iain had no experience with babes or how to guide them, but he had readily agreed to the honor.

Strangely, even as he added another emotional tether, Cairndow seemed a world away. Iain drove to town with the windows of the pickup down, returning the waves of several new friends. Even the heat and humidity had become a mere nuisance instead of an unholy trial of survival.

After loading up the bed of the truck with hay for the animals, he stopped by the hardware store for sandpaper, screws, and a sundry of items he needed to replenish. Parking close to Maitland Dance Studio, he avoided the front door, circling around to the back like he was a burglar casing the building, except instead of a crowbar, he held a drill. Music pumped out of the speakers, and he could hear Anna counting down the start of a dance.

As stealthily as possible, he climbed the rickety stairs leading to her flat, stopping at the first loose anchor point. Using the fittings he bought at the hardware store, he drove anchors into the brick and screwed the staircase into the wall. At the bottom, he gave it a shake. It didn't budge. Satisfied Anna would be safe for years to come, he slipped back around the building to the truck and retreated to Stonehaven.

After working in the barn all afternoon and into the

cooling evening, the gloaming drove him inside for a shower and food. As he was examining the meager contents of the refrigerator, a perfunctory knock sounded on the front door, followed by a familiar voice calling his name.

Anna hadn't waited for him to answer the door, but barged inside. She wore a flirty skirt and white blouse and held two plastic grocery sacks.

"You," she said. The word held a wealth of emotion, but he couldn't tell how much was accusatory.

Bereft of a response, he backed out of the entry hall. She brushed past him and set the bags on the kitchen island.

"You fixed the stairs to my apartment." She leaned against the counter and crossed her arms over her chest.

"Aye."

"That was . . ." Her gaze floated to the ceiling, searching for a word.

He searched for his own and came out with, "Overstepping," the same time she said, "Sweet."

"Sweet?" he repeated dumbly.

She turned to the bags and unpacked a variety of items, including bread, bright red tomatoes, and a packet of bacon. She paused, but didn't turn to look at him. "It's been a long time since someone took care of me. You've done it twice now."

She lifted a skillet off the overhead rack and set it on the stove, tossing a glance at him over her shoulder. "You haven't eaten yet, have you?"

"I was just foraging for something when you arrived."

"Good. I'm making you BLTs. I even ran by Dr. Jameson's and begged tomatoes from his garden." Her movements were economical yet graceful.

Iain slipped onto one of the chairs at the island to watch. The smell of the crackling bacon made his mouth water. While the bacon cooked, she sliced the tomatoes.

"I thought you couldn't cook," Iain said.

Her laugh was infectious enough to bring a smile to his face. "Frying bacon is not cooking."

"I appreciate the meal. I'm famished."

"You've been working hard and deserve more than a measly sandwich. I'll admit I was resistant at first, but your help has been invaluable. Poor Ozzie and Harriet would have been in trouble with me as their caretaker."

"I can do more than feed and water two beasties, you know. If you need me to make calls or run down deposits and whatnot, I'm available."

"Okay." Her back was to him as she tended the bacon.

Iain cocked his head. "Did you say, 'okay'?"

"Aye, Highlander. I said, 'okay.'" The Scottish burr she adopted was still inflected with her Southern accent. It was equal parts terrible and adorable.

"One sandwich or two?" she asked him.

"Is three an option?"

"Good thinking. You'll need the energy for tonight."

A zing of awareness had him sitting up straighter. "What's happening tonight?"

"Our second dance lesson, of course." Her voice was brisk and teacher-like.

Of course. He slumped on his seat, fighting off disappointment he had no right to. After all, she had been the one to label their kiss as a mistake. He'd thoroughly enjoyed the blistering kiss, but had worried he was being too aggressive. Basically, he'd attempted to act like a gentleman, and it had backfired.

She slid a stack of sandwiches in front of him. His first bite was a revelation. He made a noise of appreciation and took another bite and another until all three sandwiches were gone in the time it had taken Anna to eat one.

Her smile was bemused but pleased. "I'm going to assume that means you enjoyed them."

"Aye." He patted his belly, then folded his arms on the counter to wait for her to finish.

"What do you think of our goddaughter?" She raised her eyebrows.

"*Our* goddaughter?"

"Izzy asked me to be godmother." She pulled her phone out. "She also sent pictures. Do you want to see?"

"I do. Alasdair didn't think to send me any."

She huffed. "Boys. Here."

The baby was exactly how his da had described, except for less squally looking. He scrolled through the pictures. Alasdair looked happier and more content than Iain had ever seen him. He stared into the babe's clear gray eyes. His heart beat through the warm gooeyness filling his chest. A sense of protectiveness washed over him. "She's a bonny little thing, isn't she?"

Anna wiped her fingers on a napkin and came to look over his shoulder. "She really is. Although, I don't have much experience with babies. I don't take them on until they can dance, and I prefer them out of diapers."

"Do you want kids?" As soon as the question exited his mouth, he wanted to stuff it back in.

"I haven't thought about it much, to be honest. It's a mind warp to realize I'm teaching kids of girls I graduated high school with." She shrugged. "Back then, I was focused on making it in New York, not making babies.

You can see how well that worked out for me. What about you? Thought about kids someday?"

"I've never settled down long enough to consider it. Plus, I don't know that I want to bring a child into this world." He closed his eyes to attempt to blank out his memories.

"That's depressingly pessimistic." Her tone shifted into an unusually serious gear, and he could sense her hesitation. "Is that because of your time in the service?"

"Aye. It was the worst time of my life." He chuffed a laugh devoid of humor. "Also the best."

"So far," Anna added with raised eyebrows. "Who's to say what's just around the corner?"

"That's shockingly optimistic."

She merely gave him a slight smile before turning serious once more. "What made it the best time?"

"I joined up expecting the army would be my career. I was good at it, and it was like a huge, dysfunctional family."

"Ah-ha. You weren't lonely anymore."

It was such a simple statement but resonated like a call in a deep fissure. "I suppose I wasn't."

"What made it the worst?" When he didn't answer right away, she asked softly, "Did you have to . . . you know?"

"I mostly only fired to let the enemy know we were there. Our mission was peacekeeping, after all. My company supported humanitarian work across Afghanistan. Aid organizations needed protection as they traveled distributing books or water pumps or supplies. I was a sniper who was tasked to keep them safe."

"Was it dangerous?"

He shook his head to clear the images scrolling in his

head as vivid as the pictures of the baby earlier. "Not usually. Delivering supplies to schools were my favorite assignments."

"That sounds fulfilling."

He didn't answer.

"This is the point in the story something really bad happened, isn't it?" Her light as a feather touch on his scar brought his gaze to hers. "Is that how you got . . ."

"Ah, nay. My scar is from an accident I had on the cliffs when I was a lad. Short story is that I fell onto a ledge, broke my leg, and cut my face." The physical pain he'd experienced had faded from his memories. While the hours spent alone on the ledge still haunted his nightmares on occasion, they were nothing compared to what'd he'd experienced in the army.

Instead of looking away from him, she squared her body to his. With him sitting and her standing, their faces were level. She touched his cheek more firmly now, smoothing her palm over his scar and beard. "You don't have to—"

"It was a bloody drone. The Americans eventually took the blame. They thought it was a terrorist training camp, when it was actually a school with a playground."

"That's terrible. You were there?"

"Close enough. We lost three aid workers and two soldiers and so many kids. So many." Kids who had been playing chase or swinging on a rickety metal swing set one moment were lifeless the next. "My re-up came around, and I took my discharge."

"Do you miss it?"

The whys and wherefores of his decision to leave the army weren't entirely clear, even to him. All he knew was once he'd stepped off the base in Scotland in his civilian clothes, the bands around his chest dropped away.

Yet. There was always a yet. "Sometimes, I miss it terribly. Afghanistan was hot as hades. Beautiful and harsh. The inverse of the Highlands in many ways. I think more than anything, I miss feeling useful."

"You're useful here, and Izzy said she doesn't know what they would do without you at Cairndow."

The thought settled like a stone's weight on his chest. How could he tell his da and Gareth and Alasdair how trapped he felt at home? He didn't want to think about what happened after the festival at the moment.

He raised an eyebrow. "You think I'm useful? I was under the impression I am merely a pooper scooper."

"When we first met, I was being a . . ." She let out a huff and looked to the ceiling before refocusing on him. "What would you call me?"

"A prat," he said with twitching lips.

"Is that like a brat?"

"The grown-up, less cuddly version."

Instead of turning defensive, her eyes sparkled with humor. "I'll accept that. Are you ready for dance lesson number two?"

A nervous excitement squatted in his stomach like a horny little gnome. The last time they'd attempted a lesson, things had gone awry in the most surprising but best possible way. Was it too much to hope for a repeat performance? "I'm hopeless."

"No one is hopeless. We just need to tap into your natural rhythm." She grabbed his hands, pulled him to standing, and examined him in a clinical way. "You already sing and play. It's merely a matter of scale. What you need is confidence."

"Do you have some to spare?" he asked dryly.

"When it comes to dancing? Plenty." She rubbed her hands together and transferred her attention. "Come on and help me make room."

Together, they shifted the couch and rolled up a rug, leaving a squarish expanse of hardwood floor.

She picked up her phone and synced it with a portable speaker on a side table. Would she pick the same sexy, honeyed song as last time? A tin whistle heralded the start of the music. It was in the count of a slow waltz.

Anna's hips swayed in time, and the motion traveled up her body in an undulation that left him standing like a lump, his mouth slightly agape. She raised her arms over her head and tossed her hair over her shoulders, closing her eyes. No one was as lovely and graceful as Anna in that moment. How could she make such a traditional song so bloody sexy?

"I can't do this," he finally croaked out. "I'll tell the doc to find someone else."

"Of course you can do this." She grabbed his hips, forcing him to match her movements. "Let's count together. One-two-three."

Although, it was a toddler-level skill, he stumbled over the numbers. His arms hung useless at his sides. She maneuvered his hands like he was a doll, one on her side, the other she took in her hand.

"First, we sidestep and stamp." She took a step and he followed half a beat behind. "Now, the other way."

He performed the simple sidestep adequately, but then she said, "Now, the classic waltz."

He shuffled his feet to keep up with her without even trying to remain on the beat.

"And, a twirl." She stepped away and performed a

flawless spin under his arm, her hair flashing around her shoulders. He stepped forward at the same time she returned to her original position, leaving them in a pseudo embrace. Or was it an actual embrace?

Her arms snaked around his neck, her fingers playing in the hair at his nape. He slipped his arm around her waist and drew her onto her toes and into him. His other hand landed between her shoulder blades.

She tilted her head back and their gazes clashed, hers emitting an unmistakable challenge he was afraid to accept. What he had to offer was simple and solid and . . . boring. A woman like Anna would tire of him. But what if . . . ? What if he fed the spark between them? What if he took her to bed? The end of the festival offered an expiration date. She wouldn't have time to tire of him.

He felt unsteady and insecure like the seemingly solid cliff rocks that had crumbled under his grasp and left him alone and in pain so long ago. The last year had left him reeling in confusion. His vision for his future destroyed as surely as the school in Afghanistan had been.

Things were changing. His tether to Cairndow had weakened, and he scrambled for purchase. But, ever so slowly, he was finding his footing in Highland. He was becoming more comfortable in his own skin, and the feeling became even stronger in her arms.

As if it were the most natural thing in his world, his hand migrated south and smoothed over Anna's bum. Her intake of breath was halfway between a gasp and a sigh.

"Too much?" He squeezed slightly.

"In the middle of our dance in front of all of Highland? Yes." Her whisper was an invitation. "But here and now? Nope."

Casting off his reservations, he accepted. Dipping his head, he brushed his lips across hers, once and then twice. On the third pass, his mouth stayed to sup on hers, pulling her bottom lip between his teeth. She tightened her arms around his neck and pressed herself tight against him. She was lean and muscular from her job, but her breasts were soft and her curves inviting. Her tongue touched his then retreated as if coaxing him out to play, and he tightened his grip on her arse as he deepened the kiss.

The beat of the music had him swaying, and the back of his knees hit the arm of the couch, halting him. Before he could maneuver them into open space, she skimmed her hand to the middle of his chest and pushed. It didn't take much to upset his balance. He toppled backward onto the couch, his kilt flipping high on his thighs. He didn't have time to take a breath or repair his kilt before she straddled his hips.

She wrapped her hands around his wrists and pushed his arms above his head. He could take control with ease—he knew it and she knew it—but he didn't.

"Too much?" She boomeranged his question back at him.

He smiled. "Not nearly enough, lass."

She didn't return his smile. Lowering herself slowly, she kissed him, shimmying her hips against him. It was wild and reckless and left his breathing ragged. Finally, he couldn't take any more. She wasn't positioned where he needed her to be. He grabbed her hips and scooted her down. She gasped against his mouth.

The song ended, and the ensuing silence left them in a

strange stasis. The pulse of his heart was its own primitive sort of music, and he bucked his hips against her. Like it was the jumpstart she needed, she moved against him. He tightened his grip on her hips, forcing her into a rhythm that drove his desire higher.

With the fingernails of one of her hands finding purchase in his shoulder, she arched and pulled his kilt up with her other. He cursed the practical streak that'd had him pull on a pair of boxer briefs after his shower. If her pout was any indication, she was cursing him too.

"Underwear?"

"I don't want to shock the residents of Highland."

She sat up and traced the hard ridge outlined by the thin layer of cotton. Desperation had his hips pressing against her hand. "Shock and awe. Yep, that's the truth of it. I swear it's even bigger."

"You weren't grinding on me when you stole a peek under my kilt earlier, love. Do I need to explain how this works?"

A blush raced up her neck and into her cheeks. "I meant, bigger than I imagined."

He'd never been a practiced flirt, but he rather liked teasing her and making her blush. "Ach, so you've imagined me in this state for you?"

Her blush intensified, but her voice was coy and a smile quivered on her lips. "Perhaps."

He wanted to know if the pink extended to her chest. Nay, he *needed* to know. He went to work on the buttons of her shirt, but his big hands weren't made for such delicate work. The delay was excruciating in the best possible way. The release of each button revealed a few more inches of her pinkened skin.

"I've dreamed of you every night since I arrived, lass.

Every. Night." Finally, he was able to push her shirt over her shoulders. Her bra was made of thin lace. It took both his hands and all his dexterity to release the clasp at her back. She held the bra to her chest, the straps falling down her shoulders.

Her eyes were wide and seeking encouragement. "Iain?"

He sat up with her still straddling him and brushed his lips along the top curve of her right breast. "You're lovely. Lovely," he rumbled.

She dropped her hands and he swept the bra aside. Her breasts weren't large, but they were perfect. He covered one with his hand, her budded nipple pressing against his palm. He repositioned them, so he was sitting and she was on his lap.

"Is it weird that we're both wearing skirts?" She peppered kisses down his scar until she reached his mouth.

He pulled away to give her a stern look. "A curse on you for even thinking of my kilt as a skirt. That sort of insult would merit punishment in the olden days."

She waggled her eyebrows. "Yeah? What kind of punishment?"

"It would be up to the Highlander insulted." Their banter was playful but intensely sexual. "I'm thinking something along the lines of . . ." He scooped his arms along her back and brought her breast to his mouth.

She speared her fingers through his hair and held on tight. The tingles traveled at warp speed from his scalp to escalate the desperate situation brewing between his legs. He alternated flicks with his tongue and gentle sucks.

"Is this torture by pleasure?" she asked in a hoarse voice.

"A torture that will end with a little death, I hope."

She startled. "Death? I think I'll pass."

His laughter came easy and natural. "It's an old-fashioned way of referring to an orgasm. *La petite mort.*"

She relaxed back into his touch, and he resumed his attentions, this time on her other breast. "How do you know that?"

"I read a lot as a lad. Not much else to do during the long winters." With her arms firmly around his neck, he transferred his hands to her knees and smoothed them up her thighs, taking her skirt along for the ride. Once he reached her arse, he scooted her closer, until his erection pressed against her belly.

"What's your favorite book?" She was breathless. Her body was aroused, of that he had no doubt, but her questions signaled an uncertainty that gave him pause. He raised his head to look in her eyes.

"Do you want this, Anna?"

"I'm the one that climbed on top of you."

"Answer the question." He stroked her hair and wrapped his hand around her nape.

"Yes. I want this. I want you." Her mouth parted, and he could hear the word she left unsaid.

"But?"

Her throat worked on a hard swallow. "I'm scared."

"Why?" He didn't think anything could scare her. She seemed indomitable. "Is it my size?"

One corner of her mouth quirked up. "Aren't you full of yourself all of a sudden?"

Now it was his turn to blush. "Not the size of my . . . Other women have found me rather intimidating, but I would never hurt you."

"Oh, Iain." Her face softened, and she leaned in to

kiss his temple, his cheek, his lips. "I'm not scared you'll hurt me like that."

He forgot to ask what was she afraid of because her kisses turned wild and her hips ground against him. He forgot everything except the driving need building between them.

Her hands slipped under his T-shirt and tugged upward. He grabbed the back and pulled it off, leaving them both topless. She explored his chest and shoulders, and surprised him by following the path of her fingers along his pectoral muscles with her lips.

He ran his hands down her back, his thumbs tracing her spine and slipping into the waistband of her skirt. She arched her back and wiggled in encouragement. Anna was gorgeous, but what made her electric was how comfortable she was with herself, which in turn made him comfortable.

Iain tugged her panties to one side and slipped a finger along her core. A moaning gasp escaped as she popped her legs farther apart. "Do you have protection?"

He had no protection against the welling emotional deluge she inspired in him, but how could he admit the weakness to her?

"A condom?" Her clarification both relieved and embarrassed him, and he shook his head. "I'll bet Izzy has a stash in her room. Want to come upstairs and check with me?"

He nodded like a caveman. He was a kiss away from having to draw on walls to communicate. She shimmied backward off his lap and held out a hand. He took it and stood, looking down at her. Unable to keep himself from touching her, he hauled her closer, their naked torsos creating enough friction to start a fire.

"Hang on to me." He sounded as if he hadn't spoken in days. He lifted her, cupping her bum.

She wrapped her legs around his hips and her arms around his shoulders. Her budded nipples rubbed against him with each stair step, and she tugged his earlobe between her teeth, her hot breath liquefying his knees. He made it as far as the landing and pressed her against the wall, lifting her higher to take her breast into his mouth.

After regaining his footing and climbing the remainder of the stairs, he toed open the door to his bedroom and walked straight to the bed. He took her waist, peeled her away from him, and plopped her on the mattress. The bounce incited breathless soft giggles from her.

She pointed to the room next door. "Check Izzy's nightstand."

He stalked through the connecting bathroom and rummaged through the nightstand like a thief desperate to find the crown jewels before MI-5 showed up. Finally, his fingers brushed a familiar packet. He retrieved two and returned to Anna.

He expected to find her under the covers, but she was at the window, opening the curtains to let moonlight flood the room. It glanced off her pale skin and gave her a magical quality. She turned and he was struck even dumber by her beauty.

"Did you find one?"

He held out the two condoms like offerings to the old druid gods.

"Excellent." She took them both and tossed them on the coverlet. "Sit, Highlander."

If there was a world record for fastest sitting, he broke it. She put her hands lightly on his shoulders and stepped closer, her breasts close to his mouth. He was more than happy to oblige her desire.

He ran his teeth along her nipple before flicking it with his tongue. He fit his palm to the soft curve of the other and squeezed slightly. She turned around and he was momentarily bereft, until she bent over, her bottom swaying. Again, her physical cues were simple and obvious, and he was grateful.

He flipped her skirt up, grabbed her knickers, and peeled them down her thighs. Then, he leaned in to do something he'd never even thought about doing to a woman. He gently bit the cheek of her bum, then kissed the spot he bit. A fine tremble ran through her like a mini-earthquake. Slipping his hand between her legs, he could play unimpeded.

With an abruptness that unbalanced him, she stepped away, kicked off her knickers, and faced him. Had he done something wrong? Misread her signals?

She hooked her fingers into the waist of her skirt and wiggled her hips while pushing it to her ankles. She stood illuminated by moonlight, naked and proud and confident. Still emanating power, she dropped to her knees.

"Your turn, Highlander. Off with your kilt." Her hand cut through the air like a queen calling for someone's head.

As if following an order from a commanding officer, he obeyed, tossing the kilt and his underpants aside. She ran her fingertips lightly up his thighs. His erection jumped in reaction, and he prayed her fingers would continue their trek.

She glanced up at him. "You can speak, you know. Tell me what you like."

He swallowed and tried to produce words. "I like you."

As soon as the childish words left his mouth, he closed his eyes and shook his head. The devil take it, he really was rubbish when it came to women.

Her laugh had none of the sarcasm she normally wielded like a rapier. "I like you too, you big, sexy beast."

She smiled up at him, and he cupped her cheek, his fingers tangling in her hair. He wished he was better with flowery compliments and expressing himself. He wanted to tell her she was challenging and beautiful and brought out a side of him he hadn't known existed. One he rather liked.

Instead, he went with a simpler truth. "I'm afraid I'll say the wrong thing."

"You can say whatever you want with me." Her hand stole around his shoulders and she pulled him down for a kiss. It was brief, but firm as if punctuating her promise. Then, her attention turned to his erection and any need or ability to speak deserted him.

"By the way, I especially like this." Her voice danced with a tease her lips mimicked as they played along the tip of his erection.

Her mouth was hot and wet and foretold even greater pleasures to come. With a strong pull, she lifted her head and reached for one of the packets at his hip. When he tried to take control, she pushed his hands away.

"No, I'll do it." At the sound of the wrapper tearing, he closed his eyes and fell backward on the bed.

It was odd for a woman to take charge. Or maybe it wasn't. Had his experiences been warped? She scrambled on top of him. "Are you ready?"

He opened his eyes and couldn't look away. Her hair

was wildly tangled around her shoulders, only glints of red visible in the moonlight. Her body was lithe and strong on top of his. She bit her bottom lip, poised to take him, yet she waited for him to answer.

He caught her hips and drove her down as his answer. Their moans rang out in the sweetest of harmonies. He'd never been so in tune with a woman before. He let her set the rhythm, slow with a hip roll that drove him too close to the brink. He didn't want it to end.

She lowered her chest to his and kissed him while continuing the chase for her own climax. Her body tightened and jerked, and she let out a long sighing moan of satisfaction, almost panting. Her limbs grew lax and heavy. He flipped her to her back, positioning himself between her legs and fitting himself at her entrance.

Now, it was his turn. He thrust deep and hard. Her back arched and her eyes closed, but she grabbed his biceps and her nails spurred him on. His rhythm was fast and intense and scooted her up the bed and into the pillows.

Her internal muscles clamped him once more as a harsh cry was wrung from her throat. He followed with a low groan, his toes curling and his legs shaking, no longer able to support his weight. He collapsed at her side and disposed of the condom, breathing hard as he stared up at the ceiling.

She notched herself into his side and nudged his face with her nose like a cat. Even her voice purred. "Wow, Highlander. That was good." In her honeyed accent, she drew the word "good" out into at least three syllables.

"No, it wasn't."

"It wasn't?" She popped up on her elbow. Even in the shadows, her glare singed him.

As usual, his response had been woefully inappropriate and not at all what he meant to convey. He winced and tried to regain his verbal footing, his words stumbling out. "I meant, it was better than good. It was bloody amazing. You're amazing."

"Not as amazing as you." She kissed his cheek, the gesture endearing.

He waited for her to leave him. Once women got what they wanted, they tended to come up with excuses not to have to actually hang around. He didn't have to wait long.

"I'm going to clean up." She slid from his side, leaving him chilled in the air-con. How could such a small woman generate so much heat?

She disappeared into the bathroom. If she wanted to make a clean escape, she could slip out the other bedroom and not even see him again until morning.

Morning. How awkward would the next morning be? They still had to tackle a mountain of details before the festival kickoff, not to mention the festival itself.

He maneuvered under the covers. Inexplicably, after the most intimate moment of his life, he fought a crushing loneliness. The toilet flushed and water ran, then nothing. He strained to hear the creak of boards as she snuck away.

Instead, he heard the creak of the door and the pad of footsteps growing closer. He raised his head to watch her climb under the covers and reattach herself to his side. Her toes were cold and his leg jerked in response.

"Sorry, my feet are always cold." Anna yawned and snuggled closer.

"I don't mind." He wrapped his arm around her, daring to kiss the top of her head.

"We're batting zero for two."

"What's that mean?" he asked.

"It's a baseball reference. It means I've tried to teach you to dance twice and gotten distracted."

"Maybe it's not meant to be."

"You give up too easily."

Did he? Not usually. If a mothering ewe was in distress or a complicated project landed on his lap, he would worry and work until the birth or the project was complete and successful. Unfortunately, he'd never possessed the same tenacity or confidence when it came to relationships. He had been easily discouraged. Perhaps his failures couldn't be laid at anyone else's feet but his own.

Still ruminating on facts and fallacies, he drifted to sleep with Anna locked in his arms.

Chapter Fourteen

Anna started awake in the dark, disoriented and with her heart pounding in her ears. Unfamiliar shadows surrounded her. The bed and window were in the wrong place in relation to each other. The room was cool, yet heat emanated next to her, grounding her in time and place. Rolling to her side to face Iain, she relaxed into the comfy mattress and pulled the covers to her neck.

It was a good thing she didn't take up much room. Iain was sprawled on his back, his massive frame taking up a majority of the bed. He breathed deeply and snuffled slightly on each exhale. She liked learning new things about him.

The birds hadn't even begun their warm-up for the morning's dawn concert. She had time. *They* had time. The sex had been a revelation. Physically, he could have dominated her. And he had later, but he'd allowed her to take charge at the beginning when she'd needed to assert herself.

Iain alternated between confidence and uncertainty in a way she found captivating. Did he realize how smitten she was with him? It wasn't just the physical—although she had zero complaints with what was under his kilt—it was the vulnerability he hid under his stoic gruffness.

It would be better if he never found out how she felt. Actually, it would be best if she wasn't smitten at all and could enjoy the simple pleasure he offered in bed. No, not simple. The dynamic between them was complex. One she'd never experienced, but found undeniably attractive.

Speaking of undeniably attractive, she eyed the unused condom on the night stand. If condoms could talk, it was definitely cheering her on. She slipped her hand under the covers to cup him between the legs, surprised to find him semi-erect. It didn't take many strokes for semi-erect to turn fully erect. *Go, team Anna!*

"What mischief are you getting up to, lass?" His rumbly brogue was a turn-on in and of itself.

"Unless you have an objection, I'm going to take wild advantage of you." She moved half on top of him and brushed her sensitive breasts against his hair-covered chest.

She stifled a moan at the friction. She'd never been with a man with plentiful hair on his chest. Actually, compared to Iain, she wasn't sure any of her past boyfriends qualified as men.

"I do object." He rolled and reversed their positions, his chest pressing her into the mattress, his erection against her hip. "It's my turn."

"I didn't realize this was a turn-taking kind of situation. Anyway, you had a turn last night." Her voice lilted up as his fingers found her and stroked gently.

"I can be stubborn and selfish with my turn."

"Like a toddler?" Her words strangled when his thumb found the apex of nerves throbbing for his attention.

"Exactly. I like to get my way."

"And what do you want?"

"I want you to lose control."

He had an instinct about what she needed and where. And if he fumbled, she was ready with a circle of her hips or a gentle nudge to where she needed his touch. He kissed her, the dual sensations enough to shove her over the edge into an intense orgasm.

Iain didn't wait for her spiral back to earth. He maneuvered her onto her hands and knees and positioned himself behind her. The stretch of him entering her extended the trembling pleasure throughout her body. His thrusts were hard and deep and satisfying in a way sex had never been for her. Her brain had switched off worries of the festival and the studio and her ambition to be mayor. It could only process the physical and wallow in the pleasure signals zipping around her body.

Iain gave one last push and held still inside of her, his erection pulsing. Anna's trembling limbs gave out, and she slipped to lay on her belly like she'd been flattened by a truck. The darkness outside had lightened to gray and birds trilled. Her list of things to do was an arm's length long, yet she couldn't summon an ounce of urgency. She could have wallowed in bed with Iain all day, making love and talking.

Iain gave her bare butt a playful slap before rising. She turned her head to watch him stretch, his back muscles shifting.

"Are you leaving?" The question came out more plaintive than she intended.

"I have the animals to tend." He paused in the door of the bathroom. "You're welcome to stay as long as you want."

He disappeared and she sat up with a huff. Had he just pulled the "I've got an important meeting" card in order to escape? No, he simply had work to do, and so did she. She pressed the palms of her hands to her forehead, all the warm fuzziness imparted from their dawn sex vanishing.

After making her escape from Stonehaven in what was less a walk of shame and more like a sprint, she settled in behind her desk at the studio. She had classes to teach before she could shift gears to the festival.

The toddlers came and went with the usual amount of chaos. She suspected wrangling the animals was less difficult than herding the kids. The high school girls entered and took their places. When she started the traditional Scottish music, a collective groan went up among the girls. She switched the music off.

"What's wrong?" She turned to face the girls with her hands on her hips.

"We've practiced so much, I've started dreaming the routine. We know it, and we'll still practice, but can we do something else. Something fun?" Keisha piped up from her usual position at the front. Several of the other girls nodded.

If Anna's mother had been in charge, she would have stamped out any independence with a cutting remark that put the girls in their places. Anna wasn't her mother, though, and recognized herself in Keisha. The girl was a natural leader and had a confidence Anna didn't want to see squashed.

Without answering, Anna dialed up a current song with a thumping bass beat. "Okay, line up and try to keep up with me."

Anna moved to the front of the class, all of them

facing the mirrors. Smiles and high fives from the girls framed her. Soon Anna was caught up in the technicalities of the moves, counting them off and repeating until the girls picked up on the intricacies.

They took ten minutes at the end of class to run through the routine for the games, and the girls looked more in sync and energetic than they had in weeks. What was the lesson? That it was healthy to switch things up and have a little fun? Was sex with Iain a distraction or a stress relief?

Waving the girls out of the front door of the studio, she spotted Gabby's dad strolling on the other side of the street. Without second-guessing herself, she scooted out the door and stepped into the road, waiting not-so-patiently for a break in traffic.

She caught up to him next to an alleyway that had been bricked in to form a small courtyard between shops. A mural of the actual Highlands was painted along the back wall and a fountain added to the ambiance.

"Mr. Donaldson. Could I have a quick word?" She was out of breath from a combination of the sprint across the street and down the sidewalk, and nerves.

Mr. Donaldson turned, his only answer a brusque nod. On the surface, he was intimidating—did the man know how to smile?—but was his stoicism merely a product of grief and worry?

"I want to apologize for the other day. I had no right to tell you how to parent your daughter. You know what's best for her and for your family." Was that a slight softening around his mouth? Anna cleared her throat and continued. "My goal with dance is to instill something I lacked as a child. Confidence. A belief in oneself. Setting a goal and achieving it. My approach to dance isn't sexualized. My girls are different shapes and sizes and talent levels, but they all crave the same thing—someone to cheer them on. That's me. That's what I do."

Mr. Donaldson's eyes narrowed, and he pulled at his bottom lip, considering her like she were an insect to be classified.

She made one last ditch effort. "Yes, Gabby could win Lass of the Games, but this is not about a competition. After her mother—your wife—died, she got quieter in class. More reserved. She's never talked about her mother with me, but that's when her dancing changed."

"How so?" he asked.

His interest, no matter how mild, galvanized Anna. "Her dancing became emotive. A safe way for her to experience love and grief. I guess that sounds silly to you, but—"

"No." He let out a long exhale and looked toward the mural. "I feel the same way in church when the organ plays and I sing the old hymns Margie loved. Makes me feel close to her and less sad. I've hoped Gabby would find the same peace through church."

"I understand. I truly hope she does."

He scratched the gray stubble along his jaw. "Let me think on what you said."

She would take it as a win. "Have a good day, Mr. Donaldson."

He touched the frayed brim of his ball cap with a John Deere emblem on the front and continued down the sidewalk, disappearing into the hardware store. She wasn't sure she had made a difference, but she was satisfied she'd done all she could do for now.

A truck with an animal trailer attached rumbled to a

stop next to her. Holt rolled down the window and hollered her name.

She hopped off the curb and poked her head through the passenger window. The AC was refreshing. "What's up?"

"I was headed out to Stonehaven to drop off Mom's goats. Best if they have a chance to get acclimated. Is Iain out at the house?" Holt's blue jeans were broken-in and dirty, and his black T-shirt had a tear at a shoulder seam. The Highland motto on the pocket was peeling off. His ball cap was sweat-stained, and his stubble was veering into a beard. He looked exhausted.

"As far as I know, he is." When the window was halfway up, Anna rapped on it, and Holt let it back down, pushing the brim of his hat up. "How about I grab a couple of to-go plates from the Highland Lass and bring them out for you two?"

"That would be great, actually. I haven't had a chance to sit all day, much less eat." Holt shot her a smile, but it only emphasized how grim he'd been before.

Not only did she get three to-go plates of the fried chicken special from the Highland Lass, but an entire pecan pie. After stopping for a six-pack of beer, she made her way to Stonehaven, wishing she'd had time for a shower.

This would be the first time she and Iain saw each other after the weirdness of their morning-after parting. In keeping with her level up in maturity for the day, she promised herself to handle the moment with grace, no matter what happened. After all, they still had the festival to get through.

By the time she reached Stonehaven, the trailer on the

back of Holt's truck was empty and the sounds of animals from the barn was louder. Two pairs of dirt-caked boots graced the stoop. Juggling the to-go boxes, pie, and beer, she rang the doorbell with her elbow.

Footsteps sounded on the other side, and she froze with a smile on her face, determined to look unaffected. The door swung open and revealed Iain. His sweat-splotched T-shirt clung to him and his kilt was one of his durable gray utility versions.

She swallowed but kept the smile mostly intact.

His eyes narrowed. "What's wrong? Did something happen?"

"What do you mean?"

"You look funny."

"Not 'funny' ha-ha, I assume." Her cheek muscles felt sore, and she let her smile drop. How crazed had she looked? "Nothing happened. It's just . . . you. And me. And stuff."

He took the pie off the top of the boxes and the six-pack from her hand. "I should have called you or texted you today. I apologize. I wasn't sure what the proper etiquette was."

"It's fine." Was it really? She didn't want to play the polite Southerner with Iain. "Actually, I felt like you were trying to escape this morning, and I have no idea where I stand with you. Do you want to forget last night ever happened?"

She took a deep breath, the burden of the day somewhat relieved, even though waiting for his answer was its own torture.

He huffed something resembling a laugh, but his expression veered rueful. "Usually, it's the woman who can't get away fast enough from me the morning after. I'm sorry. I will never forget it happened, and I hope it might happen again this evening?" His voice lilted up.

The man was so adorably charming, she was lost. "If I were a Magic 8-Ball, I'd say your chances are favorable." She stood on tiptoe to press a chaste kiss on his cheek and scooted around him.

She set the to-go boxes on the table where Holt sprawled in a chair, his head resting on the back. His eyes fluttered open, and Anna noted the dark circles underneath.

"What's going on, Holt?" Anna set one of the plates in front of him.

"Same old, same old." Holt heaved himself up and popped the lid off. "Smells amazing."

Iain doled out a beer for each of them, and they dug in, the conversation meandering around festival goings-on.

"Are you ready for the Laird of the Games competitions?" Anna asked Holt.

"I haven't had as much time to practice this year—Dad is slowing down—but working the farm keeps me in decent shape. I suppose I'll do okay." Holt used his biscuit to sop up the pot liquor from the greens and didn't look up.

"Is the farm doing well?" Anna asked.

"Well enough, I suppose."

"Then what's wrong?" Anna pushed her plate away and crossed her arms on the table.

Holt finally looked up, but his gaze skated toward the window and the field beyond. The mowers were coming soon to clear the wildflowers and grass away. "Why would you think something is wrong?"

"You're usually Mr. Optimistic. Lately, you've been downright mopey."

Holt let out a groan. "It's nothing. I mean, it's crazy. It's what I planned to do anyway. I don't know why I'm freaking out about it."

"Freaking out about what?" Anna asked.

"Dad is ready to retire and hand the farm over to me. He wants to take Mom on an extended RV trip this fall."

Even in high school, everyone had known Holt was going into the family business. He'd been president of the Future Farmers of America club three years running. "And you don't want to anymore?"

"No. I do. I think. I expected to be more settled by now. Happier." He ran a hand through his disheveled blond hair. "I sound pathetic."

"Of course you don't." What he sounded was lonely, but Anna wasn't about to tell him that.

"Family obligations are complicated," Iain said.

"You got 'em too?" Holt asked.

"My da is Cairndow's groundskeeper, and I'm expected to take over for him. My family has always served the Blackmoors."

"That sounds medieval." Anna didn't like the connotation of Iain serving anyone, even if they were friends.

"Is that what you'll do after the festival? Go back to Cairndow until it's time to take over?" Holt asked.

Iain gave a small shake of his head and did his own staring out the window. She wasn't sure if his head shake was a yes or a no or a maybe. If only answers were as easily plucked out of the field as the flowers.

Anna cut them all a piece of pecan pie and the conversation veered to less weighty topics, including how Izzy and Alasdair were getting on with baby Annie. By the time they finished, the sun was sending streaks of orange and yellow and pink across the sky. Anna walked Holt to the door while Iain cleaned off the table.

Holt shot her a half smile as they stepped onto the front porch. "Don't tell me you're going to desert us for the real Highlands too?"

Her heart played her ribs like a xylophone. "What are you talking about?"

"You and Iain couldn't keep your eyes off each other. Is he going to drag you back to Scotland like Alasdair did to Izzy?"

She grabbed Holt's arm and pulled him around to face her. "I'm not leaving Georgia. I've worked hard to build my studio into something I'm proud of."

"Doesn't sound like Iain is ready to cut the cord with Scotland. Unless . . ."

"Unless what?"

Holt snorted. "And here I thought I was the class dunce. Not what; *who*."

"Me?" She squeaked out the word.

"Lord have mercy." Holt looked to the heavens. "You'll figure it out eventually, Einstein."

Anna watched him drive away, turning over the possibility. No, the *impossibility*. Iain wouldn't stay in Highland. Not for her.

She backed inside the house and turned around. His outline filled the other end of the hall, steady and stable and sexy as hell. They still had time, and she wouldn't squander it on questions of staying or leaving, because she already knew the answer.

She took a step and then another until she was in his arms, winding her hands into his hair and hiking her leg

up on his hip. Their kiss was combustible and charred
her worries to ash. As soon they hit the mattress upstairs,
she went up in flames and didn't think about anything
except the next kiss.

Chapter Fifteen

With only two days until the Friday kickoff parade and whisky tasting, Highland was filling up with tourists. Not a parking space was to be had on the street, a line of customers snaked out of the Brown Cow Coffee and Creamery, and dodging families on the sidewalk was a given.

The Bluegrass Jacobites, with Anna as the guest dancer, were performing at the Dancing Jig pub as the evening's entertainment. Anna's body hummed with expectation tinged with nerves. It had been months since she'd danced for an audience. Having Iain there was an added shot of excitement.

The mowers had sheared the field of flowers and grass, and workers were setting up the vendor stalls and the stage where the pipers and dancers and the band would perform. In five days, the festival would be over. The field would empty, and Iain would return to Scotland.

Neither of them had mentioned the approaching expiration date, but the seconds were counting down like a doomsday clock. Every moment took on an urgency, from the personal stories they shared, to the sex they had every night after falling into bed. And once in the barn, bent over a sawhorse. And another time on the couch.

Regular classes at the studio had been canceled for the week to allow the girls competing extra practice time. It also freed Anna up to tackle any last-minute issues. Iain had finished the enclosures and was organizing the barn to handle the influx of tourists who would be wandering through. He was also coordinating the athletic events with Dr. Jameson.

Anna thought she worked hard, but Iain put her to shame. Even more, he seemed to enjoy the work. When he wasn't building fences or helping townspeople with odd jobs, he was carving wood for fun. His animals had a cartoon quality that made her smile, and she'd encouraged him to commission with Loretta to sell them at All Things Bright and Beautiful.

Anna dressed for the performance in the studio, throwing a tartan shawl around her shoulders. She flicked the lock, whipped the front door open, and gasped. Gabby stood with her hand up to knock. They froze for a moment, then Anna pulled Gabby into a hug.

"How are you feeling?" Anna leaned back and grinned.

"Bored." Gabby's smile was small and disappeared entirely as she tucked her hair behind an ear. "You're not mad at me?"

"What? Of course not." Anna bit her lip. The last thing she'd wanted to do was make Gabby feel any guilt over not dancing. It held shades of Anna's mother, which made her shudder. "I wanted you to dance for you, not me. I'm sorry if I put pressure on you or made things difficult with your dad."

"He told me he ran into you the other day." A slow

smile curled her lips. "I don't know what you said, but he changed his mind about me dancing."

"That's great!" Anna tempered the excitement in her voice. "As long as it's what you want."

"I want to compete so bad. Is it too late?"

"It's not, but even if it were, I happen to know the lady in charge pretty well." Anna winked, and Gabby giggled like any other teenager. Anna's heart swelled, and she fought the urge to pull Gabby into another hug. "We need to make sure your costume fits, though. Can you come by in the morning?"

"I can be here around nine after I finish my chores."

"Perfect." Anna gestured out the door and joined Gabby on the sidewalk after locking up the studio. "I've got a performance of my own down at the pub with the Jacobites."

"Sounds fun. Wish I could come watch, but the girls are waiting for me. I'll see you tomorrow." Gabby waved then skip-ran down the street, disappearing into the Brown Cow. Keisha's head popped out, and she gave a thumbs-up. Anna returned a crisp salute. With a dad who wanted her to be happy and friends like Keisha at her back, Gabby would be fine. Anna would make sure of it.

She stepped into the Dancing Jig pub and took a deep breath of whisky-soaked air. Dark wood covered every surface and swallowed the light, leaving the space dim and intimate. The bar was packed with a combination of locals and tourists. The members of the Bluegrass Jacobites, including Iain, were gathered around a table in the back. While Iain wasn't in the thick of the story-telling, his face creased into a genuine smile that made her heart soar. All of them wore kilts, but Iain wore his best. Granted, she might be a tiny bit biased.

She weaved through the tables, and Iain looked up, homing in on her in the crowd as if she emitted a signal only for his internal antennae. She smiled. He didn't return it, but stood and circled around the table to meet her halfway.

Without thought to anyone who might see, he folded her in his arms, tucking her head under his chin. While he'd been a huge help with the animals and vendors, his ability to stay calm was his superpower. She was a bird come home to roost, and her stress melted away.

"Everything good?" he asked.

She would tell him about Gabby later. "More than good. You?"

He made a chesty sound she had learned to take as an agreement and led her over to the table, where Robert gave her a subtle thumbs-up.

The bartender hopped on stage and introduced her and the band. After the players were settled, the Jacobites warmed the crowd up with a couple of rousing drinking songs. Iain's concentration was inward on the music and his part to play, so she was free to study him.

While not traditionally handsome with his aggressively masculine features, strong brow, and scar, he attracted her like no other man. His spirit was solid. Izzy had said he was a sticker, and Anna was beginning to understand what that meant. She could lean on him, and he wouldn't crumple. She could count on him.

To a point. She couldn't let herself forget he was leaving.

The song ended, and Robert gestured toward her, announcing her to the crowd. She took a deep breath and stepped into the same zone Iain had entered. The space on the floor was limited, but she laid her heart and soul out for the crowd during the performance. As the last strains of music faded, silence filled the space before clapping and whistles erupted.

Anna took a deep curtsey before performing her second dance number with the band, then she took a seat and sipped on lemon water, enjoying the rest of the set from the Jacobites. Burn's classic "Auld Lang Syne" wrapped up the entertainment, and the bar patrons sang along, arms thrown around shoulders and voices raised enthusiastically if a little off-key.

Another half hour of socializing followed. Anna considered it a warm-up for the hand-shaking and baby-kissing of her campaign for mayor. Finally, though, she grabbed Iain's hand and pulled him toward the exit.

"Where are we headed?" he asked.

"My place is closer."

He raised his eyebrow, but his pace quickened. Anna unlocked the door to her apartment, and Iain ducked his head to enter. He filled the room to bursting. With her body still humming from the performance, she threw herself at him—literally. He caught her to him, his hands cupping her bottom. She twined her arms around his neck and her legs clamped his hips.

"Take me to bed, Highlander." She smoothed a hand over his cheek and beard and smiled. He didn't smile back. Without closing her eyes, she kissed him, a simple brush of her lips. The moment was sharp with an intimacy unfamiliar to Anna.

He moved toward her bed, bumping his head on the top of the doorframe and scraping her back along the side. Finally, they collapsed side by side on her mattress. The creak of her bed frame did not bode well for the activities Anna had planned. Laughter burst the serious mood.

"I'm not sure my place is going to survive the fallout of what I want to do to you. It might end up a pile of rubble." She pushed him to his back and straddled his hips, leaning over him, her hair a curtain around his face.

"Isn't that how everything eventually ends?" The question twisted with meaning beyond the physical.

She hung still above him, not sure what to do or say in response. As the moment veered awkward, a pounding came from the door.

"Anna? Are you there? Please!" It was Loretta's voice, but imbued with an unfamiliar tremor.

Anna scrambled off Iain and skip-ran to the door. "What is it? What's wrong?"

Loretta's panic transferred to Anna with a shot of adrenaline. "A leak from the sink in the bathroom. My inventory. The floors. I didn't know where else to go."

She didn't need to say any more. Any business owner lived in fear of water and fire. Acts of God weren't welcome unless they involved a plague of customers with full wallets. Any loss would hit especially hard right before the Highland games.

Iain had come up behind Anna. "Let's go."

Loretta led the way into the back of All Things Bright and Beautiful. Iain strode to the bathroom to stem the leak. Anna stacked boxes out of the way of the creeping water. Loretta watched the destruction as if she had already given up.

"Do you have any quilts or towels?"

"Yes. Yes, I think so." Still, Loretta watched the rivulets of water snake closer to her inventory. Her face was drawn in deep lines of worry and shock. She wasn't the formidable opponent Anna dreaded crossing swords with but a neighbor in need.

Anna took Loretta's shoulders, squeezed, and turned her toward the store floor. "Go get them while Iain works on the leak. I'll move your inventory out of harm's way."

Loretta did as she was told. Anna returned to moving the boxes and furniture and knickknacks outside, where they would be safe for the time being.

Iain emerged from the bathroom, his shirt and kilt wet. "Water's stopped."

Loretta returned with an armful of quilts. Anna helped her form a makeshift dam to buy some time. "It's going to be okay. We're going to keep your inventory dry and safe. I promise."

Loretta nodded even as she fought tears. "Thank you. You didn't have to come help me."

"Of course I did." Anna put her hand over Loretta's and squeezed. "I know we have different visions for the town, but you can always count on me."

The three of them continued to work on moving vulnerable inventory, but the water was soaking through the quilts. They needed something to actually remove the water. "Do you have Mr. Timmerman's number?"

Loretta pulled out her cell phone with a shaking hand and scrolled to the right number. Anna took the phone and stepped outside. She explained the situation, and as she suspected, Mr. Timmerman had a wet-dry vacuum in his shop.

She handed the phone back to Loretta. "The cavalry is coming in the form of Mr. Timmerman and his wet-dry vac. Let's concentrate on getting the stuff closest to the bathroom shifted. Did any water make it to the shop floor?"

"Not that I could tell, but . . ." Loretta covered her mouth.

"Good thing these floors are concrete," Iain said as he strode by with a nightstand.

They continued to work until Mr. Timmerman appeared at the back door, out of breath and wearing, not a kilt, but loose-fitting jeans.

Anna and Loretta stood back while Iain maneuvered the vacuum into the storeroom. Anna found a small smile in spite of the situation. "I don't think I've ever seen you in anything other than a kilt, Mr. Timmerman."

"I didn't realize this was a fancy emergency cleanup party." The twinkle in Mr. Timmerman's eyes brought a much-needed sense of optimism to the situation. "I must admit I enjoy wearing something other than a kilt when I'm off the clock. Don't tell anyone."

"Being the keeper of dark secrets is my jam. Don't forget that I work with teenage girls," Anna teased before turning serious. "Thanks for coming to our rescue."

"Thank you all for coming to *my* rescue," Loretta said.

Mr. Timmerman put a bracing arm around her shoulders.

Iain fired the vacuum up, and the hum filled the need for further conversation.

After the boxes were moved and the standing water had been vacuumed up and dumped under the trees lining the alley, the four of them evaluated the situation.

"The floor is still damp," Iain said.

"I'd recommend getting your insurance man out here

first thing in the morning to do an evaluation," Mr. Timmerman added.

Anna propped her hands on her hips and surveyed the boxes and furniture clogging the alley. "In the meantime, let's move everything to my place. We can store what we can in my office and the overflow in a corner of the studio."

"But you have classes and the games to plan." Loretta turned her faded blue eyes to Anna.

"I've been working at Stonehaven with Iain." Her face heated even though it was mostly the truth. "And I don't have my regular classes this week."

It took another hour for the four of them to move everything to her studio. While not ideal, the situation was workable for the time being. Loretta gave Anna a tight hug. Shock held Anna immobile in the woman's embrace.

"Your mother would be proud of you, dear," Loretta whispered.

Anna pulled away. "Would she?"

"Of course, she was always so proud of you."

Anna jerked backward and Loretta's arms fell away. "Proud of me? I don't think so."

Loretta tilted her head, grit coming back into her voice. "Anna Maitland, your mother thought the sun rose and set in you. She was always bragging about how talented you are."

"She's never said anything like that to me."

"Did she need to?"

Anna harrumphed. "It would have made a nice change."

Iain came up next to Anna and dropped his arm around her shoulders. His wet shirt sent her squealing away. "We've got to get you out of those wet clothes."

The irony was she hadn't even meant the sentiment sexually, but the height of Loretta's and Mr. Timmerman's eyebrows made heat burst in her cheeks.

Mr. Timmerman cleared his throat and sidestepped toward the studio's back door. "Unless you need me for something else, I'll be going."

Loretta wasn't far behind. Anna accompanied her to the door. "Iain and I are, you know, friends."

Loretta's laugh was throaty and had a mocking edge. "Friends? That would be a darn shame." When Iain stopped a few feet behind Anna, Loretta transferred her attention to him. "Thank you, Iain. You're becoming invaluable to the town."

"Glad I could be of some help," he said.

The door closed, leaving her and Iain alone. The silence that followed made Anna's stomach squirm. She searched for something to say but found only blank pages.

Finally, Iain said haltingly, "I need a hot shower and dry clothes. Do you . . . want to come back to Stonehaven with me?"

"Yes." She clung to the easy answer.

He waited at the foot of the stairs leading to her apartment while she gathered a change of clothes and toiletries. When she stepped onto the landing and looked down at him, a sense of vertigo spun her head, and she couldn't make it to his side fast enough.

After stumbling the last couple of steps, she grabbed his arm and tried a nonchalant laugh. "I guess we'll have to wait to turn everything to rubble."

"Yes. We should put it off as long as possible."

A hundred questions scrolled. He turned to the pickup, opening the door for her. She hesitated with one foot in and one out. Did she really want to know the answers? Giving him a small, tight smile, she climbed in. By the time he slid behind the wheel, the moment had passed, but the doomsday clock's hands moved ever closer to midnight. How long did they have left?

Chapter Sixteen

The ringing of his mobile on the counter brought Iain out of his three-count waltzing trance. He had been practicing without Anna. While avoiding total humiliation would be nice, more than anything, he wanted to make Anna proud. He didn't want her to be embarrassed to be with him. Progress had been made, but as the whisky tasting was in mere hours, time was running short.

He grabbed his mobile. It was his da. A zing of worry shortened his greeting. "Everything all right, Da?"

"Hullo, lad. How're you making out? Melted away yet?" The timbre of his da's voice was so comforting and familiar, Iain's lips curled into a smile.

"Not yet. How are things at Cairndow? No issues, I hope."

"Everything is puttering along. Alasdair and Isabel are head over heels for the wee babe. Nothing much is getting done besides routine maintenance." While his da might not admit it, he had a soft heart under the gruff exterior and would be wrapped around little Annie's finger in no time.

"There'll be more time for big projects in a season or two. How is Tommy working out?" Iain had handpicked one of the village boys to take care of the herd while he was gone.

"He's a hard worker and isn't a complainer." High praise indeed from his da. "Doesn't know his arse from a hammer, though. Rose tells me the festival is this weekend. You're still flying home Monday, I hope?"

"I need to double-check my flight time. I'll send you the details." He didn't need to double-check. He'd stared at his return ticket so often, he had it memorized. "I've been busy."

"I need you home, lad." The somber shift had Iain clutching his mobile tighter.

"What's wrong?"

"I didn't realize how much I'd come to rely on you the last year until you left this summer. If I'm being truthful . . . I can't keep up, and that's without the extra projects Isabel and Alasdair have envisioned. It's time to pass the mantle to my son." The pride in his da's voice wasn't diminished by the physical distance between them.

If his life hadn't taken a detour though Highland, Georgia, he would have been, if not exactly happy or content, then resigned to follow in his da's footsteps. He'd spent the last year convincing himself he could and would stay on at Cairndow. He couldn't allow the last weeks in Highland with Anna to instill doubt.

"I'll be home next week as planned. I'll send on my arrival times."

"I'll meet you at the airport." Silence full of love and pride stretched between them. "I've missed you, son. It was always just the two of us, wasn't it?"

"Aye. The two of us." Iain disconnected and closed his eyes. How could he abandon his da like his mum had? It would break his da's heart and do irreparable damage to Iain's.

The front door opened, and Anna rushed the room, a ball of nervous energy. She commenced pacing. "Are we ready? What are we forgetting?"

Iain set aside the heaviness of his conversation with his da as best he could. If his time with Anna was short, he planned to savor every minute with her, and at the moment, he was enjoying the way energy spun around her like sugar.

"The animals have settled in. Ribbons are ready. Portables are in place. Final touches are going on the vendor stalls. The stage will be completed by this evening. Dr. Jameson and I organized the field for the athletic competition yesterday. I'll stake out the parking area this afternoon." He ticked the items off on his fingers. "What's your checklist say?"

"It says we've got everything under control, but you can't stake out the parking this afternoon. I'll be marching in the parade with my classes, and you must come and watch."

Of course, he wanted to watch Anna strut down the center of town. His protest was weak. "I have too much to do."

"You can't miss the parade." She slipped her hand in his and smiled up at him. "Trust me, okay?"

If he had the talent of Robert Burns, he would compose a ballad about her smile. She held nothing back when she smiled. Her smile lit her up from the inside like a beacon, and he would follow her like a sailor being drawn to the cliffs even if it meant certain destruction.

"If we're going to the parade, I'd better take care of the parking now." He leaned down to brush his lips against her smiling mouth, a jolt running straight to his heart.

The conversation with his da hung like storm clouds on the horizon. As he worked in the hot sun to set stakes and cording out for the parking area, he felt both like a foreigner and a native. He'd come to get a job done, and while he'd never imagined himself feeling at home in Highland, Georgia, somehow that was exactly what had happened.

It was because of Anna. She made it feel like home. She *was* home. Yet, so was his da and Cairndow, and Iain had promises to keep, even if the promises weighed on him like shackles.

Iain finished the mindless work with enough time to take a cool shower before the parade. He told her he'd be watching from Maitland Studio, but found himself having to park several streets away. He strode past several families herding their children toward Main Street and exchanged polite greetings, ignoring their double take at his accent.

Bagpipes echoed through the trees. The haunting sound filled his chest with longing, but what did he long for?

He stood behind a row of people already in front of the studio, his height a distinct advantage. First came a firetruck with the fire and police chiefs waving. Next were several floats decorated with banners filled with Boy and Girl Scouts and church groups.

Mr. Timmerman materialized beside him, wiping his forehead with a pristine white handkerchief. "Good day, Iain. I trust the festival is on track to be a great success?"

"That's the plan. I hope we've done Isabel and Rose proud."

Mr. Timmerman grinned. "If you haven't, then how will they know?"

A laugh stumbled out of Iain. "I'm sure a dozen locals will be on the line first thing to let them know how we did."

"True." Mr. Timmerman slapped him on the shoulder and did a turn with his hands up. "What do you think of my creation?"

Iain shifted his attention to the kilt Mr. Timmerman wore. Made of a durable twill, it was similar to Iain's utility kilts, but with more bells and whistles. Removable cargo pouches attached to loops at the belt and could be moved from hips to back to front depending on convenience. Metal latches for small tools like a tape measure attached to various points and could be adjusted. The pleating was kept to a minimum but would allow for easy movement.

"How do I get one?" Iain asked.

"I have one waiting for you made to the measurements of the kilt you lent me."

"I'll pay top dollar."

"It's on the house. I can't wait to begin marketing them online. I expect to attract a younger generation to the kilthood."

Iain and Mr. Timmerman exchanged a handshake. Girls and a few lads marched toward them in neat lines from the smallest to the tallest, turning and leaping in unison. At the front was Anna, performing the same moves but backward as she faced her pupils.

Smiles dominated, and in the back, Gabby's smile was incandescent. Anna had been right to steer the girl back to dance. On the opposite side of the street, Gabby's father surveyed the organized chaos with a stern expression. Iain could tell the moment Gabby's father spotted her because his face softened, not into a smile perhaps, but into an expression Iain had seen often enough on his da's face. It was combination of love and pride.

Anna drew even with him, her attention briefly settling on him. Relief banished the uncertainty he sensed in her eyes. With a start, he realized she too knew their time together was short. The street and sidewalks were full of people, yet in that pinprick of time, it was the two of them standing on opposite sides of a vastness neither one could breech.

She broke the connection and concentrated on leading her dancers like the Pied Piper. Iain took a step back, then another, retreating from the parade to the accompaniment of "Scotland the Brave." Irony was his specialty.

After arriving back at Stonehaven, he checked in with the contractors and confirmed the vendor stalls and stage would be ready by the morning. Another shower followed to prepare for the whisky tasting party. He was straightening his sporran when a knock sounded on his bedroom door.

"You disappeared this afternoon." With her shoulder propped against the frame and her arms crossed, Anna emitted both exasperation and affection.

She was lovely in a strapless bodice and full skirt, both in emerald green. An intricate gold brooch held a length of green and black plaid draped over her shoulder in a traditional touch. Her red hair was pinned up loosely, tendrils curling around her face and at the nape of her neck.

"I needed to make sure we stayed on schedule here."

The lameness of the excuse made him wince a smile. "You look beautiful."

"Thank you." She performed a graceful twirl into the room. "You're looking mighty fine yourself. Are you ready?"

"I hope I don't embarrass you during the waltz." He took her hands and rubbed his thumbs along the soft skin of her palms. Steely strength in a delicate package.

"Don't worry, I'm not easily embarrassed. As long as you don't spin and show everyone what you *don't* wear under your kilt, I'll be happy."

He groaned. "That was one time, and it was hot. I am covered tonight."

"That's a darn shame." She tilted her head back to grin up at him. "I had inappropriate plans to take advantage of you in some dark corner."

His laugh was half-hearted. "Will you respect me in the morning if I admit that I'm terrified of a bloody dance?"

She tucked her hand in the crook of his elbow and tugged him toward the door. "No need to be scared. We'll muddle through it together. I won't leave you hanging, I promise."

Her lighthearted promise reminded him of other promises made, and his mood spiraled further into nerves and dread.

A crowd had gathered outside of the venue. Most of the men were in their finest Scottish regalia and the women were in fancy dresses with vibrant touches of plaid. Dr. Jameson stood at the door, a whisky-soaked smile on his face, and greeted everyone as they entered. Anna knitted her fingers with Iain's and drew him forward.

While they had done nothing to hide their relationship,

neither had they flaunted it through town. Iain's surprise was doused by a flooding warmth that made him stand taller. Any man would be proud to be at Anna's side and thankful to be invited into her bed. Dr. Jameson pumped his hand in an enthusiastic shake at the same time he leaned in to kiss Anna's cheek.

Anna laughed. "You're feeling no pain, are you, Dr. Jameson?"

"Great whisky makes you forget all your troubles, eh, Iain?"

"That's the right of it, sir." Iain and Anna continued inside, where conversation buzzed around the room. The short bar area was three deep. A curtain separated the main room from the back. A peek behind the curtain showed a group gathered around small tables while servers delivered tastings of exclusive whiskies to the people who had paid extra for the pleasure.

"I'm surprised you didn't want to attend the tasting." Anna lifted her face to speak close to his ear.

"If I could nurse my head in the morning, I might have, but you need me in tip-top shape tomorrow."

She stole an arm around his waist and grinned up at him. "I need you in tip-top shape tonight too."

He brushed his lips over hers. He used to second-guess every move with a woman, but not with Anna. With Anna, he followed his instincts and shockingly, they hadn't steered him wrong.

Anxiety in large social gatherings had also haunted him for years, and he couldn't deny a feeling of being on edge tonight, but when he might have retreated to a shadowy corner to observe everyone else having a grand time, Anna kept him by her side, circulating around the room as the unofficial hostess.

Even more shockingly, Iain held up his end of the hosting duties, contributing to more conversations than he could count. A half hour of socializing sped by, ending when Dr. Jameson hopped on a dais in the corner, announced the start of the festival to cheers, and took up his bagpipes.

It was time. Nerves inflated Iain like air to the pipes. Then, Anna took his hands and drew him into the circle of the spotlight. The brightness blinded him to anyone but her. She stole his nerves away as easily as she'd claimed his heart.

The music lifted around them, and he took her in his arms and led her into the waltz. No one would ever accuse him of being a professional dancer, but he didn't embarrass himself or Anna during the few minutes they spent on the floor.

Other couples joined them, and the spotlight shifted away from them. Iain drew her closer. All he wanted was to take her home and strip her bare, body and soul.

"You did great, Highlander," she said in his ear.

"Only because of you."

"Half the town is here." She chewed her bottom lip and glanced around them.

"A good chance to garner some votes, eh?"

"I was thinking the same thing."

"You go on. I'll be at the bar with a celebratory drink." She leaned up on her toes and kissed his cheek. "As soon as I finish schmoozing the room, we'll head home for an early night."

Home. If only he could take her home every night. He retreated to the bar and nursed a whisky while he watched her from the sidelines.

Holt Pierson joined him, propping his foot on the

bottom rail of the bar. "Anna is a firecracker. I have no doubt she'll be Highland's next mayor."

Iain shot him a look before continuing to track her progress around the room. "Will Highland's old guard agree?"

"They'll be overrun by her charm." Holt angled himself toward Iain. "What about you?"

"What about me?"

"Have you been overrun by her charm?" While teasing lightened Holt's voice, his face was serious.

"I have been bloody gobsmacked, but there's nothing to be done about it. I'm needed at Cairndow."

"So, you're leaving." It landed somewhere between a statement and question.

"I have my return flight booked for Monday." It was a non-answer to Holt's non-question.

"I see." Holt stared into his whisky before drinking.

Iain wanted to know what Holt saw in the amber depths. Could he divine the future?

A tap on Iain's shoulder had him whirling around. Anna smiled up at him. "Ready to blow this joint?" Without waiting for a response, she tugged him toward the door. "See you tomorrow, Holt."

Anna's urgency infected Iain like a spark to dry tinder. His truck was several streets away. Too far. As if she could read his mind, Anna kept hold of his hand and steered him toward the stairs to her flat.

"We need to make a pit stop," she said softly. The dim light of a half-moon illuminated the narrow alley. She climbed two stairs and turned, leaving them almost at eye level.

Her kiss unlocked a wildness in him to match hers. They scrambled higher, kissing and pulling and clanging up the metal stairs. She unlocked the door and dropped her clutch and keys on the floor.

Her hands were under his kilt and tugging his underwear down before he got the front door kicked closed. He pushed the plaid off her shoulder and pulled her bodice down, her breasts coming out of the top.

It took some work getting his underwear over his boots, but finally he was free. She wrapped her leg around his, not needing to articulate what she wanted from him in this moment. He'd become fluent in her body language.

He pressed her against the wall next to the door, hooked a finger in her knickers, and pulled them aside. She tilted her hips, and in one smooth move, he was inside of her. His knees trembled, not from the effort of holding her against the wall but because of the way she clamped him tight with her body.

Her nails dug into his shoulder, and he slapped the wall beside her head, spurred to go faster and harder. She shuddered around him, and his control slipped to hang by fingertips. He knew just enough to withdraw before he released.

After the tumultuous sex, the aftermath was strangely serene. Anna slid between him and the wall until her weight left him and returned to earth. He let his forehead fall to the wall and breathed heavily.

Anna dropped to her hands and knees and crawled to the couch, flopping onto the cushions. He turned, still using the wall to steady himself.

"I'm tingly all over," she said. "And officially exhausted."

He found the strength to shuffle to the couch, leaning over the back to give her a kiss. "The beasties need their nightly watering. I should go."

She took hold of his shirt, but her grip was weak. "I'll come with you."

He pushed her hair off her forehead. "If you come with me, we won't get any sleep, lass, and we'll need it to face tomorrow. I'll see you at dawn?"

Anna nuzzled her lips against his palm, her eyes already closed. "If not before."

His feet were almost as heavy as his heart as he retreated. He wanted nothing more than to spend his last weekend in Highland in bed with Anna, but the festival was his responsibility, and he would see it through even if it heralded the end of the best thing that had ever happened to him.

Chapter Seventeen

Anna's day started before dawn when she woke on her couch, her bodice still pulled low and her body sore in the best possible ways. By the time she'd cleaned up and made it to Stonehaven, purples and pinks streaked the cloudless sky. Iain was already up and working.

From the moment she stepped out of her car, she didn't stop, not even to eat a sandwich while walking from the food trucks to the athletic fields. Only a few bumps marred an otherwise smooth day. The temperature had soared into the low nineties, and Anna had scrambled to put together some sort of cooling station for the attendees. The same company who had provided the portable potties had answered her desperate calls and brought out a misting station that not only cooled bodies but tempers too. The kids in particular loved it.

Iain had finagled the food vendors to offer free refills of water, and it had turned into a win-win with people more often than not purchasing food if they were already standing in line. The athletic events wrapped up as expected with Holt Pierson taking the ribbon for Laird of the Games, and the husbandry exhibit had been a fun, if pungent, addition to the day. Harriet, in particular, had proved popular with kids and grown-ups alike. The dancing competitions would take place the next day.

All that was left to wrap up day one was a concert by the Scunners, a band that melded traditional Scottish music with a rock beat. They'd been a hit the year before, and Isabel and Rose had booked them months ago. The lead singer was a petite woman with short, spiky, bright red hair and an oversized stage presence. The rest of the members, men from what Anna could discern, were wallpaper in comparison.

The stalking tension that had been a constant companion for weeks stepped to the sideline. She had done it. No, *they* had done it, because as much as she had railed about not needing help at first, she would have fallen on her face without Iain.

A hand tapped her shoulder, and she spun around, expecting to see the man who haunted her psyche in the flesh. Instead, Holt's dad stood with his hat in hand.

"Mr. Pierson. I can't thank you enough for—"

"Ozzie is gone." Grooves bracketed his mouth.

"Gone? How? When?" She fell into step next to him as they strode toward the barn. "Where's Iain?"

"Radioed him, but he's dealing with two young boys who smuggled alcohol in and are now sicker than dogs. I was on my way to find Elijah, but I spotted you first."

Standing next to the open door to Ozzie's stall was a young blond girl crying into her mother's waist. The mother's grimace held an apology. "Emily thought she was helping."

Anna put her experience teaching all sorts of children into practice and dropped to a knee, bringing them eye-to-eye. "What was wrong with Ozzie, Emily? Why did she need help?"

The girl lifted her head, her tear-stained face grubby after a long, tiring day at the festival. "The music was scaring her. I only opened the door a little bit to give her a pat, but she knocked me down and left that way."

Emily pointed toward the barn door facing the parking areas and not the main field. On the plus side, the sheep had less of a chance to trample a festivalgoer, but a higher chance of getting trampled itself by a truck.

"It's okay, sweetie. Ozzie and I have a special bond. I'll find her and get her home safely." Anna's fake confidence dried the girl's tears.

"Really?"

"Really." Anna stood. "Why don't you two go and enjoy the music for a bit."

Once the mother and daughter were gone, Anna turned to Mr. Pierson. "Any advice?"

He pulled a carrot and an apple out of a bucket on the floor. "Bribes might help."

"Good thinking." Anna sent a quick SOS text to Iain before setting out.

With no sign of Ozzie in the parking areas, Anna headed toward the line of trees that bordered Stonehaven. The gloaming wasn't quite upon the land, but the shadows under the trees were long and deep. Anna shuffled forward, a shiver raising the hairs along her arms.

She took a step into a spider's web and squealed, high-stepping into something squishy and very stinky. A pile of fresh sheep excrement.

Muttering curses, she wiped her shoe off on the grass and leaves. At least she was headed in the right direction. She gazed into the trees then looked over her shoulder, hoping to see Iain charging in to save the day, but only spotted a few people headed for their cars and a swarm of gnats.

Hunching her shoulders, she took a step into the forest, then another and another. When neither a giant spider web nor Bigfoot attacked, her stride lengthened and she called for Ozzie while brandishing the carrot.

The sound of running water quickened her step. The sound made Anna thirsty, and if she knew sheep—which she didn't *at all*—then maybe Ozzie was near the river because she was hot and thirsty too.

Anna followed along the bank until something white caught her eye. Ozzie stood in a small clearing, munching on sparse grass. The sheep's underbelly was dripping water. Keeping her voice cajoling and holding the carrot out in one hand and the apple in the other, Anna crept forward. "Come on, you little terror. You've been a thorn in my butt since the moment you showed up at Stonehaven."

Ozzie chewed and stared as if she understood the insults leveled by Anna. She tried again, this time with a stiff smile. "I'm kidding. You're a frigging delight. Doesn't this apple look delicious?"

Anna crept forward a few steps. Ozzie paced backward, keeping out of her reach. Anna halted and considered the situation. The sheep had no harness on because it had been in the stall, so even if Anna could get close enough, how would she control the sheep and get it moving in the right direction?

The image of old-timey cowboys came to mind. Could she herd Ozzie back in the right direction? She made a sweeping motion with her hands and stepped toward the sheep. "Shoo!"

Ozzie did shoo, but not in the right direction. She skittered toward the water, keeping Anna in her sights. Anna peered toward the river. It marked the boundary between Stonehaven and a state forest. The woods beyond the river were dense and the shadows were deepening by the minute as the sun crept toward the horizon.

If Ozzie spooked and bolted over the river, she might be lost forever. Or she might get chased by coyotes. What if the rumors of bobcats were true? Ozzie would be easy, delicious pickings.

Anna sidled between Ozzie and the river. Watery mud squelched around her tennis shoes and leaked inside. She ignored the grit and clammy cold, and waved her arms like she was directing an airplane in to landing.

"Go on! Get!" Making herself as big as possible, she stomped forward.

Ozzie scrambled away from her and the river. Anna breathed a sigh, but didn't let her arms drop. She continued forward yelling nonsense. Ozzie turned and trotted toward Stonehaven. Anna followed, barely able to keep up. Ozzie wasn't on a cleared path, but blazed her own trail through the woods. Anna slipped on dead leaves in her wet, dirty shoes. Low branches clawed at her hair and brambles snagged her clothes and scratched her legs, but onward she stumbled, keeping Ozzie's white haunches in view between trees.

The woods seemed never-ending. Surely they would break through to the grounds of Stonehaven at any step. The music seemed louder, didn't it? Or was it merely a trick of the ears? Just when she was beginning to worry they had circled back toward the river, the trees thinned and strobe lights from the stage quickened her step, but she wasn't quick enough.

Ozzie broke through first and took off in a trot across the athletic field. Luckily, the competitions were over, and the field was mostly deserted. The festival attendees were crowded in front of the stage . . . which, *of course*, was exactly the direction Ozzie was headed.

Anna kicked into a squelching sprint as soon as she was in the open. Ozzie increased the difficulty by zigging and zagging. The sheep was scared. Fear made animals unpredictable. People too for that matter.

From the corner of her eye, she spotted Iain running hell-bent in from the parking area. Math wasn't her strong suit, but in that moment, she turned into a savant, her mind estimating angles, trajectories, speed, and acceleration. Iain wouldn't intercept Ozzie in time. It was up to Anna.

She kicked into high gear, trying to predict the sheep's erratic path. Ozzie zagged, and Anna took a risk, keeping her line. It paid off when Ozzie zigged back into her path. She'd closed the distance and grabbed hold of the wool at the scruff of her neck, using her weight as an anchor.

Ozzie slowed, but didn't stop, dragging her along, but it was enough to allow Iain to catch up. Breathless, Iain took control of Ozzie, slipping a halter with leads over the sheep's head. Anna let go and fell to her back on the ground. A smattering of applause sounded, and as the music played on, she could only assume it was for the spectacle they'd made.

The carrot in her back pocket was a pain in her butt. She pulled it out, and as if nothing unusual had transpired, Ozzie leaned over and took the carrot out of her hand, leaving behind a wet trail of saliva. Anna wiped her hand on the grass and laughed with the limited amount of breath she had left. What else could she do in such a situation?

"That was quite something." Iain loomed over her, his hands on his knees, looking both worried and amused. Then, his eyebrow quirked up in a totally Iain-like way.

The words popped out of her mouth before she had time to consider them or worry over them or weigh the consequences. "You should stay."

"What?" The crinkle between his eyes erased his amusement.

"Stay in Highland after the festival." Her swallow was painful, but she couldn't stop now. "With me."

He straightened and said nothing. Each second that ticked off was like a tiny splinter driven into her heart with the force of a sledgehammer. If enough seconds passed, would she bleed out on the ground?

"Nope. Forget I said anything. It was a stupid idea. Why would you want to stay? There's nothing for you here." Now it was her turn to zig and zag out of fear. She scrambled to her feet to try to put them on even footing. His silence bothered her more than an out-and-out rejection would have. "Say something. Anything."

"Anna, love, I'm not sure what to say." His gaze remained anywhere but on hers.

It wasn't necessary to read between the lines. He might as well have been yelling through a megaphone. "I get it. You don't need to say anything. Let's wipe the last minute from our memories. We still have tonight and tomorrow to get through. Can you take Ozzie back to the barn and do something to prevent little girls with big hearts from setting the animals free?"

She walked away and refused to look over her shoulder until she was hidden in the back of the crowd watching the concert. Iain had disappeared into the barn. The concert would be ending soon. Not that her night would be over. Izzy had left her with an extensive checklist to finish before bed, so the grounds would be ready for the next day.

In the midst of people clapping and swaying, Anna stood still and alone. Lonely. It was a revelation. She had a full life and meaningful connections with her students and a handful of friends. She was making a difference in Highland.

Yet, until Iain had bulldozed his way into her life—and heart—she hadn't realized how lonely she'd been and for how long. It had been weeks, months, *years*.

She blinked back tears and barked a laugh. The last person she'd asked to stay had been her dad. She'd been eight. The moment carved itself in her memories with a clarity she wished she could blur. Her dad walking out the door with a suitcase. Anna crying and begging him not to leave her. He had left anyway.

Someone bumped her shoulder, and she whipped her head around to find Holt standing next to her. Anna sensed his thoughts were directed not at the redheaded singer of the Scunners, whom he watched strut and shimmy her way across the stage, but on her.

"You look like you've been dragged through the river bottoms," he said.

Anna looked down at her mud-splattered legs and formerly white-and-pink tennis shoes. Her hand went to her hair. She pulled out a twig and snapped it in two, holding the broken pieces in her hand so tightly, it hurt.

When she didn't say anything, he continued, "Did a festival-related disaster occur?"

"More like a life disaster."

"A love-life disaster?"

She shrugged but then turned toward him. "Actually, it's kind of your fault, considering you're the one who told me to take a chance with Iain."

"You told him how you feel?" Holt finally peeled his wide-eyed gaze off the singer.

"Yes. I mean, no. Not exactly, but I asked him to stay in Highland. With me."

"And?"

"And he said he didn't know what to say, which is basically a rejection."

"That's all you said? Stay in Highland? Why would he take such a huge risk without knowing how you feel?"

"When the hell did you become the 'enlightened male'?" Anna imbued as much sarcasm as possible into her air quotes. "I seem to recall you ditching your prom date when Monica crooked her little finger in your direction."

Holt had the grace to wince. "Monica was hot, and I was horny. That was a decade ago. I've learned a little something since then."

"Oh, really? Next you're going to tell me that you're putting in to be the next advice columnist for the *Highland Sentinel*."

Holt leveled her a look that shriveled her mockery. "I've learned what loneliness is, Anna, and if you care for Iain—if you love him—you need to tell him. Or you'll regret it."

The rush of tears to her eyes burned, and she wiped an escapee away with the heel of her hand—angrily, defiantly, resigned. "What if he tells me he doesn't feel the same way? That I was simply a fun distraction?"

"At least you tried." Holt put a bracing arm around her

shoulders. "If the worst happens, give me a call, and we can soak our feelings in rum."

The sound coming out of her was half laugh, half sob. "Like a big, pathetic cake?"

The lead singer of the Scunners took a bow, invited everyone back the next day for the dancing and pipe competitions, and headed off stage. Anna had too many details to handle to have an existential crisis of the heart.

People milled about. Anna left Holt and acted like a sheepdog for the second time that evening, herding people toward the exit with a smile. High spirits abounded. The weather had held for the day, but the updated hourly forecast called for thunderstorms the next afternoon. Anna could only cross her fingers the lightning held off until after the ribbon ceremony.

Two hours later, the parking areas were cleared, the crew had hauled off the trash, and the generators were shut down. Full darkness had overtaken the sky, and the chirp and buzz of insects replaced the crowds and music. It was both eerie and peaceful to see the once-crowded space empty.

Anna gathered her courage and made her way toward the barn, where Iain cast a long shadow in the portable light. He had mucked the stalls, the product of which was in a wheelbarrow, and was distributing hay and oats to the animals.

His T-shirt stuck to his back and the hair at his nape curled damply from his exertions. He paused when he caught sight of her at the door, then continued his work. The awkwardness that had sprung up between them was something new and unwelcome.

Their relationship had gone through a gamut, beginning with shades of hostility, morphing into friendship, and finally culminating in a physical relationship. Her emotions had gotten tangled up along the journey, and the void he would leave behind would never be filled, no matter how many men came after him.

"Hey." It was as eloquent as she could manage at the moment.

"The day went well enough, excepting Ozzie's jailbreak." His lips pulled into an expression that didn't come close to qualifying as a smile.

"The forecast has thunderstorms rolling in tomorrow afternoon. It'll be touch-and-go."

"We'll make it work."

She couldn't stand the stilted atmosphere another second. She'd never admit it to Holt, but he was right. If she didn't speak now . . . "Listen, about earlier—"

"No. Let me." Iain turned to her. "These last weeks in Highland—with you—have been like a dream. I've never felt like this."

Anna's heart filled with helium and her lips trembled into a smile as he closed the distance between them.

"*But*." The word was a stiletto into her chest, bursting the lightness. "Cairndow is my home and where I belong."

"Highland is my home." Why had she felt the need to say it out loud? It's not like Iain had asked her to come with him.

"I know. Highland needs you. You're going to be mayor."

"You don't know that."

"The town would be fools if they don't elect you." He raised his hand, but dropped it to his side before making contact with her cheek. An invisible barrier had come between them.

Anna took a step backward. "Has Ozzie recovered from her adventure?"

"She's no worse for wear, and I fixed the door so it's not easily opened. The other option is a padlock."

"I don't think that's necessary. It wasn't a malicious act." Anna looked down at the list on her tablet and tapped randomly as if Iain were just another completed task. "I have Izzy's checklist to finish, and then I think I'll head back to my place for a solid night's sleep."

At the spate of silence, her hands tightened on her tablet. She waited for the rising tension to break one of them, determined not to be the weak one. Finally, he said, "Aye. That's probably for the best."

She smiled—at least she hoped it resembled a smile because her lips felt distorted and trembly—and walked off with as much dignity as she could muster, which would have barely registered on the Southern Scale of Steel Spines considering her squelchy sneakers, dirt-streaked shorts, and grassy hair.

Somehow, she got through the list without having to speak to Iain again. Now, she just had to get through the rest of her life without him.

Chapter Eighteen

Anna parked at the back of Stonehaven at dawn. She wasn't sure whether to blame Iain or the festival or both for her restless night's sleep. Of course, he was already working with the animals in the barn.

On the plus side, she would be so busy and there would be so many people around, she didn't have to worry about being alone with him. Once the day was done, she could go back to her life, and he would go back to Scotland. Monday morning, she would work on forgetting him like it was her job. But, for now, she had to muddle through the day.

The dancing and pipes competition would start in a few hours, and Anna was a bundle of nerves and excitement to see her pupils perform. Most of them wouldn't place, but she was proud of every girl who had the courage to get on the stage. In class, she emphasized finding as much joy in the performance as possibly winning a ribbon.

Anna acted as the stage manager, herding participants

to the proper areas, and even gave pep talks to dancers fighting nerves, whether they were part of her studio or not.

Keisha and Gabby ran up to her arm-in-arm. Keisha grinned, her body nearly vibrating with excitement. "Hey, Anna! We are here to dominate."

Anna laughed, slightly jealous of Keisha's unshakable confidence.

Gabby's smile was more tremulous. "Hi, Miss Maitland. The competition looks fierce."

Anna leaned in to give them a quick group hug, but kept a hand on each of their arms. "I only have one directive as your teacher. Have fun up on stage today."

"I *always* have fun," Keisha said before sashaying to the warm-up area.

Gabby gnawed on her bottom lip. "I'm super nervous. I feel like there's a lot riding on this performance."

"No pressure from me." At Gabby's continued silence, Anna asked hesitantly, "Are you worried about your dad?"

Gabby's gaze slid off to the side as she raised one shoulder. "He's coming to watch."

"Let muscle memory take over. You concentrate on injecting emotion into your dance."

"I don't want to disappoint you. Or him."

Anna shook Gabby's arm until the girl met her eyes. "No matter what happens on that stage—even if you fall on your face—no one will be disappointed. We'll all still love you. As long as you dance with your heart, the blue ribbons don't matter."

Gabby gave her a quick, tight hug before she skipped off to join Keisha. When it was time for Keisha to dance, Anna moved toward the center of the crowd to watch, fighting her own nerves. She bumped someone's shoulder and turned to apologize.

It was Mr. Donaldson. "Hello, Miss Maitland." His voice was reserved and formal.

"I swear I'm more nervous watching them than I ever have been to dance myself."

"I'm nervous too." Standing with his arms crossed and his work boots braced wide, he looked as nervous as an oak tree, but she didn't doubt him.

Keisha was first and put on an electric performance that got the crowd clapping along. It was her gift, and she could easily win the blue ribbon and Lass of the Games. Gabby took the stage next with a quiet grace that was just as enthralling. Her music was slower and more melancholy, and her dance wrung every ounce of emotion from the moment.

When the music faded and she stilled in her final position, a moment of breathless silence hung in the air before the crowd erupted in claps and whistles.

"She's beautiful, isn't she? Reminds me of her mother." Mr. Donaldson's voice was reverent.

"She's beautiful inside and out, Mr. Donaldson." Anna lay her hand on his arm and hoped she wasn't overreaching. "You should be very proud."

He nodded, his mouth screwing into a grimace. His work-calloused hand wiped at a tear from the corner of his eye. "I wish her mother were here to see what a fine young lady she's growing up to be."

"Maybe she is here, looking down and smiling."

His mouth relaxed into a small, uncertain smile. "Maybe she is. Is it okay if I go around back to see her?"

"Of course it is." Watching him go to his daughter, Anna fought back her own tears.

She took a deep breath and consulted her tablet. No time to get overrun by emotion. She had bigger problems, like Iain and the weather. She checked the radar. The line of thunderstorms was creeping ever closer like an invading army.

She made her way over to the stables, to find Iain and Holt in conversation. Holt spotted her first, raised his eyebrows, and spoke low to Iain before exiting like a rabbit on the run. She cursed him under her breath. She could have used a Holt-sized buffer.

"All the animals are staying put, I hope." She prayed her casualness covered her hurt.

"So far."

"We have a problem. The weather front is on the move."

"What's the ETA?"

"Looks like it might hold off until three, maybe four if we're lucky, but I think we should shut things down at two to give people a chance to get to their cars and on the road."

"Agreed. What will we have to compress?"

"Just the awards for the dancing and piping and husbandry. And we should give the vendors a heads-up in case they aren't watching the forecast."

"The husbandry awards are scheduled for one, so we should be fine. After they're given out, I'll get the animals sheltered. I can alert the vendors if you want to handle the food trucks and the ribbon ceremony for the dancing and piping." His voice was calm and assured.

She was proud how professional she was acting, when inside she wanted to curl up on her bed, burrow under the covers, and cry for twenty-four to forty-eight hours.

Shooting a polite smile in his direction, she spun

around, but was stopped when he took her wrist, his grip firm but not painful.

"Was there something else?" she asked brusquely.

"I want to . . ." Words seemed to desert him. "I don't want things to end like this, Anna. Please."

Please what? she wanted to ask. Was he seeking her absolution? Had he wronged her? They both knew at the outset their relationship was temporary. She'd gotten too attached to him and had only herself to blame.

"It's fine, Iain. I understand. This was never meant to be anything permanent. I didn't have any illusions otherwise. What I asked last night was stupid and impractical."

"No, it wasn't." A huff escaped. "Perhaps impractical, but not stupid. I've come to . . . care for you very much, Anna."

"Yeah, me too." Tears clawed up her throat, but she swallowed them down before they could make a bid for escape from her eyes. "Asking you to stay was totally spur-of-the-moment, and I regretted it as soon as it was out of my mouth." At least that wasn't a lie.

"You're okay?"

Her cheeks hurt from the force of her faked okayness. "I'm peachy. Let's get through the storm, okay?"

This time he let her go. She made a beeline back to the judges' table and waited until the head judge looked up from scoring her sheet. Imparting the need to shift the ribbon ceremony up incited mild panic, but Anna corralled two volunteers to begin the tally of the previous contestants.

At two o'clock, with storm clouds amassing in the western sky, Anna climbed the stage to give out ribbons and award Lass of the Games. She didn't let herself peek at the cards, but as she announced the fifth, fourth, and third places in the dance competition, her nerves and excitement grew for Keisha and Gabby.

The two girls stood below the stage, their faces up-turned, clutching each other's hands. Mr. Donaldson and Keisha's mom stood behind them, looking as anxious as the girls, although they weren't clinging to each other.

"The second place ribbon goes to . . ." Anna flipped the card over. "Keisha Johnson!"

Keisha squealed and skip-ran up on stage. Anna handed over the ribbon, hugged Keisha, and whispered, "I'm so proud of you."

A grin on her face, Keisha stepped to line up with the other ribbon winners, waving at the crowd.

"The Lass of the Games is . . ." Anna already knew what the card would say, but flipped it over anyway. "Gabrielle Donaldson!"

Gabby clasped her hands together and bowed her head for a moment before looking up with a radiant smile. She hugged her dad before making her way on stage. Gabby took her ribbon and the trophy in one hand and clasped Anna around the shoulders with the other.

Before Anna could congratulate her, Gabby said, "Thank you for everything, Miss Maitland. This means more than you can know."

This was why Anna loved to teach, and she wiped a tear away as she shooed Gabby to center stage to bask in the cheers. Once they died down, Anna stepped forward and made her prepared announcement thanking everyone for coming out, inviting them back next year, and added on a warning about the incoming inclement weather.

As soon as Anna made the announcement, the con-tractors jumped into action, beginning to disassemble the stage and vendor booths. The next two hours were a race to get the field cleared of festivalgoers as well as vendors. The food trucks packed up and lumbered off, leaving crushed grass in their wake.

Iain and Anna passed each other several times, but only to exchange the briefest of updates from their respective tasks.

A crack of thunder opened the sky. As a few fat drops of rain hit the top of her head, she tucked her tablet under her shirt and headed toward the house, but only made it a few steps before the drops turned into a torrent.

The closest cover was the back porch overhang. Iain was already there. She stuttered to a stop to keep from jostling into him. Breathing hard, she checked the tablet and wiped it dry as best she could. The festival was officially over. The contractors would be back in the morning to finish hauling everything away. Ditto for the portable potty people.

"The animals?" she asked.

"Holt is coming with a trailer in the morning. He'll keep Ozzie and Harriet at his farm until Gareth gets home and decides what to do with them."

"So that's it, then. It's over." The sentiment encompassed more than the festival. The thought of never seeing Iain again felt surreal. A rivulet of rainwater slipped down her spine and made her shiver.

"Come in and take a hot shower." He opened the door to the house and the cool air only increased her shivers. "I grabbed an assortment of food from the vendors before they closed up shop so we'd have something to eat. I noticed you skipped lunch."

How had he noticed that? For a moment, she blinked at him, nonplussed. She shouldn't stay. She should get in her car and drive home to her apartment. Her empty apartment. Was it weak to want a little more time with him?

"I *am* cold and hungry."

"Go on and take your time. I'll be waiting."

Anna dripped her way to the upstairs bathroom. Under the hot spray of water, the tension she'd carried over the last weeks drained away. The festival was finished. Her case for mayor was strengthened by the success. Why then were tears leaking out of her eyes?

She borrowed a pair of yoga pants and a tank top from Izzy's drawers, leaving her wet underwear to dry over the towel rack. Iain had seen her in less. On the way down the stairs, she gave herself a pep talk, determined not to embarrass herself by crying or begging him for something he couldn't give her.

The storm cast a premature dusk outside. She paused at the edge of the kitchen. Iain had set the table and laid out a variety of food from burritos to scones. His movements betrayed his own nerves, which in turn tamped Anna's down. They stood on either side of a fault line, preparing themselves for the inevitable quake and fissure.

He caught sight of her and stopped fussing with the napkins. Electricity arced through the air between them. She took a step forward the same time lightning flashed outside, the thunder cracking on its heels. The lights snapped out and the drum of rain on the windows quickened its cadence.

"Thank goodness the storm held off," she said.

"Aye. This would have put a damper on the festival." Iain used his phone as a flashlight and located matches in the ubiquitous junk drawer in the Buchanans' kitchen.

He lit the two white tapers on the table. The ambience veered painfully romantic.

He gestured her over, and she sat next to him at the table. Faced with a cornucopia of food, her stomach begged to be filled. "I didn't realize how hungry I was."

For a few minutes, they concentrated on the fundamental need for food after two long, difficult days, physically and emotionally.

"Tell me more about growing up in Scotland," she said.

His stories settled the mood into the vicinity of comfortable, and they split a blackberry scone.

"This is tasty, but nothing can touch Mrs. Mac's scones hot from the AGA." Iain wiped his fingers on a napkin.

As if they were dancing and she was following his lead, when he rose, so did she. Somehow it seemed the most natural thing in the world to step into his arms. She rested her cheek on his chest, his heart thumping hard and fast.

"I missed you last night. I barely slept." A sigh rumbled through him with an aching melancholy.

"Me too. On both counts," she whispered.

"Will you stay tonight?" His muscles tensed.

Was she going to miss being with Iain one last time because of pride?

She slid her hand into the back of his hair and pulled his face down for a kiss. A desperate kiss tinged with foolish hope. His chesty groan vibrated against her, and he swept her into a cradle hold, making toward the stairs without breaking the kiss.

He lay her on the bed with an unexpected gentleness, his lips leaving hers to catalogue her cheek and temple and forehead. "Anna, love, I wish . . ."

Would his wish mirror hers? She wasn't sure she wanted to know. He stood and stripped his clothes off, then worked her pants and tank top off. This time, he took charge, holding her wrists above her head in one of his big hands.

His other hand traversed her body, followed by his mouth. The hum of need quickly escalated into a primal scream to be satisfied. Finally, he moved between her legs and pushed inside her, slowly, inexorably, like the tide.

He let go of her hands, and she clutched him close, his weight and warmth pressing her into the mattress. The sex was slow and sweet, and when she climaxed, a single tear trailed into the hair at her temple.

He shuddered over her, and she held on to him with all her strength. Exhaustion swamped her, and she was only dimly aware when he shifted them under the covers. She fell asleep in his arms and dreamed impossible dreams.

Anna stirred awake and reached for Iain, finding only cool bed sheets. Bright sunshine had replaced the stormy night. The birds had long concluded their dawn song. The clock next to the bed was blinking perpetual midnight. The power had come back on sometime during her coma-like sleep. Like being doused with ice water, she bolted upright.

Iain was gone.

It was a fact she fundamentally accepted like the sun rising in the east. The world still turned despite the crater in her chest where her heart had been. Somehow, in spite of knowing better, she'd held on to the thin hope he might change his mind and stay. Not only did he not stay, but he'd skulked out without even telling her goodbye.

Anger galvanized her and drove her out of bed. Dressing in her now-dry clothes from the day before, she clomped down the stairs, needing to fill the suffocating silence. She had no time to fume or rail. A dozen final details had to be finished before she could crawl into bed with a gallon of ice cream and a pecan pie.

A clang on the driveway drew her outside. The steamy humidity was as suffocating as the silence had been. Would she ever be able to take a deep breath again?

Holt was leaning out of the driver's side window backing his trailer up to the barn. He climbed out, took one look at her, and hauled her in for a brotherly hug. Anna clung to him and squeezed her eyes shut, but a couple of tears still managed to escape.

"He's gone," she managed to choke out. "He snuck out in the middle of the night, the damned coward."

"I know. I took him to the airport."

Anna jerked back and slapped Holt's shoulder. "I swear if we weren't grown, I'd give you the biggest, deepest wedgie in history. You'd still be singing soprano on Sunday."

He high-stepped out of her reach, swatting her with his ball cap. "Damn, woman! Don't kill the messenger. Or the transporter, in this case."

"His flight must have been early."

"He's somewhere over the Atlantic by now."

Anna pressed the heels of her hands against her brow, forcing the tears to stay dammed. "Why did I have to fall for a hot Highlander?"

"I'm sorry if I gave you terrible advice. Although, to

be fair, you're the one who took advice from a bachelor who hasn't had a serious girlfriend in longer than I'd care to admit. I know nothing about love."

Anna dropped her hands and shook her head. "No, you were right. I'm glad I put myself out there. At least I won't wonder if there was something else I could have done."

"I really am sorry, Anna. I thought you crazy kids had a chance."

"Me too." She didn't even try to fake a smile, but with Holt, she didn't feel the need to. "I guess you're here for the animals."

"Yep. Mom is missing her goats." Holt got to work loading the animals, starting with the goats.

When Holt led Ozzie out, Anna was beset by a fit of affection. She reached out to rub the top of the sheep's head, but Ozzie snapped at her hand. "You little . . ."

Holt laughed and put Ozzie in the trailer followed by Harriet. With one last hug and invitation for a drink later at the pub to drown her sorrows, Holt drove off. She turned in a slow circle.

The barn was empty. The house was empty. Her heart was empty.

Chapter Nineteen

Iain worked a finger between his neck and collar. Being strangled by a tie would be preferable to what he would have to endure today. Anna Maitland had arrived at Cairndow for the christening of Annie Blackmoor. He was godfather, and Anna was godmother. They were bound together, just not in the way he had dreamed they might be.

Wearing his finest kilt in the Blackmoor colors, his da knocked on his doorframe and stepped into the bedroom without having to stoop like he had when Iain was a child. His shoulders hunched forward and his back was slightly rounded. When had that happened? He'd been larger than life when Iain was young. Even more, he'd been the center of Iain's life.

"Aren't you looking smart?" His da's smile was a rare and bonny sight.

"Smart or strangled to death?"

"A bit of both, I suppose." His da's smile faded and his expression turned pensive. "It's been good to have you home."

"It's good to be home." His tongue stumbled over the words even though it was true—to an extent. He missed Anna like he'd left a limb in Highland. Phantom pains woke him from dreams of her or hit him when he stood on the cliffs and looked out at the endlessness of the ocean separating them.

Now she was here and he wasn't sure how he was going to keep himself from falling to his knees and begging her for . . . what exactly? Forgiveness? The last night with Anna had been intense and heartbreaking. He'd had to leave her.

But perhaps he shouldn't have snuck out before dawn. He'd thought there was nothing else to say, but he found himself wanting to talk to her as soon as he woke and before he went to sleep and all the minutes in between.

"I met the American lass earlier. Pretty little thing."

Iain stilled, his breath shuddering out. He could feel his da's eyes on him, and he tried to assemble a sense of normalcy from his frayed emotions. "Anna is indeed lovely, but she's so much more than that."

"Aye. She's a spitfire. A doer, my old man would say. She whisked little Annie away and sent Isabel for a nap before the ceremony. It's not often Isabel gets bossed around." Was that admiration in his da's slight laugh?

His da wasn't keen on ladies in general, probably because of his history, but also because he wasn't one for making polite conversation. Only Mrs. Mac and Isabel had worked their way into his da's heart since his wife's desertion thirty odd years ago.

"I suppose we'd better get on to the big house, eh?" Iain didn't wait for his da to answer, but slipped on a tweed jacket that strained across his shoulders but was his only option and led the way to the door.

Autumn had crept closer to Cairndow, but a warm breeze rose from the south as if Annie Blackmoor was bringing life to the old stones and mortar. Iain took a deep breath. He fought both anticipation and dread at his first sight of Anna.

Following on his da's heels, he entered the house through the kitchens out of habit and convenience. Mrs. Mac was stirring a soup over the burner on a new gas stovetop and directing a young girl who was buttering the top of scones ready to go in the AGA.

"Ta-ta, Mrs. Mac." His da whipped off his hat and ran a hand through his still-thick, more-salt-than-pepper hair.

"They're in the drawing room. I'll be up in a tick with tea." Mrs. Mac had her best dress on under her apron.

They ascended the narrow stone staircase meant for servants to the wide second-floor hallway. The door to the drawing room was open, and the hum of conversation and laughter echoed off the stone walls.

His da sidled into the room but remained along the edge like a hare avoiding a snare. He'd always be more comfortable in the gardens or on the moor than in the big stone castle, even after all the years he'd worked at Cairndow.

Iain hesitated in the doorway, his gaze bouncing around the room until it landed on Anna. Her tartan wool skirt was a feminine version of a kilt. Paired with dark brown riding boots, tights, and a thin, emerald-green jumper, she could have graced the pages of *Town and Country* and looked right at home at Cairndow.

She was holding Annie and pretending to eat one of her chubby fists much to the delight of the baby, who squirmed with laughter.

Why was Iain at all surprised that Anna had charmed a baby when she had so easily put a spell on him? How was he to bear this? He rocked back a step, but it was too late, Isabel had spotted him.

"There you are." Isabel tucked her arm in his and drew him toward the baby.

Anna's brilliant smile trembled, but she was made of stern stuff, as well he knew, and her voice was steady. "Hello, Iain. Good to see you."

"Hello, Anna." He savored her name on his tongue. While her name had been on repeat in his head and heart, he had done his best to avoid speaking of her, lest his da or Isabel guess at the depth and breadth of his feelings.

Their gazes caught and held. He had no idea what she was thinking. Did she want to punch him in the gut? Or lower? Did she want to yell at him? Did she want to kiss him as much as he wanted to kiss her?

Isabel glanced between them, obviously trying to put the puzzle of their disquiet together in her mind. Iain was surprised Anna hadn't told her best friend everything, but it had become clear soon after returning to Cairndow that Isabel didn't know about Anna and Iain.

While he'd been relieved not to bear the brunt of Isabel's anger over the way he'd left Highland, he'd been disappointed as well. Not being able to talk about Anna had made him question the reality. Had the feelings been real?

Standing in front of her quelled all his doubts. In fact, time and distance had only strengthened his longing for her, and making polite conversation was torture when he wanted to pull her aside and confess everything weighing on his heart.

"How is everyone in Highland?" he asked.

"Good." She was giving him crumbs.

"How is your campaign for mayor progressing?"

"Fine." Stale crumbs at that.

With her brows drawn down, Isabel added, "A bit more than fine, I'd say. She got an endorsement from the local paper and from Baxter down at the Chamber of Commerce."

Anna gave a one-shouldered shrug. "They're on board with my progressive platform. The Burns Night Christmas festival will be a go. If I'm elected."

"Is Loretta putting up a good fight?" Iain asked.

"Not really. She seems content to lose, if I'm being honest. Since the almost-flooding of her shop, things have been good between us."

Isabel let out an unladylike snort. "Better you than me. I'll be honest, Loretta scares me."

"She puts on an intimidating front because she's the one who's scared." The philosophical edge to Anna's words was new. "Loretta is becoming—and I can't believe I'm saying this—a friend."

A commotion at the door heralded the arrival of tea and fresh-from-the-AGA scones. Isabel touched the baby's cheek. "Are you okay with Annie for a bit longer?"

"Of course I am. I'm going to take full advantage of holding her while I'm here. Video chats will be all I get soon enough." Anna nuzzled the baby closer. Isabel hurried off to help Mrs. Mac.

Iain was alone with Anna. The baby cooed at him. Almost alone. He held out a finger and the baby caught it in a surprisingly hearty grip and pulled it to her mouth to gum.

"Have you been asked to babysit?" Anna asked.

"Not yet. I'm not sure I'd be any good at it." The baby grinned and drooled up at him.

Anna made a scoffing sound. "Please. You're good at everything. You'll be great with kids."

"I need to talk to you."

"Isn't that what we're doing right now?"

Damn, he'd missed her teasing, sarcastic bite. "Alone."

Her lips thinned, and she glanced around them. "Later tonight. If I'm not too tired."

He wanted to say more, but the clink of a spoon against a teacup stalled him. Everyone gathered around and shared tea and scones before walking to the small family chapel that was hundreds of years old and had overseen countless Blackmoor christenings and deaths. The ceremony was at times touching and funny, especially when Annie bawled her dismay at getting cold water poured over her head.

Iain made more promises, this time to keep Annie safe, which he had already vowed to himself. Even as everyone else's attention was on the babe, Iain basked in Anna's presence and etched every nuance of her expression and the sound of her husky laughter in his memories. These moments would have to live forever to be revisited, because nothing had fundamentally changed in their situation.

Dinner followed, and he was seated next to Anna at the polished dining table. Conversation at the table was lively, but he barely contributed, unable to concentrate on anyone other than Anna. His knee bumped hers, and his hand glanced across her wrist while reaching for the bread. It was a glorious torture.

"How's your mom doing, Anna? Still loving Florida?" Isabel asked.

Iain stared at Anna's profile, surprised to see her mouth tip up into a slight smile. "I think some of the glamour has worn off, to be honest. She wants to spend Christmas in Highland. With me."

Surprise drew Isabel's brows up. "Is she homesick?"

"She said she misses me." Anna shrugged and gave a little laugh. "I think she's mellowing. Plus"—she cast a lightning-fast look toward Iain—"I've learned people are more complicated than I gave them credit for. My mom included."

As dinner wrapped up, Iain's da made motions to leave. This was a wild night out for his da. He leaned closer to Anna and whispered, "I should walk Da back to the cottage. Can we meet in a quarter hour?"

"I'm in the green bedroom. I assume you know where that is?"

"Aye."

After congratulations and goodbyes were made, Iain and his da walked shoulder to shoulder toward the cottage. "Let's take the cliff path," his da said.

It was the long way around. Iain quelled his impatience and took the right fork of the path. After ten minutes of brisk walking, the breeze quickened and the inky expanse of the ocean came into view, stretching to the horizon. His da stopped and stared out at the water. Iain joined him.

"Cairndow has been the great love of my life," his da said.

"I love it too, Da." It wasn't a lie.

"Your mum hated it here. She wanted all of us to start

a new life in Glasgow together, but . . . I couldn't abandon my first love. I insisted you remain with me until she could get on her feet. Looking back, it was selfish of me, but I couldn't leave Cairndow. Not even for her."

Iain blinked and reordered his history. "She wanted me?"

"Aye."

"But she never came back to visit."

"She came back a half dozen times. Things hadn't turned out like she expected in the big city. I tried to get her to move home, but she had gotten mixed up with some bad people. She knew leaving you with me was the only choice. Eventually, she stopped coming home."

"She's dead, isn't she?" He'd known in his heart she was lost to him forever.

"Not long after you turned three. An overdose. I should have been more bendable for her. I should have been stronger and told you the truth of the matter years ago." A note he'd never heard weaved through his da's voice. Regret.

"If you had it to do over, would you have gone with her?"

"Nay. I belong here." His da heaved a sigh. "But I would have fought harder to make Cairndow a home for her too. Now, what about you?"

"What about me?" Iain shifted his gaze off the water to his da.

"I kept a close watch on you today. I knew something in your heart had changed after you came home, but I couldn't put my finger on it until today. You love the Maitland woman."

Iain was tired of denying his heart, even to himself. "Aye, I love her, but there's nothing to be done about it. I can't leave Cairndow."

His da's jaw worked before he found words. "I didn't try hard enough to make your mum stay, and I live with the regret every day. When you left for the army, I only wanted one thing: to have you safely back at Cairndow. Now I see, it's not so simple. While you may be safe, you're not happy."

Iain tried to protest, but his da held up a hand. "Only when I saw you with Miss Maitland did I understand the cause."

"She can't pick up her life and move to Scotland, Da." Iain's voice was thick with conflicting emotions. Surprise, sadness, resignation.

"Nay, I don't expect she could." His da clapped him on the shoulder and squeezed. "But you could pick up and move to the States. You've never wanted to be Cairndow's groundskeeper, have you?"

Iain swallowed down the lie that sprang to his lips. He'd come this far. He owed himself and his da the truth. "I haven't. I love Cairndow and the life you gave me, but I've never truly belonged. Even in the short time I was in Highland, I carved a place for myself. The people welcomed me, and I was able to contribute in ways I never dreamed of."

"And Anna Maitland?"

"Anna feels like home."

"Then you must win her back, lad. Whatever the cost. Learn from your old da's mistakes." His da tilted his head back and sniffed. "I've always wanted to see the States."

His da hated to travel, but he would make the sacrifice to see his son happy. Iain pulled his da into a tight hug, fighting the burn of tears himself. His da had offered him a much-needed benediction.

"Go talk to her, son." His da broke away.

"I'll see you to the cottage before I—"

"No. I'll find my own way, so you can find yours." His da patted his arm, then walked away, his footing sure on the path he'd treaded hundreds of times.

Only when his da faded into the darkness and out of sight did Iain turn toward the castle. Everything had changed. He was free to follow his heart. Was it too late?

Bypassing the kitchen entrance, he entered through the mudroom door, wanting to avoid being drawn into polite conversation. Padding up the stairs, he made for Anna's room. With his fist raised to knock, he hesitated. The next few minutes might well change the course of his life.

"I never pegged you for being indecisive, Highlander." Anna's voice came from over his shoulder.

Shock had him slapping his hand on the door and spinning around. Anna leaned against the wall on the opposite side of the hall, her legs crossed at the ankle.

"You gave me a fright, lass. I was just . . ." He gestured toward the door then ran a hand through his hair and gave a humorless laugh. "Gathering my courage, I suppose. I deserve a good tongue-lashing for the way I left."

"A tongue-lashing? You wish." Anna swept by him, trailing the scent of magnolias, and entered her room to lean against the nearest post of the four-poster bed.

He followed. The moth-eaten curtains and musty rugs had been replaced since he and Alasdair had engaged in one of their sweeping games of hide-and-seek twenty-odd years earlier. Perhaps he'd been inside since to change a lightbulb, but with Anna in the room, he took in every detail with fresh eyes.

The green bedding brought out the red glints in her hair. The stone walls were softened by faded tapestries. The lemony scent of wood polish sharpened the air. In olden days, a fire would have burned in the massive fireplace, but now, only a brace of unlit candles stood on the hearth.

"You deserved better than to have me sneak out. It was cowardly." Iain remained standing in the middle of the room.

"Yes, it was. I was mad and hurt and wanted to beat you senseless that morning. And the day after and the day after that and—"

"I get the picture." Nerves shuffled him into a short pace, hemmed in by the bed and the hearth. "I wanted to stay, but I made promises and was honor bound to keep them."

"Promises to who? I thought you didn't have a girlfriend." Anna straightened and crossed her arms under her breasts.

Iain barked a laugh and pivoted toward her. "Not to another woman. To my da. I couldn't abandon him the way my mum had. Besides Cairndow, I'm all he has."

"He's a nice man with kind eyes. The kind of dad I always wished for." Her smile was tight and watery. "I understand. I even forgive you. Is that what you want?"

"There's something else I want even more."

"What?"

"*You.* I want you. Do you still want me?" His jaw was clamped so tight, he was sure all his teeth would crack.

A laugh stuttered out, even as a tear escaped her eye and trailed down her cheek. She wiped it away. "Of course I want you, but nothing has changed. I can't leave Highland."

"My da released me from my promise. He wants me to be happy and knows you will make me happy."

"What are you saying exactly? I need you to spell it out like I'm the village idiot." She took a step toward him, closing the distance by half.

He met her in the middle and took her hand in a grip that was desperate and too tight, but she didn't pull away. "Wherever you are is my home. I'll happily move to Highland. If you'll have me."

"You'd move halfway around the world just to be with me?" The wistful incredulousness in her voice made his heart swell.

When words were hard to come by, Burns never deserted him. "'My heart's in the Highlands, my heart is not here; My heart's in the Highlands a-chasing the deer.'"

"Am I your deer?" she asked.

"You're my everything. I love you."

Her mouth opened and closed, but only a strangled sound emerged. She threw her arms around his neck, and her weight fell into him. He closed his eyes and wrapped her close, knowing he didn't have to let go.

"What will you do in Highland?" she asked.

"Hire myself out as a contractor. I'm good with my hands and based on my experience with Loretta and her friends, there's plenty of work around town. What do you think?"

"You are definitely good with your hands." The sexual tease in her voice kindled a heat in his stomach. She pulled back to look at him, her hands tight on his shoulders. "Do you want to know what I really think?"

He nodded brusquely.

"I think we'll have to find a house together. You don't

fit in my apartment. And what about a work visa and immigration and—"

"We'll figure it out. Together." Unspeakable relief flooded him. "I was afraid I lost my chance."

"You came awfully close. By the way, I love you too." Anna examined him from head to toe before shoving him backward by his shoulders. The unexpectedness of the move caught him off guard, and he toppled, landing on the soft mattress.

Anna unzipped her boots and kicked them to the side, then she climbed over him, straddling his hips. "It's time for your tongue-lashing," she said in a decidedly wicked voice.

"You're going to make me pay for my idiocy, aren't you?"

"It's going to be absolute torture, Highlander. I'm going to make you scream and beg for mercy." She smiled as she shimmied down his body and flipped up his kilt.

And it was the best sort of torture he could imagine.

Epilogue

Holt Pierson ran a hand through his hair and adjusted his ball cap so the brim rode low, making it easier to avoid eye contact. He wasn't in the mood to make polite small talk, and it seemed like the entire town had come out to watch Highland's new mayor, Anna Maitland, cut the ribbon on the new shop on Main Street, Highland Antiques. Even the brisk November wind cutting through the crowd couldn't diminish the current of excitement.

Holt had forgotten about the ribbon cutting. He'd only come to town to replenish his beer supply and to grab some easy frozen foods. His parents were leaf peeping in Vermont in their RV. They had been as giddy as newlyweds on their last call home. Was Highland still their home? They had broached the possibility of heading to a Florida RV park for the winter. His mom thought the warm weather might help her arthritis.

Iain Connors stood at the back of the crowd, leaning against the brick storefront of the Dapper Highlander. He had opted for jeans over a kilt in deference to the cool day.

Holt sidled up next to him. "Anna has really energized the town."

His smile held a quality Holt couldn't identify but left him with a strange sort of emptiness. "She's a rare one. Her enthusiasm will drive the town to new heights."

"The Christmas party the town is putting on sounds like fun."

"It's a bastardized version of Burns Night. Good food, great songs, plenty of fun. The lads and I are already practicing." Since making his move to Highland, Iain had become a permanent member of the Bluegrass Jacobites.

Iain had also launched a renovation business specializing in bringing out the classic beauty of older homes. His first project was the craftsman-style house he and Anna had bought on a quiet tree-lined street within walking distance of downtown.

Meanwhile, Holt was living in the same one-bedroom cabin on the farm he'd moved into after high school graduation. Back then, the autonomy had made him feel like a big-shot bachelor. At some point in the intervening years, the feeling had turned to melancholy and then loneliness as he watched friend after friend pair off.

Anna finished her speech and cut the ribbon to a wave of applause. The crowd milled about, some pushing into the antiques store, some clogging the sidewalks and street to socialize. Rose Buchanan and Gareth Blackmoor backed out of the crowd.

Rose gave him a half hug while Gareth shook Holt's hand. "Where are your parents, Holt?" Rose asked.

"Traveling the backroads of Vermont at the moment."

"Oh, how nice. I would take Gareth up north to sightsee, but his blood has gotten too thin from living in

Georgia, hasn't it, darling?" Rose tossed her silver hair and sent Gareth a teasing smile.

"That is has, Rosie." Gareth wrapped an arm around Rose's waist.

"How's little Annie doing?" Holt asked politely.

"She's grand. Already rolling over. She has Isabel and Alasdair wrapped around her little finger." Gareth beamed. "It's good to hear a child's laughter echo through the castle again. We're going to spend Christmas at Cairndow."

"That's great. Really great." And it was. Holt didn't begrudge Izzy and Alasdair their happiness. In fact, he'd been integral to getting them back together after Alasdair had nearly screwed it up.

A woman stepped out of the Highland Drug and Dime. Holt's gaze homed in on the petite figure, a vague feeling of familiarity washing over him, but his churning brain failed to catalogue her. She pulled her hoodie up and darted down the sidewalk with her face down.

For the first time in weeks, energy zinged through his body. Smiling absently at Rose and Gareth, Holt excused himself and set off in the direction of the woman. The two stuffed grocery bags slowed her down, and he was able to close the distance to a dozen feet.

She darted to the right, down an alley between buildings on Main Street. He hesitated at the street, questioning his sanity in following a strange woman into an alley. One of her bags brushed against the brick wall, snagged, and ripped open, sending items scattering along the concrete.

Her hoodie fell back, revealing a set of pixie-like features framed by choppy, dark brown-red hair. While she looked like a disheveled Tinker Bell, the curses falling from her lips weren't Disney-approved. The memory clicked the pieces into place.

She was the lead singer of the Scunners, the Scottish rock band that had performed during the last two summer Highland festivals. He'd spent both concerts admiring her energy and spirit onstage. The bright red hair she'd sported over the summer had dimmed like her spirit. Dark circles under her eyes marked her fatigue, and her cheekbones cut sharply in her face. She sniffed and worked to gather her purchases. Was she . . . crying?

Stepping forward, he said, "May I help?"

She startled and stepped away from him, holding a bottle of generic aspirin to her chest. "What do you want?" Her Scottish accent still counted as unusual in Highland even with Gareth and Iain officially transplanted.

Holt held his hands up and spoke as if she were a spooked horse. "Just offering to help you gather your things."

"Were you following me?" Her shoulders hunched inward. She wore several T-shirts under the hoodie. So many, in fact, she was shapeless.

"Of course not." He forced his wince into a hopefully non-creepy smile and held out a can of soup that had rolled to his feet. "Thought you looked familiar and I was trying to place you."

She snatched it out of his hand and juggled the bags. A jar of peanut butter cracked against the concrete, the plastic lid splitting in two. She squatted to scoop it up, her head down, but not before he noticed her chin wobbling.

"Let me—"

"I don't need your help." Her steely tone was weakened by the sound of the bag rending further.

He scooped the torn bag out of the crook of her arm
and tipped it up so nothing else would escape. "Of course
you don't, but my mama would tan my hide if I didn't
help anyway."

They faced off in an impasse before she shrugged and
spun on her heel, heading to the narrow alley that ran
behind the Main Street shops. A bike with a front basket and a canvas saddlebag leaned against the brick wall.
The rims were rusty, and one side of the handlebar had
lost its grip, leaving an exposed metal rod.

She repacked the items from her bag into the front basket, including a loaf of white bread, a half-gallon of milk,
and tea bags among other staples. Nothing that could be
considered an indulgence, except for maybe the tea.

She plucked the items out of the bag he held and filled
the back satchel. This included the peanut butter, baking
potatoes, cans of soup, and an assortment of ramen noodle packages. She straddled the bike. "I guess I should
thank you," she said grudgingly.

Without another word or a backward glance, she
peddled off, making the turn onto Maple Street and
disappearing through the dancing yellow leaves.

Holt shook his head and strolled to his truck, trying and failing not to wonder how the lead singer of the
Scunners had landed back in Highland after the festival.
Surely the Scunners were touring or had gigs or whatever. Questions niggled at him.

With his own meager supplies of food, which included plenty of indulgences like beer and frozen pizza
and a banana cream pie from the Highland Lass restaurant, on the passenger seat, he pointed his truck toward
the farm and his evening chores. Even with the harvest

in, he had to make sure the cows got milked and the animals fed.

A small, hunched figure walked on the narrow shoulder of the road ahead of him, pushing a bike. The front tire was flat. He rolled the passenger window down and crept along beside her. She stared straight ahead as if his diesel truck was a gnat she could ignore.

"Can I give you a ride?"

"No." Her voice clipped any hint of her Scottish accent.

"I'm basically harmless. I promise." He tried on his best Boy Scout smile even though it had been a while.

She cocked her eyebrows and heaved a sigh. "*Basically* harmless? Not exactly a resounding recommendation. I find it creepy that you're following me."

"I'm not following you." This time he could state it as fact. "I live five or six miles down the road."

She stared straight ahead and ignored him.

"I can't rightly drive off and leave you here. People fly up and down this road, and there's no shoulder. Either you let me give you a ride, or I'll trail you until you get home. How far do you have to go?"

She shot him an assessing glance. "Not far."

"It will go faster if you let me give you a lift. How 'bout it?"

Her nod was reluctant and nearly imperceptible. He sped up, pulled halfway off the road into knee-high scrub grass, and climbed out. After loading her bike into the bed of his truck, he opened the passenger door, pushing his own shopping bags to the side.

With her dark brown eyes full of suspicion, she grabbed the side of the seat and attempted to climb in.

The lift kit plus the mud tires made it a difficult distance for her. After watching her try twice and fail, he picked her up by the waist and set her on the seat, making sure his hands didn't linger.

She gasped and turned on him like a half-feral cat ready to strike even the kindest hand. He took two stumbling steps backward, windmilling when his heel caught a divot of soft ground. After he regained his balance, they regarded each other like prey and predator. There was no doubt what she considered him.

He held his hands up as if surrendering. "I didn't mean to scare you, miss."

"Keep your bloody hands to yourself next time." She slammed his truck door shut.

He was just relieved she hadn't bolted for the woods. Instinctively, he knew she'd be more comfortable keeping him in view at all times, and he circled around the front of the truck to climb into the driver's seat.

Once he got them back on the road, he kept his voice casual when he asked, "Where am I dropping you?"

"At the top of Meadows Lane."

His foot jerked on the gas pedal. "Are you staying with old Ms. Meadows?"

"Aye." While her body remained as still as a mouse not wanting to attract the gaze of a circling hawk, he didn't miss the surreptitious glances she aimed in his direction from the corner of her eye. What had made her so skittish and suspicious?

A widow and recluse, Ms. Meadows lived in an old house on a sliver of woods and hills along a creek surrounded by Pierson land. His dad had been trying to buy the property from her for decades.

"I'm Holt Pierson, by the way. What's your name?" he asked.

She hesitated as if she was loath to surrender any more information than she already had, meager though it was. "Claire."

"Nice to meet you."

She made a throaty sound of acknowledgment, but didn't return the sentiment. "Do I take it your skills don't extend to the kitchen?"

"And what would you know about my skills?" He couldn't keep the tease out of his voice.

Color rushed her cheeks. "I watched you compete at the games this summer. That's all I was referring to, I can assure you."

"I watched you perform too." He tossed a glance toward her, but she didn't react as far as he could tell. "Are you sticking around Highland for a while?"

"Here it is. You can let me out at the top, thanks."

Overgrown bushes camouflaged the start of a gravel lane. Holt had driven past hundreds of times and never paid it any mind. The old mailbox needed a coat of paint and legible numbers and the red flag dangled toward the ground like the standard of a defeated army. He hadn't seen the old house in years even though as the crow flew, it was a half mile or less from his cabin. Based on the overgrown state of the lane and the dilapidated mailbox, he could only imagine what shape the house was in. Last time his dad had gone out to make yet another offer to the old lady, she'd run him off with a shotgun.

When he was young, he'd see Ms. Meadows some-times at church. She sat on the opposite side of the sanc-tuary, wearing an old-fashioned pillbox hat and clutching a black patent leather handbag with a tarnished silver clasp. Holt's father and Ms. Meadows observed a cease-fire while in the house of the Lord. Holt had followed his dad's lead and ignored the old lady. He supposed it had become a habit. A bad one.

Holt beat Claire to the truck bed and lifted her bike out, replacing the grocery items that had fallen out. Her hands brushed his when she took the handles from him. Her fingers were thin and cold, and when he'd lifted her into the truck, he couldn't help but notice her physical fragility. In contrast, strength radiated from her eyes and the set of her jaw.

"Thanks for the ride." She ducked between the bushes and out of sight.

"Maybe I'll see you around Highland!" Holt called out.

"Maybe." Her voice lilted to him.

He stood there for a moment, wondering if he'd imagined her. Wired like he'd slammed an energy drink, he headed to his cabin on the farm. He couldn't stop wondering what had happened to her since the summer and what she was doing with old Ms. Meadows. Did his fascination stem from the fact Claire wasn't someone he'd known all his life? She was a mystery, and in a town as small as Highland, not many mysteries remained.

Carrying his last bag of groceries into the cabin, he noticed the jar of peanut butter with the cracked lid rolling between the grooves in the bed liner. Debris stuck to the peanut butter inside. Looked like he owed either Claire or Ms. Meadows a jar of peanut butter.

Worry worked its way into his psyche like a splinter. When was the last time Ms. Meadows had been to church? He couldn't remember. Was she ill or injured?

Was Claire taking care of Ms. Meadows or taking advantage of an old lady? While he had a hard time believing Claire was up to no good, the air around her had been rank with desperation. Desperate people often couldn't afford morals.

Holt tossed the peanut butter into the air and caught it, a decision snapping into place. He would stop by Ms. Meadows's house tomorrow with a new jar of peanut butter in hand as a peace offering. It would be as good an excuse as any to check on Ms. Meadows and to see Claire again. His curiosity was aroused.

With an anticipation he hadn't felt in months, Holt couldn't wait for the morning.

Coming soon . . .

Don't miss the next title in **Laura Trentham**'s
heartwarming Highland, Georgia series

A HIGHLANDER IS COMING TO TOWN

"Romance that is both extremely
sensual and phenomenal."
—*Fresh Fiction*

**Available in October 2020 from
St. Martin's Paperbacks**